AERIE

A MAGONIA NOVEL

ALSO BY MARIA DAHVANA HEADLEY
Magonia

AERIE

A MAGONIA NOVEL

MARIA DAHVANA HEADLEY

HARPER

An Imprint of HarperCollins *Publishers*

Library of Congress Control Number: 2016942319
ISBN 978-0-06-232055-1

Typography by Ellice M. Lee
16 17 18 19 20   CG/RRDH   10 9 8 7 6 5 4 3 2 1
❖
First Edition

FOR JASPER, ROWEN, AND HAZEL ANNE,
WHO ARE STILL TOO LITTLE FOR THIS BOOK,
BUT WHO ARE CLEARLY SKY SAILORS
{{{{ &! &! &! }}}}

I listen to the sound of singing. Everything, everywhere. The world inside my house. The world outside my house. Birds and wind and trees. Electricity, and water through pipes, and people walking up and down the stairs, ice cracking outside, something being chopped in the kitchen. The world is all voice, all the time, and if I'm here, being quiet, I'm still not silent. I can hear my heart beating and I can hear the distance between me and everyone else on earth, because no one, not anywhere, sings the way I do. I seem to be the only one with a voice like this, and the only one who carries this song.

So I listen with all my might, wondering if one day, I'll hear another voice like mine, someone else singing the notes only I can sing.

But if there's anyone out there like me, I can't hear them. My voice is like an instrument meant to play in an orchestra, but instead it's playing solo, a repertoire of songs no one's written yet. This must be what it would be like to be an inventor of a new instrument, the only one who knows how to play it.

That sounds like it would be fun, but—

This must be what it would be like to be the last of a species of birds.

I listen.

I listen.

I listen.

CHAPTER 1

{AZA}

Good evening, Boyle residence. It's 11:30 p.m. on the night before your eldest daughter's seventeenth birthday, and said daughter is creeping through the house like a roaming shadow, lurking her way to the back door.

How much does she wish she could sing a (silent, yet effective) version of *invisible* and/or *teleport*? Much. But, sadly, there's no song for that.

There's bike + rain, sleet, snow. All very typical for a night on which I've decided to embark into the outdoors.

I'm wearing layers. It's long underwear meets furry boots, and I'm basically looking like a tiny wrong lumberjack, with a rain poncho over the whole thing. Maybe in the movie version of the Imaginary Life of Aza Ray I'd be wearing . . . I don't know what. A dress of some kind?

I'm never pretty in pink, though. It's far more likely that I'd be wearing overalls than a frilly party dress. But, as ever on birthdays, I'm questioning my aesthetics. Should I be a different kind of person? Should I attempt it? Should there be some version of Cupcake Aza rather than Captain?

Historically, this kind of questioning took place in an

attempt to avoid counting down the days remaining in my life. Now? It's just . . . how I live.

I'm not the kind of girl, generally, who frills it up, even on special occasions. I was born backward from the rest of the world, and backward I remain. Three parts pirate, one part alien.

So I'm wearing all the layers of clothing, and one really major, integral layer that isn't clothing, exactly, but might as well be.

It's the shell. The skin I took from the skyship. The one that covers my Magonian body.

That's right. Magonian.

Does that sound not-from-Earth to you? Well, congratulations, game-show contestants! You win a bona fide alien. Or maybe the opposite of bona fide. Mala fide. Yes, that's real. Nobody ever uses it, which surprises me, because it's useful.

As a result of this skin, I look nothing like who I really am. I mean, I never do, not since last year. But I look *especially* nothing like it right now. The skin makes me look like a person I'm not.

Of course, mind you, I'm not a person at all.

Aza Ray Boyle's been dead a year, and yet here I am, still alive.

Aza Ray Quel is known only to the kingdom of Magonia— the place I was born, high in the clouds where weather is made and squallwhales sing.

I'm also Beth Marchon—here on Earth, undercover in this skin.

Here because: my family. Here because: destiny. Here because: Every Imaginable Reason and Some Unimaginable.

My old body was the same as this one—a fake, a copy meant for someone else. A disguise to mask who I really was.

But still, for sixteen years, that body was mine.

It was dying from the moment I arrived here. And I don't miss the coughing, the choking, the drowning, the last page of the book in front of me every second, but I miss looking in the mirror and feeling like I knew who was looking back.

I still miss being Aza Ray Boyle, dying girl or not.

Aza's shell is gone, though. And if I want to stay here, then Beth it is.

In truth, doesn't matter which skin I'm in. My soul dictates who I am, and as a rule, the things the world thinks should matter to me do not even. I'm almost seventeen, and there's no prom queen hiding under this poncho. If there was?

I'd kick her out.

I was born this way, and no matter how I look, I'm Magonian.

And since I left Magonia this fact has caused certain unforeseen problems.

There's a word in German (of course it's in German) for the feeling caged birds have when it comes time to migrate. The anxious, panicky restlessness of knowing you should be flying.

Zugunruhe. Me? I have *major* and constant *zugunruhe.* I feel like I'm fluttering up at the top of my cage, trying to get to the sun. Last year on this day, the northern lights were arcing across the sky, and stars were lit up, and the whole universe was stretched out in front of me, this impossibly glorious thing.

Last year, on my birthday, I was in Magonia. And I was the chosen one. The Captain's Daughter.

This year, I'm a fake exchange student from a real city, doing nothing more than sneaking out of the house I live in.

It's a normal night, in a normal life, on which I can't outwardly celebrate the birthday that's about to happen, because it's Aza Ray Boyle's, not Beth Marchon's.

There's a picture of the girl formerly known as me in the hall of my school. It's up in the display when you walk in, my/her birth and death dates on a plaque.

MY death date.

Nothing's more fun to walk past every morning, except *everything*. The reality of my situation is so completely batshit it would be crazy-making, if it weren't so easy to confirm.

But there it is. There SHE is.

Staring at me. Right in the mirror every morning. And then, again, staring at me from that plaque. It's my birthday—it's written right there.

But it's not *my* birthday.

It's my deathday.

Except that I'm a thousand percent alive.

A year's passed since I woke up on a ship in the clouds and discovered that I wasn't human but a part of a race of people who live in the sky.

A year's passed since I discovered the door in my chest—yes, an actual door—and the space that was supposed to be filled by my songbird, my canwr, Milekt, and the song of my arranged partner, Dai.

Both of them betrayed me.

A year since I discovered that my mother, Zal, wanted to use the power of my Magonian song to transform landmasses into water and flood the earth, destroying it in the name of the Magonians who'd starved at the unwitting hands of humanity.

All in the name of revenge.

I was moments away from doing it, raising the level of the ocean, bringing on an ice melt and environmental collapse. The end of the world as we know it. But I didn't.

A year's passed since Jason kept me from becoming a monster—the real monster my mother intended. A year since Zal and my Magonian *intended* were hauled up into the Magonian capital and taken to prison.

Does it feel like a year?

Nope. Like yesterday. But here we are. Almost 365 yesterdays from that one.

I was one person, but now I'm another. That's true in the literal AND the figurative.

And everything I knew about little things like, oh, *this planet* and *life in general* turned out to be not-so-much.

The plaque in the hall of my high school says all of the above, in incorrect shorthand. I have to shut my eyes and fumble by sound to get around it, every single day.

I creep in the dark through the kitchen.

The lights go on. I squint, busted.

My sister, Eli, is standing at the counter wearing leg warmers and drinking a green smoothie, despite it being almost midnight. She's giving me an eyebrow and the eyebrow is made of *dream on, Aza Ray, you're not getting past the sentinel.* Sometimes having Eli for a sister is like having a moat around the house. There are no clandestine anythings when she's here. Never have been. It took me years to realize that my sister knows all, sees all, is all.

Which, when you're not trying to sneak out of the house, is not uncool. When you are, however—

"Are you worried you're going to turn into a pumpkin at midnight?" Eli asks. "Is that why you're trying to get out the door before your birthday? Or is this just a strange coincidence?"

"More like I'm worried I'm going to turn back into Cinderella," I say. "I was never a pumpkin."

"Cinderella wanted to be a prince's wife and wear high heels made of glass. Apparently you haven't read that fairy tale lately. You weren't ever Cinderella," she says. "Unless there's a geek-brained Cinderella who wears—"

She looks down at my fur-lined, knee-high, snowshoe-bottomed boots, bought at a flea market, thank you.

"—whatever those are—and has nothing to do with princes."

"Maybe I'm trying to have a rendezvous," I surrender. "With a handsome stranger."

"Ew," she says. "*Rendezvous*, Aza? Seriously?"

I grin at her. "So seriously."

"You're not as discreet as I'd be," she says.

"No one's as discreet as you'd be," I say.

"Truth." My sister smiles a smile that says I don't know everything about her activities. If Eli ever goes wild, I don't know if anyone will be aware enough to clock it. Nothing shows on her face. Just green smoothie.

She's next to the terrarium. Some of my mom's experiment mice are on a weekend visit because a lab tech is out. They basically just run giddily around their domain, periodically jumping into their pond, where they hold their breath for an hour at a stretch. At first it was nerve-racking. They looked like they were drowning themselves, but now it's kind of gorgeous. Little sea monkey mice.

The experiments have been going better. The mice used to die before their time.

These lucky mice are the product of my mother's refusal to give up, even on a daughter whom she was told wouldn't last past her first birthday.

When I was a baby, I couldn't breathe, so my scientist mom researched ways to make breathing less . . . relevant.

I watch a particularly accomplished rodent breaststroke and wonder if I'll need that again—the medicine my mother is developing. I might. This skin is only a skin, and the serum in these mice is the reason I'm still in the world at all.

I feel all kinds of tender toward them.

Eli slides a package across the kitchen counter.

"Since you seem to be leaving the house before the stroke of midnight, when I was planning to give this to you, we're doing your birthday present now," she says, and clears her throat. "Two years' worth of birthdays."

For about five seconds, my little sister and I stare at each other across the kitchen counter, tears streaming down our faces, like we're different people than we are. Then, because we're ourselves, we get it together.

I tear the wrapping paper, opening the box, pulling out folds of leather. And fur. And . . . zippers?

Then I'm crying again, because Eli got me a flight suit. An old one, like the kind military pilots used. Vintage. World War II, I'm guessing? It's pretty much the match to the boots.

I look up from my teary embarrassingness, and Eli is grinning like I've never seen her grin. She cackles. "It's electric!"

She flips a switch and activates its battery pack. It's heated. I don't even. Eli's crowing.

"Put it on," she says. She already has it unzipped and open for me, and for a second, I'm scared to put a flight suit on, because what if I suddenly get snatched into the sky? It feels like tempting fate.

But no. This is too amazing to worry about fate.

I step out of my layers and into it. I zip it up. It has a million pockets. It's much, MUCH better than overalls. Much better than a lumberjack in a poncho. Much better than anything else I've ever owned.

"That looks perfect on you," Eli says.

"But I don't know how to fly."

She gives me a very Eli look.

"Not on a plane." And there's so much we don't actually need to say. Eli knows all about the ships and Magonia. She knows about the half-bird, half-human Rostrae, the slave class there, some of them my friends.

She knows about my mother. She knows about who they say I'm supposed to be. And now she's given me a flight suit.

"This represents five long months of me babysitting puking toddlers. Make it worth my while," says my sister.

There are words embroidered on the pocket, gold thread, a few silver stars around it.

"I couldn't do your name, because obviously."

"Carpe omnia," I say.

Not carpe diem. Not *Seize the Day*.

No, this says *Seize Everything*.

I'll take it.

I grab my sister and hug her so hard she makes a sound of suffocation. I let her go.

"No big deal," she says, and tugs at her leg warmers.

"No big deal," I say, and tug at my many zippy pockets.

"Listen though," says Eli. "Something happened. I have to tell you."

"Yeah?"

"Julie told me she thought she saw you at school today."

I take a second. "I was there, so."

"No. *You* you. The old you. Aza."

We're both silent for a moment. I know what Eli's thinking, because I'm thinking the same thing.

Heyward.

The human girl who I was a poor copy of. The one they took to Magonia when they hid me here on earth. Eli's biological sister.

"She was standing across the street from the gym, looking at the building," Eli adds. "Julie thought she was seeing a ghost. She's wrong, isn't she? There's no way?"

"She must've imagined it," I say.

"Should I tell Mom and Dad?" asks Eli.

I shake my head. "If she was really down here, we'd know."

I'd have felt it through Caru, my heartbird. I'm sure of that much, at least.

"Don't tell Jason either," I say. "I don't want to freak him out. I'll deal with it. Okay?"

Eli nods, but I'm not sure I trust her to keep her mouth shut. I run out the door, convincing myself all the way that nothing bad's going to happen.

It's about to be my birthday and nothing, nothing bad is going to happen today.

I bike through the rain-sleet-snow-muck-storm, pretending that I'm singing on a skyship, capable of taking care of everyone I love with just an exhale and a note. I try to pretend it's all simple, that I want only this life I have, that there's nothing else out there for me.

But I know better.

I consider Jason's front door, decide on romantic gestures instead, and climb the drainpipe outside his window. Halfway up, I have frozen fingers and a bruised knee, but once you commit to climbing a drainpipe, you can't stop or you die of shame.

I'm having pretty clear visions of said drainpipe falling off the side of the house, another version of our long-ago hoax flight off the garage. It wouldn't only be mortifying, it'd be ridiculous for someone who can control the elements to fall off the side of a house and break her ankle.

When I finally haul myself up to Jason's window, I stop. I can see him in there, sleeping. I don't usually see him that way, because he's an insomniac, especially since last year, when they took me.

So this is *whoa*. I'm loath to interrupt whatever he's dreaming.

I want Jason to sleep like he's sleeping now, certain of everything, no panic, like nothing I'm doing is making him worried.

Everything I do makes him worried, though. I keep seeing his eyes focused internally, running stats on something, or writing an endless list of something, or calculating the probability of—

I don't know what.

He's not *with* me sometimes, even when he's with me. And maybe that's partly my fault. Maybe I'm not with him.

The chosen one, they called me, not those exact words, but that's what they meant. It's tempting bullshit. A million years of myths. They can convince you to be some kind of believer, tell you that you have a Destiny.

But what happens when the chosen one makes choices of her own? What happens when she walks away?

I look at Jason. I'm *his* chosen one. And he's mine.

Jason's sleeping face is sharp-planed, shadows beneath his cheekbones, a nose maybe bigger than it should be, and more crooked too, given the four times he's broken it.

I witnessed all of them. Three times I was the cause. (What can I say? Errors.) I'm looking at his too-long eyelashes, the only part of him that still seems like it belongs to a little kid. I know every mark on his skin. I know everything he was born with, and every scar that came in the years since.

I know Jason Kerwin as well as I know myself. Probably better, given everything that's happened. He, unlike me, looks the same as he always has. Though maybe somewhat better to casual observers.

Time passes. Some people get pretty. Others change bodies entirely.

Him, though? No matter what he looks like, he's an alligator on the inside, the same one that crashed my birthday in a reptile costume with a long scaly tail.

Twelve years later . . .

Here he is.

Here I am.

Here *we* are.

I wedge my fingers under the sash and pull.

CHAPTER 2

{JASON}

I wake to the sound of someone trying to sound like no one, my bedroom window opening, a scratching creak. I'm reaching my arm down to grab the telescope beside the bed—a telescope, Kerwin, really?!—when . . .

My girlfriend (fine, fine, this still sounds impossible to me, still sounds like far more than I could ever deserve in any universe not science fictional) tumbles head over heels onto my floor, and lands in a pile of knees and elbows. She's managed to climb my drainpipe in the middle of December. It's not everyone who can shinny straight up two stories.

Aza Ray, of course, isn't everyone.

Aza Ray is the *only* one.

I clamp my mouth shut because 1) She's trying to surprise me and 2) Every time I even glance at her I want to grab both of her hands and never let go.

This is what happens when you lose someone once. You never really feel safe again. Complication: having that someone be a girl who is always running as fast as she can, not necessarily away from me, but in nine directions at once. Three of them straight up. Causes anxieties.

She mutters a string of colorful swear words as my window shuts on her forgotten-on-the-sill foot, but she's fine. She's just Aza, the superspy version. Yep, she hums a scrap of *Pink Panther* theme. She can't help herself. Triumph makes her talkative.

I pretend I'm beyond asleep so she can have the satisfaction of sneaking up on me.

Not that I ever sleep. Would anyone?

Imagine your girlfriend making the water rise up out of a wading pool, and turning it midair into rocks. Imagine her singing a piece of the sidewalk into a sudden lake, and then imagine that lake has no bottom. Imagine this amazing, not-of-this-earth mind, this girl who tells me casually about silver tentacles reaching out of clouds, who sings me notes of Magonian song, who one day made me something out of rain that shimmered green and gray. It wasn't a gemstone, nor anything I'd ever seen before, and when I asked, Aza shrugged, and said, "Minor meteor, blah-de-blah."

Imagine loving *her*.

Imagine losing her.

Everyone thought she was dead. Everyone but me. Someone like Aza couldn't die.

I was right, in the end. She hadn't. She'd become—already was—something else. Something *more*.

Now imagine being the guy who has to worry about that, about losing her all over again to a country in the sky.

My eyes are open to slits. I watch Aza tiptoe across my bedroom. She shakes her hair out of her hat, and tries to silently unzip her—what is she wearing?—and get out of her boots at the same time, which results in another near collapse of tangled limbs. Aza's failing to navigate her new skin. She's still not used to this version of herself.

"Damn it," she says, bending over me, her clothes half off, her hair standing straight up. "You're totally awake now, aren't you?"

I laugh. "When have I ever not been totally awake?"

"There was that one time you slept through the night five years ago."

"An aberration."

She puts an icy, questing hand on my skin, clearly considering jabbing it into my armpit, and so I grab it and roll her under the covers with me, until I can wrap her up completely.

I get her into my arms, face-to-face, and she's cracking up.

"You could've come in the front door, you know." I hide my twitchiness over her being out at night alone (during a storm, no less) with no one watching her, no one even knowing where she is.

Aza doesn't ever follow rules. If I try to point out even basic things, she transgresses double time. Storms make me nervous. Every time the sky darkens, I think it's Aza's last day of this life, and the first day of something much worse.

"It's not like my parents don't know you sleep over."

"It isn't like Magonians like to use the front door," she protests, and puts her frozen nose into my neck. "It was a misjudge, though. It's icy out there. And disgusting. Like, sleet city disgusting." She shivers. "I don't have toes anymore."

I hold her despite her cold feet trying to sap all the warmth from my body. Like I care about cold feet. Like I care about anything beyond Aza in my bed. Even a year later, I'm still in shock every time. All those years of me being lamentably, silently, secretly in love. All those years of not knowing. She clamps around my ankle bones.

"Nope, don't worry, you still have toes," I say. I feel her smiling into my skin. She wriggles closer. I kiss her, forehead, nose, mouth. I run a hand down her spine and feel the familiar lines of her shoulders, her rib cage, the bones beneath the skin the same ones as ever. Different body, same girl. Same voice.

Same Aza.

Why am I so stressed out then? There's a list of give or take fifty terrible things I keep expecting, chief among them anchors falling out of the sky and a crew of warriors bringing Aza straight back up to Magonia.

Maybe everyone spends a big part of their time afraid they're about to lose the love of their life. Maybe most people live like that and it never shows.

Not everyone's hiding an alien in their skin, obviously, but everyone's hiding something. I try to convince myself that it's normal to be this paranoid, but my life feels like I'm standing on a cliff, the camera panning out to discover Niagara Falls.

I mean, I'm okay. I'm not saying I'm not. *Pi* has been largely backgrounded in the last few months, due to a better regimen of pills. They manage anxiety loops efficiently, so I don't end up spending half of every day caught in a spiral of infinite digit recitation. I still have the kind of mind I have, though, which means I have to map out every bad eventuality and then make plans to evade said eventualities.

I used to know that the only person I'd ever love was going to die at any moment.

Now I have hope. Hope, it turns out, is problematic.

"*Hope is the thing with feathers,*" says Emily Dickinson

inside my head. *"That perches in the soul—and sings the tune without the words—and never stops at all—"*

Yeah, *the thing with feathers*. I want hope to have zero feathers. No feathers, or plumage of any sort, anywhere.

When we got back from Svalbard last year, I tried to hire someone to guard Aza's house. I wanted protection, surveillance, but that costs like $3,500 a day. I'm serious. Just for some low-rent service, the kind of thing you hire to see if someone's husband is cheating, or if someone is stealing from someone else's business. So THAT was obviously impossible. I had to do other things.

Those things are what have me sleepless these days.

In theoretical math there's a concept called the pea and sun paradox. The Banach-Tarski paradox, if official is what you want. Basically, it's the idea that you could reorganize the molecules of a pea into something the size of the sun, or the sun into something the size of a pea. The universe is elastic.

Aza is elastic.

I want her pea-close, like she is right now. But there are forces that want to turn her into the sun.

I glance at the clock. Midnight. I pull out a book of matches. "Shut your eyes," I tell her.

She does, though she makes a patented Aza Ray face at me that says I can never surprise her, because *hello*, she knows everything about everything.

Not this time.

"Hold on to this." I put something in her hand. "Over the floor, not the bed."

I strike the match, and then there's sizzling and spitting. "Open."

She opens her eyes. She's holding a sparkler in the shape of an ampersand.

"Happy birthday, Aza Ray," I say.

It sends off tiny "&" fireworks in the dark of the bedroom. The look on her face says I got it right.

&, is what I want. & more. &, &, &.

I hand Aza a little package and she opens it. A compass. A really good one, engraved with a tiny winged ship. I don't fool around when it comes to birthdays.

"It goes all directions."

"All?"

"Should work down here," I tell her. "AND up there. Just in case." It has a spinning orb in the center, with arrows pointing every possible way.

She points it at me.

She smiles. "Seriously, Kerwin?"

Yeah. So maybe I had a high-tech modification put in. So maybe north is not actually north, but *me*, all the time.

It took some doing.

Minor sensor installed under my skin.

I know, I know. Untested hackology. But once I learned I could do something like that, was I really *not* going to do it? I scoured all the clandestine message boards, and I was willing to pay for it. It was already reality, just not in the larger world.

"Just in case," I say. She looks at me. Her eyes, even in the dark, are ridiculous, ink with fire underneath.

"Where do you think I'm going?" Aza asks.

What if she just decides to go out yondering (I don't care, it should be a word) into the wild blue?

"Nowhere, but you never know. It also has a flashlight inside it," I say. "And other things. It's like . . . one of those multi-tools."

"So if I'm lost in the dark, I can always point north, turn on the flashlight, and find you?" she says.

"Correct," I say.

I've run the stats on catastrophe, and I've run the stats on love. Lost love, smashed love, messed-up love, star-crossed love. And finally, love *as* catastrophe. I'm trying to determine if the two are inevitably, inextricably linked. Thus far, my studies are inconclusive.

"So . . . ," I say.

"So," she says, and smiles at me.

"So, do you hate it?"

"Are you real right now?" she asks. "How could I hate it? In what universe could I possibly hate it?"

"Because I can return it," I say. I try to take it back. She grabs it from me.

"How do you return a compass that has YOU programmed into it as north? Do you think I want other people northing at you, Kerwin?" She looks into my face, and smiles.

"Maybe not," I say.

She kisses me hard and presses herself so close to me that there's no space between us at all. We're like two pieces of a very particular puzzle.

Optimistic data to counteract the catastrophic data: my parents are still madly in love. They chose it every day for years, even when the world felt impossible, or at least, that's what Carol said when I asked her a few months ago. Carol isn't the romantic one of my moms. Carol's the realist. Eve would tell me nice things about how love saves you from the rest of the darkness of living. Carol would never go there.

"Eve has my back," Carol told me. "Even when I'm at the hospital twenty hours a day, even when my patients are so sick that I feel like I'm failing, and I'm worrying about you at the same time—"

She gave me a Significant Look. It was ignored. I can't deal with my moms being worried about me at the same time I'm worried about the fate of the world and more particularly, the fate of Aza.

"—she can make me crazy. I can make her crazy too. But we're still here. Nobody better on earth for either of us, far as I can tell."

Carol, of course, was saying this with no knowledge of anything that'd gone on lately.

This is a universe of choosing. Aza chose me. That was a year ago, but here she still is, choosing me, climbing in my window in the middle of a dark and stormy night.

She sings very quietly, a little scrap of Magonian song. In my bedroom a tiny star appears, floating overhead. It's blue at the center and red around the edges. It's so bright I kind of can't look, except that all I want is to look at it forever.

I pull out my phone and video her song and the little star. I'm compiling records of the ways her notes bend the air, the ways Magonian sonics can shift matter.

Seems unreal at first, till you know about breaking glass with a high note, for example. You can also put out a fire with a certain kind of loud note, which displaces all the oxygen in the air. Truth.

For now, Aza's song isn't shaking the world. It's just a tiny star in my bedroom. She's getting better at singing and controlling her song.

"Why do you look like that?" she asks me.

"Because I'm in love with you, stupid," I tell her.

She runs a hand down my side and kisses me again. After a moment, I kiss her back. I try to live in that for the moment. It turns out, I can.

"I'm in love with you, stupid, too," she says.

I roll over and feel her underneath me, her hip bones and ribs and elbows. I can smell the smoke from the ampersand star I gave her, and I can see her face in the light of the Magonian star she's sung into being.

I kiss this girl who is mine because of some miracle. I keep my back to the star.

I only want to look at Aza, and try to forget she might belong somewhere that isn't with me.

CHAPTER 3

{AZA}

So—first hours of seventeen, I'm beside the person I love more than anyone else in the universe.

And, yeah, I say that with full knowledge of the size of the universe. I know the options. There's a whole sky out there, a whole starry map of minds and wings.

Jason's the only one who's ever believed everything about me without me having to convince him. The one who heard. The one who's been beside me since we were five, and who never left.

He was holding my hand when I died. He was holding my hand when I wasn't sure I was worth resurrecting, an alien, a lost singer who'd just almost destroyed all the people on earth.

He's been next to me almost since the beginning, and he'll be beside me at the end, wherever and whenever that is.

I'm thinking about Heyward. Let me stop. Let me not think about what might be starting to happen. Let me just be here—

Jason & Aza.

Just [{{   }} & {{   }}]

It's simple, that "&."

Except, it isn't.

Nothing is.

I try to medicate by putting my face into Jason's shoulder and pressing it against his skin. It's nice there, looking at the insides of my eyelids.

I could pretend that I came innocently to his bed, where I planned to sleep holding his hand, but how likely is that? We're red-blooded . . . blue-blooded . . . oh, I don't know. An indigo-blooded Magonian, and a Jason Kerwin.

Which is to say, we've been having sex for a few months now. Sex isn't quite how one thinks it's going to be when one is hearing about it and thinking that it's the ONLY CATEGORY on earth.

It's only *one* of the onlys (as opposed to *"only one of the lonelies,"* which is what I used to call myself, because hello, admittedly, drama).

I thought love + sex would = electric dizzy, some kind of mixed-up pop song, plus great poets, stomach butterflies, blushing-Christmas-morning-meets-new-museum-full-of-previously-undiscovered-flying-insects situation. But in reality, it didn't look like it was going to be any kind of triumph, the first time. There was no factoid expertise. There's no learn-one-scrap-of-information-and-pretend-you-know-everything when it comes to sex, or at least, there's not a successful version of that which ensures both parties have fun.

I knew exactly nothing about anything and neither did Jason. So, the first time, six months ago, it was . . . less than spectacular.

As in both of us were nervous—

and *ow* (mostly me with ow),

but also *ow* for him because I was SO nervous I flailed and whacked him ferociously in the nose (again, poor nose) and then we were both like SORRY I'M SORRY OH GOD VERY SORRY.

Sex is not unfraught in the first place. I had the added worry there'd be some kind of alien surprise. There wasn't. It was just your typical weird and awkward and uncertain. At least, I assume it's typical. I don't know, but probably, even given every teenage movie ever made, no one starts out with candlelight and a bed covered in rose petals, and if they do? Well, it's probably still a whole lot of kneecaps and um.

The second time we attempted, we both ended up taking a step back and asking questions of the universe because we didn't understand what we'd done differently.

It worked. It felt like a random miracle that'd never happen again.

The third time EFFORT + STUDY = SUCCESS. The hoped-for fireworks. The two of us saving each other's lives casually in the middle of the night. I know how that sounds, but sometimes it's like that.

Sex isn't always magic. That's lies. Sometimes, regardless of love and like, sex is a bike ride on a bike that has a flat tire.

Sometimes you get somewhere.

And sometimes . . .

Sometimes I think about singing—

—which wasn't the same, NO, but was . . . kind of . . . the same?

Especially singing with Dai. It was easy. It made the sky shake. It made the ocean rise.

And, unlike here, our song would never accidentally tangent off onto some long, wrong discussion about things like

FOR EXAMPLE SURELY THIS NEVER HAPPENED, the item of legend that has fallen from the sky since at least the fourteenth century, which is called star jelly.

Run-on sentence. Forgive. Only way to get that out.

Star jelly. Seriously?! No, surely no one named Jason Kerwin would ever bring that unsexiness up IN THE MIDDLE OF HOOKING UP WITH ME, and surely I would never have to stop everything in order to do internet research, because dear god. Star jelly??

Yes.

Star jelly, it turns out, is little blobs full of random, probably poisonous bacteria, which exist all the time environmentally, but are apparently activated only by rainfall. They drop to earth in globs.

Oh, there are other names for it. Star rot, anyone? Star slubber? Because that's romantic.

Or, if you speak Welsh (I do not; Jason, of course, does), *pwdre ser.* In Latin (also Jason) *stella terrae,* or star of the earth.

There's a horrific school of thought that says that shooting stars are sperm trying to impregnate the eggs of the planets, and here, I die, because in that scenario, this star jelly is . . . well. Exactly what it sounds like.

Or, how about another horrible theory?—

The boy beside me opens his eyes.

"Stop thinking, Aza Ray," he says sleepily. "I feel you thinking."

"I can't," I say. "I'm made of thinking."

So he figures out a way to, if not *stop* me, at least to put my thinking on pause. And it's a pretty perfect non-flat-tire way.

Maybe this is how love is. I don't know any other version. I try not to worry about a version in which something goes very wrong, in which we're alive and not together.

But even as we're kissing, I'm worried.

About singing.

About Heyward.

I'm worried and worried and worried.

At 5:30 a.m., as I'm slinking out of Jason's house, I run smack into his mom. Eve's sitting on the front steps drinking coffee. At least she's not Carol, Jason's other mom, whose attitude is far more depth-charged. Eve's way more accepting of the inevitability of girlfriends.

She grins at me, her precision-wicked grin, a grin that doesn't remotely belong on the face of anyone's mom. Eve has gray eyes, dark brown skin, and dreads, which she rocks in varying ways, depending on what she's doing in the world, be it talking to the UN or digging in the compost, with either cargo pants or a suit. Her expertise is the kind of thing that makes other scientists sit down and shut up, but people who don't know anything assume she's, like, a really killer gardener, rather than an expert on genetic modification, plant plagues, and world hunger strategy, among other things.

Jason comes by his brain honestly. Eve usually just factoid-slays everyone who misjudges her. And then hands them a giant organic pumpkin so they're confused all over again. The Kerwin garden is legendary.

Eve's casually like: "So, Beth, you spent the night?"

And I'm casually like: ". . ."

I didn't spend the entirety of the night in Jason's bed. Like, really, NONE of the night. Only the early morning hours. But she has the look that says we're about to have a Discussion.

"Condoms?" says Eve, and I wriggle throughout my entire hidden self. *"Protection"* is the preferred parental euphemism, hello!

"Yeah," I say. "Obviously. The prophylactics and the et cetera et cetera ET! CET! ERA!"

She looks at me for slightly longer than she should be looking. I realize I've just Aza Rayed that answer. I grab up the London accent I've been using.

"I mean . . . we're definitely using the rubbers, so . . ."

Oh god. Did I say that? Is that what I said? Where did it even come from? Why would I use that word?! Why would I add a "the" to the already wrongful term?! Why would I be hunting British birth control slang in the back of my memory and find *that*?

Eve agrees. She's giving me a look that clearly says *You Have Broken the Code of Euphemism, Dear Son's Girlfriend. Now: Further Questions.*

It's not like there hasn't been, FOR YEARS, a giant jar of condoms in the hall closet, which they pretended they weren't checking in on, so much so that when we actually did start having sex, we didn't even use any of those, but bought our own secretly on the internet.

"The Rubbers?" Eve says. "Do we need to do a review? Because, kiddo, that sounds like a band, not birth control."

I die.

Eve is staring at me, waiting for a real response.

"We're using tons AND TONS of protection," I say. This is the wrong set of words. I smile in a way that I hope is convincing, but which probably has never convinced any parent ever.

"There will be no accidental babies!"

We could have parents who'd lose their minds over this. I guess they figure it's better to have us having sex at home than, for example, in a certain person's orange Camaro.

"Without fail," says Eve, sounding exactly like Jason.

"Without fail," I repeat.

She toasts me suspiciously with her coffee cup, and I walk home, texting Jason on the way.

He texts back the woeful and unsurprising lines: *BOTH MOMS HERE NOW. IN DEPTH SEX-ED REVIEW, WITH FOOT-NOTES AND READING LIST.*

For a second, we're, like, normal people who are normally in love, and normally being suspected of sins by our parents. There's a script for this version. We both feel calmer when there's a script.

I take one last glance at the sky as I walk into my house, but even though today is Aza Ray's birthday/deathday there's nothing to suggest that today's anything but ordinary.

So why is every nerve in my body screaming that something's about to change?

CHAPTER 4

{JASON}

I scan the sky with my anomaly app before I drive to pick Aza and Eli up for school. Nothing wrong up there, or at least nothing my phone wants to report. Still, I'm on edge. This doesn't feel like any kind of birthday to me.

By which, I mean, it does.

Every birthday of Aza's has been a countdown toward something bad, and every year I've been hanging streamers and making cake. The only birthday party at which I remember feeling clueless and thus hopeful was the first one I went to, when we were five. By the time we were six, I'd learned about death, and I knew it was going to try to steal Aza from me. By the time we were seven, I'd started writing my apology list, and by the time we were fifteen, it was forty pages long. Not that I ever read it to her. Not that she ever knew.

It's not like I haven't been faking celebration all these years, while going home after every birthday dinner to scan the entirety of the internet for ways to cure someone incurable.

In some ways, freaking out about just the weather is an improvement. I've spent hours looking at old tabloids, comparing them to medical research, curiosity cabinet and freak show stuff, the horrible things that happened to people unlucky enough to be born spectacular, strange, and inexplicable.

Aza is, of course, all of the above. There are things I wish I didn't know: Magonian ships yanked out of the sky, experiments in secret government labs in the desert, Magonian bodies taken apart in the name of science. Given what Aza's told me, some of them were probably thrown off ships for the crime of being mouths to feed. And that idea cracks my heart open.

Before Magonia, Aza had no good-bye mode, but there's always a preemptive good-bye on her face now. She thinks she has me fooled, but I know she's just-in-casing. Maybe she's always ten minutes away from taking hold of a skyrope and climbing.

Fine, there are things to be nervous about. Things I seem to be unable to shake.

When the girl you love says *oh, right, this guy Dai is imprinted on me as my universally fated life and song partner* it's hard to take it in stride. I'm not a jealous guy, normally, but—

Yeah, I'm full of shit. I'm completely jealous, even when Aza Ray is in my arms.

Zal and Dai want Aza up there. I want Aza down here.

Aza wants—

Aza wants everything.

But what if everything is elsewhere?

"You look way weird," Eli says to me when she gets into the car. "Aza walked. You're late."

"You look way weird too," I tell Eli, and she snorts.

"Please. Nothing about this is weird."

Eli's wearing her uniform of perfectly symmetrical every-thing, buttoned and ironed. She's like someone unrelated to the messy chaos of Aza-now-Beth, and in reality she is, except she isn't. They're sisters. Just weird sisters.

"It's not a minor day," I tell her.

She gets it. Eli was with me on the last day of Aza's life as Aza, in the ambulance in the last moments, and she was with me at Aza's funeral too. Exactly 365 days ago, I was heading to school wearing a rental alligator, and Eli was wearing wrinkled black clothing and a crooked haircut, and both of us had broken hearts.

Eli shrugs, puts her hand on my shoulder, because actually Eli's kind in the heart, and gives me a look.

"We move forward," she says. "There is no reverse when it comes to reasonable course of action. We don't freak out, Kerwin."

I actually have to turn my head to stare at her. She sounds like she's been reading something self-help. She shrugs again.

"Yoga," she says. "And meditation. And tai chi. And a ther-apist. I had to keep Magonia a major secret, but still. Ballet and gymnastics weren't enough to deal with this. I had to do some-thing or I was gonna spend all my time staring at the sky. No one else has that problem, I'm sure."

She gives me her own version of a Significant Look. It's not fair.

"I have a new place I'm working out. You could come too, you know. Like, leave your computer behind and see the sun. Stop thinking for up to ten minutes at a time."

I'm not sure how I got roped into a friendship with my girlfriend's little sister, except that she was the only one who understood the loss and return of Aza. No one else can talk to me about it. Her parents are way too sensitive, and it's a secret from the rest of the world. Eli and I have a survivor bond. But since when does she get to shame me for being housebound?

"You're looking badly pitiful. And pallid," says Eli.

"Pallid?" I say.

"I thought I'd speak your language," she says. "Today I can actually see your brain oozing out your ears. It's not a good look. Also, you have wrinkles in your forehead that're new. You didn't have those three months ago. You look way, *way* old. You're acting like somebody's dad."

I sigh. We're in the parking lot.

"Why'd she walk?" I finally ask.

"Birthday nerves," Eli says. "Neither of you are in good form today. But you're going to have to deal. There needs to be cake later, and candles, and it needs to be amazing. Not for you, for my parents. I know you love my sister, but you aren't the only one. And you can't just worry about her all day long. You're going to make her feel suffocated."

I wince at that word choice.

"She didn't say that, did she?"

"You're supposed to be her boyfriend, not her bodyguard. Get yourself together."

Then she's out of the car and into the building. I stew a moment longer.

I'm allowed to be worried. Aza's still technically dying. Just differently, wearing a degrading skin stolen from off a Magonian ship, and who knows what, or who, this skin was meant for? Beth Marchon—the identity Aza's had since last year—is an exchange student from London in America staying at the Boyle house for the next couple years. *Little Women* reference on purpose. Aza decided Beth March, who died before her time, wrapped in a blanket she didn't ask for, should get another chance at being alive. Beth March marches on.

And if Beth happens to have a voice very much like the voice of a certain deceased Aza Ray, the London accent disguises it. There are other differences too, pretty major ones on the disguise front. Aza Ray Boyle was fish-belly white tending toward pale blue. Beth Marchon's skin is brown. As a result the past year has been full of a uniquely earth-based brand of bullshit, people reacting to her in ways I'd never have imagined.

It's been a bad education in the way the human world still sees things. Particularly bad if you'd had delusions that humanity might be okay accepting someone from Magonia. Nope. Humanity isn't even okay accepting someone from *earth*.

People have had a few things to say about the fact that we're dating. Nothing I could pin down closely as a Basic Racist Comment, but still, it's there. You can feel it. And it's not like I'm from some clueless zone. My mom Eve is black, and when I was little, walking around with her—

Let's just say I thought the world had gotten better since then. Mind you, I don't actually know which of my moms is biologically my mom. Could be either of them. My skin tone is somewhere between. That's the awesomeness of my moms for you, actual awesome, not being sarcastic. They don't care what people think. They do it their way, and I do it mine.

It's not like the history of humans is full of perfect examples of how to live. Why not invent a new way?

Magonians: same deal. Tons of things about both places, fucked up. Rostrae, after all, are up there, enslaved by Magonians. There's that, and all the ways I'm trying to figure that out. The scientific ways. The daily ways.

God. I'm on high alert for everything today.

Not only am I on high alert, I suddenly remember, I'm also in high *school*. I make my way in, passing a variety of people in the hallway, all of whom give me the look that says apparently I'm not hiding anything well today.

I pass Mr. Grimm, who's been looking at me too closely ever since last year and the lightning strike. I prefer less attention.

"Jason," he says. "Don't think no one noticed you sitting in your car. You get a pass today, but that's it. Are you sick?"

Why is he everywhere?

"I'm okay," I say, but actually—

Maybe Eli was right. I've missed two class periods by sitting in my car gnawing on the universe. I didn't even feel time passing.

Once I get into the room, I look over at Aza, who's three desks away being Beth. I discover that I have no idea what's going on in her head.

She looks happy. But not like she's thinking about me.

I wasn't thinking about her either, was I? I was thinking about everything else in the sky and sea and wilderness. I was thinking about failures on every level, and about how I don't know how to fix them.

So, we're even?

Aza's staring into space.

I'm staring into Aza.

I catch a flicker of expression on her face, her forehead crinkling, her eyes far away, and I wonder if she's talking to Caru, her heartbird, or if she's got a headache. Or, maybe, she's thinking about how to go back to her sky kingdom.

Paranoid, Kerwin. Paranoid.

I change my focus and run in-brain stats on fixing the problems between Magonia and earth. All the old-school data on skyships is still part of my collation. Centuries of reports of temperature crises, and weather meltdowns. Miracle books from the 1400s, the parts that depict rains of leaves and tendrils, and other things. Triangulating that with the activities of people on earth.

I know from super plants, at least a little bit. There's no magic food crop I've hit on that can provide enough for everyone on earth and above, not without huge vulnerabilities.

I think about, alphabetically, almonds (which require too much water), bananas, catastrophic chemicals, drought, dust, garbage patches, GMO, heat waves, ice storms, Magonia, oil spills, ozone, parasites, parch, pesticides, shrivel, whirlwinds. There are plenty of other categories in the alphabet of collapse. What if they all happened at once? What if Magonia stopped making weather?

I'm trying to pluck things that're Magonian apart from things that are earth-based, and trying to figure out how much of earth knows about Magonia. Some people definitely have known over the years.

There was a rain of something called angel hair the other

day, a shiny fiber, like a ticker tape parade, falling from the sky. The official version is that it's chaff dropped by military aircraft to keep them from being recognized on radar. The reflective strips confuse things.

According to Aza, though, it's also a thing Magonian ships do, making a cloud of tiny objects around themselves so that they don't look like ships. It's a kind of surveillance camouflage. Except Magonian ships employ Rostrae and canwr to do that job, not little showers of reflective aluminum strips. I imagine standing beneath a fall of that. Imagine the confetti of camouflage falling down over you.

More things are hidden than you'd think. Camouflaged in plain sight.

I look at Aza again, but her pen is moving quickly over her paper.

She looks human. She looks like she's mine.

I know I can trust her.

I look at her, and she's writing in the handwriting she's always had, her pen moving the way it always does, and it's her birthday.

I wish there was a support group for people dating people who aren't people.

How does that sound? Wrong. And like the reverse of some seriously weird song lyrics. But still. I have a vision of a bunch of guys whose girlfriends are Magonians, all of us sitting around a table getting a turn at saying . . .

"I'm worried every time there's a storm. Every time there's weather at all. I'm worried every time she coughs. I'm worried every time she doesn't answer the phone."

But there's no support group like that. I'm the only one in it.

Just one guy, at a table, in a room alone.

Aza glances at me. She smiles. She blows me a kiss.

And like that, I'm not the only one at the table. Aza Ray's there across from me.

Breathe, Kerwin. Keep breathing.

Despite what I told Eli, the very idea that Heyward is here fills me with nervous energy for the entire day.

Because if she's here, someone sent her.

Zal, Dai, someone else. She's an assassin by training, and a Boyle by birth. If she's here, she's here to get me.

I want to go/I don't want to go/I want to fight/I don't want to fight/I miss singing/I—

I miss Magonia.

It pisses me off that I miss Magonia, but I do. I don't want to. I want it to be nothing I'd ever want again. But.

I walk to school, because I need privacy for peering into every shadow, staring at every corner, and there's no Heyward in any of them. If she came through the school, looking the way she does, she'd be insane. She has the face of a dead girl. She'd get attention, fast.

I get to class early and call to Caru.

I seek him with my mind and—

FLASH. I'm soaring directly at the sun, stretching myself to test my speed, twisting and diving, dropping with my wings folded. My body's an unidentified flying object.

Well, not *my* body. Caru's. My heartbird's. He sings to me from Magonian skies. I sing a note back to him. For a moment, me on earth, my canwr in the sky, we make a note we can only sing together. Mine's silent. His is loud. Caru flies free, at his own speed, and with his own destinations. When he connects to me, I see what he does.

Heyward? I ask him. He doesn't answer. He's more interested in flying than in thinking about the past. I, on the other hand? Am mired. It's my birthday and everything feels wrong.

Understatement. I spend the first two class periods of my birthday in the center of wrongville. It's the weirdest and saddest feeling to have to pretend that you're someone else, when on the inside you're exactly the same Aza you always were. I'm a riddle without a solution. I've always been that, except now it's a different riddle. I was a dying girl. Now I'm an alien. Not *Name That Disease*, but *Name That Species*.

I still don't know how I'm supposed to LIVE here.

In Magonia, I was a captain's daughter with a song strong enough to change the world, but on earth, I'm Teenager. Version 1.0.

People my age are considered adults in Magonia. There, I could be a captain by now. I could be anything but what I am. Rudderless.

"BETH MARCHON! ARE YOU WITH ME?"

My teacher, Mr. Grimm, is leaning over my desk, his face a hundred kinds of no. Jason's at his desk a few seats away, and I catch a glimpse of his face. He looks as spaced out as I was.

"Beth, were you . . . *singing*? Even if I were phoning this in, teacher-wise, that'd be a pretty clear indication you weren't listening to the lecture, don't you think? Are you planning to be part of this classroom's activities or are you starting an a cappella group? If it's the latter, perhaps you can make your way down the hall."

Um. Wow.

"Yes, hi, I'm here. Sorry. That was an accident."

"Don't let it happen again," says Grimm.

I still like Mr. Grimm. He's as weird as ever, that PE teacher look with a brain like a steel trap. I should know better than to drift off into the Caru-zone while I'm in his classroom. He notices.

"I'm back."

The class looks at me like I'm wrongness personified, but that's nothing new, not in this body or the former one. I have to have some sympathy. *They* haven't been flying with a heartbird. They've been stuck here on earth.

"Quiz," says Grimm.

"Pencils up!" I say, sounding a bit too Aza Ray.

Grimm sighs, and says, "Beth, maybe we can spare the lip."

Grimm has his back to me at the board, so I slip back into Caru's flight. A big pod of squallwhales pass, and I look at their gray spines as they sing their rain up toward me and down again into the world below. I'm light and strong, my feathers sleek, my wings cupping the wind, and I glide, easily. The air carries me.

This isn't confusion.

This is simple, the kind of flight Caru's wings were made for, and with him, I'm weightless.

I occasionally ask Caru to fly over Maganwetar, the capital, to confirm Zal's imprisonment, but not today. Today he goes wherever he pleases. My heartbird, no matter how strong he is, is damaged. Years in isolation with no partner left him *touched*. And touchy.

And I—

I'm damaged too.

I didn't grow up knowing how to sing with Caru. We have to make it up as we go. His bond was with my mother, but it was torn away as a punishment for her first attempt to drown the world.

Mind you, that didn't keep her from trying again—with me.

A canwr can't be without a match with which to sing. Caru spent fifteen years screaming to himself in a cage, and now he has to fly fast to keep himself from remembering the dark.

So, we're a pair.

He's shown me nests on rocky cliffs, and high ice caves at the edge of the sky. He's shown me an airkraken—a fog-topus with long, smoky tentacles, and a few flying things I have no words for.

Our atmosphere is alive. Each bit of weather created by something breathing. I wish humans, any humans, had known it sooner. Everything could have been different.

I get another quick flash of a sunset somewhere, the clouds scarlet, and Caru's path through them, lit as he sings. Even though there're things wrong in the world, there are things to be grateful for. This is one of them.

I pick up my pencil, pull out my paper, and focus myself on the realities of being on this earth, quiz-taking, even if Caru's out spinning through a sunset.

"A song sung in the Forest of Arden," says Grimm. "Lyrics. Go."

Interesting choice. Luckily, I've got this. I scratch them

in a furious scribble. Shakespeare wrote a lot about birds and weather. I like his storms especially. What was Shakespeare doing with his life that he came up with this kind of material? No one knows. So who's to say *he* wasn't wandering on a skyship?

> *Under the greenwood tree*
> *Who loves to lie with me,*
> *And turn his merry note*
> *Unto the sweet bird's throat,*
> *Come hither, come hither, come hither:*
> *Here shall he see*
> *No enemy*
> *But winter and rough weather.*

Mind you, *I* have some definite enemies, but today I sit at my desk and try to forget them. Outside the sky's gray and full of beautiful monsters, but in here it's warm, and everyone around me is writing.

I have a family who loves me. I have a boyfriend who loves me. I should be grateful.

I glance over at him.

North.

He's looking out into space, not back at me.

For a moment, inaudibly, my heartbird and I sing together, right here in the middle of the usual. Actually silently this time. We sing a quick storm, enough to drench a dry field. Magonia and earth could work together, and why the hell don't they? Rain + fields = crops. Crops + Magonia = happiness.

Instead, everyone down here is clueless and everyone up there is scared of/hates "the drowners." It's stupid. But on earth, no one shares. Half the world starves. Apparently sentient creatures have selfishness and fear in common across the universe.

Caru trills, and I get a flash of his flight beside a squallwhale, his wings tucked to his sides, the rain created by our song pouring over his falcon head.

I close my eyes and feel his pleasure. He scans the horizon, and far out at the edge, there's a black dot, very small at first, and then larger. I can't figure out what it is. Some kind of bird?

Something about it gives me a chill, and I tell Caru to stay away.

It moves in a tilted, jerking way, and then Caru banks with the squallwhale and I lose sight of it again. Just clouds and stars as the vision fades.

I shudder. Whatever that was, it wasn't anything I liked. *Be careful*, I sing silently to Caru, but he is too busy flying to respond.

I'm left with a feeling of edginess that's nothing reasonable. Caru's tough. He takes care of himself. He fights better than anything else in the sky.

So why am I on edge?

I know why. You don't have a birthday like my last one and feel calm the next time that day comes around. It's normal that I feel like this. Nothing weird about it.

I wonder for a second, though, if I should've gotten Caru to fly over Zal's prison. Just to check.

But somehow, I don't do it.

Instead, I turn to Jason and blow him a kiss, trying to

ground myself back in this world.

I just barely keep myself from blowing him not a kiss, but a tiny storm cloud.

But I don't. I'm in control.

CHAPTER 6

{JASON}

After school, Aza takes off.

"If you love something set it free," says my brain, so annoyingly, quoting off of some poster I saw when I was seven in a dentist's office, so I let her go and pretend it's not a thing. I've been off my game all day, worried, sleepless, stressed out, taking risks I shouldn't take. Distracted by the sky.

I got busted in Grimm's class for tracking mass bird deaths. Whole flocks falling, a combination of news alerts and radar. It's not bird flu. It's just death. Sometimes it's flocks that get unlucky, and end up in rocket or jet paths, but thousands of blackbirds fell from the sky six hundred miles from here this morning, and I went through every record, trying to find out why.

Could be some loser setting off fireworks near a roosting flock.

Or.

There are other things in the category of rains of birds. It rained red in Kerala, India, in 2001, and again in 2012. Apparently there was a terrestrial algae bloom in the sky, like a red tide, but cloud-based instead. Every time I think about it, there's science, and then there's Magonia.

The yellow rain political incident that took place in the early 1980s? Just like it sounds, except that it was—maybe—a battle between the US and Russia over chemical weapon supplies. When the yellow rain, which fell all over Laos and Cambodia beginning in 1975 was analyzed, it was discovered to be honeybee crap. That's the official story. It's never been unclassified.

So . . . maybe it was Magonian. And the governments, various, are just covering their collective asses.

These are the things I think about these days. I think about ways that Magonian poisons might be hidden in earth rainstorms. How easy it would be to take us, the mostly unsuspecting populace, out in pretty much exactly the way Aza's mother intended.

Good thing I wasn't the one fighting for the other side.

Grimm came up behind me as I was plotting the whole thing on my tablet, and he looked at it with way too much interest. It's graphs and grids, and mostly encoded, but . . .

"Special project, Kerwin?"

I mean, it wasn't like anyone but me would understand what I was looking for.

"Yeah, for science," I claimed.

It *was* scientific. Unfortunately it also had a variety of images of strange birds found dead in various places around the globe.

Grimm leaned forward, pointing at one of the images.

"What kind of bird is that exactly?" he asked.

It's a video of something part bird, part human, made by me with input from Aza, and a whole lot of entry-level CGI. She wanted me to understand the Rostrae. I edited an eagle together with a skydiver. She told me I got pretty close. It's amazing what you can make with basic software and a brain.

"Nothin'. Just foolin' around," I said, using a voice that could not have been more unlike my real voice. Far more in the 1950s sitcom category than the Kerwin category. "I'm working on it with Az—with Beth."

Sleep deprived. Mistakes made. Grimm walked away with the sympathy face on, and I vowed to be more careful. Not a good thing to slip like that. Not a good thing at all. No one wants a drama involving guidance counselors, parent calls, god forbid, the *school nurse*. Not on Aza's birthday.

Eli takes one look at me after school and says, "Nope."

She hijacks me to her version of working out, directing me to the edge of town, where she's found a tree with several perfectly straight limbs. I don't like it here already. It's right down the hill from the cemetery—the one where Aza was, but really wasn't, buried. It's also where I last saw Heyward.

"What?" I ask. "You couldn't go to an actual gym? Those exist, you know."

"Gyms are indoors," she says. "You need sunlight. You're like a plant dying without photosynthesis."

"I'm not a plant. I'm a person. Don't we have birthday stuff to do?"

"You're totally transparent, Kerwin," she says. "You're having a brain melt."

She gets out of the car and runs to her tree. Two seconds later, she's flipped upside down into the branches. She pokes her head out of the leaves.

"Climb out of your skull, sister's boy," she shouts.

"That's not yoga," I shout after her.

"You don't know how to do yoga anyway," she says.

I consider doing the sole pose (crane) that I learned purely to taunt Aza, but why? She's right.

"Look," she says. Eli hangs by her fingertips from a branch, and swings. She's freakishly strong and nimble. She reminds me of last year, of Heyward, and no wonder. They're biologically sisters.

Eli is benign, of course. Well, mostly.

Heyward, on the other hand, is an assassin. Or, at least, almost.

Eli's swinging on the branch like it's a bar, and she flips herself up and over into a handstand in the middle of a tree. The Boyle sisters, all three of them, two human, one not, are nothing if not capable.

"Eli," I say.

"Yeah," she says, upside down.

"I'm never going to do that."

"You need to do *something*," she says, swinging back down the other direction. "You're OCD on toast."

I shrug. "This is not news."

"Do you tell Aza what's going on in your head? Do you tell her how much you remember about her dying?"

"No," I say. "It's too terrible to talk about. I've been lying about it since it happened."

"I don't either," she says. "I do this instead. This one's called Midnight. I invented it."

She flips upside down again, into an in-tree, straight-up handstand that pretends there are no ships in the sky, no rains of birds, no polluted squallwhales, no enemy captains, no entire other civilization trying to kill us all.

"You spend too much time worrying," she says.

"Either way, there's no way I could ever do what you're doing," I say, granting her the admiration she deserves. She's an athlete, and she's good. Never mind that she's kind of inventing a sport.

"You might be able to do a modified version," she says hopefully.

"I might also be able to fly," I say.

Eli rolls her upside-down eyes, reminding me totally of Aza, and simultaneously shaming me into realizing my poor choice of words.

She swings down and looks at me.

"Look, reality. I just want another person strong enough," she says. "If they come for her. This time, we know about them. I'm not letting her go. Not again."

For a second I see Eli's worry right there on the surface. That's rare.

Then it's gone and I watch her do her whole routine on the branches, running along them barefoot to train for balance. I've seen the Breath—humans integrated into Magonia, either kidnapped from earth as babies, or rarely, adult defectors into the sky—with almost supernatural abilities. Heyward's one of them. Eli's apparently been doing her own version of Breath training out here in this field.

Okay then. We all deal differently.

I watch her kick the ass of an imaginary enemy for a while, out in this freezing field. Who but Eli works out outside in the winter? I'm huddled in my coat and hat, hunched against the wall that borders the field, thinking dark thoughts about Dai and Magonia, about fate and freak-outs.

"Up," says Eli, and I realize I'm so exhausted that I've

managed to pass out right here, completely by accident. Not a good sign. "I'm done."

"I'm awake," I say.

"Better be. You have to make a birthday cake," she says. "And one day, you'll be up in that tree with me. Mark my words."

"One day," I say, but. This is who I am. The back of my brain twitches around everything, just the way Eli's body does. We both just want to keep everyone safe. Different kinds of gymnastics.

So we get into my car, and drive. That's apparently as good as it's going to get today. It's okay. I can stay in this limbo state. I certainly have before. When I wasn't sure of Aza's feelings, I was like this 24/7, scratching notes on every surface, imagining scenarios of rejection, and never trying to plan a future with us both in it.

When we pull into the Boyle driveway, Aza's sitting on the steps wearing that flight suit. Still no clue where it came from, but it's perfect. It has a fur collar. She looks very Amelia Earhart, which gives me a qualm, which qualm I banish.

She waves at me, but her face says she's still as far away as she's been all day.

"You clearly just got carried here by a parade and nine ponies," Eli says to her.

Aza comes back to life, but in a bluish way.

"Only eight ponies," she says.

"You need cake. Both of you do. I can't be the only happy person on this birthday. Someone is gonna start baking said cake, posthaste, because there can be no more of this. Hear me," Eli says as she makes her way into the house, giving me a look.

I sit down next to Aza instead.

"Give it up," I say. "If you try to tell me you're fine, you're only going to prove to me you're not."

"I'm okay," she says, not in her most convincing voice.

"What happened?" I ask.

She sighs.

"Eli told me one of her friends thought they saw me yesterday. Meaning *me* me. Heyward."

I'm instantly on fire. How did I not know this? Who failed? Everyone? Definitely Eli, because Eli should have told me.

"But I've been all over, looking, this morning, and afternoon, and she's nowhere. If she were here, there'd be a Breath ship nearby. There's not."

"That's true," I say. No disturbances. But there are plenty of other ways Heyward could be here. Breath don't travel only by ship. She could've hitchhiked from some drop-off fifty miles from here. Breath are human. They're not limited by our atmosphere.

The last time I saw Heyward, she just showed up, no storm, no lightning, no thunder, just an Aza doppelgänger at my door, who quickly tried to exterminate me.

"How would *you* know if there were Breath ships overhead?" Aza asks, her forehead crinkled.

Oops.

I can't actually see Magonian ships with my normal eyesight. Not anymore. But I make do.

"I wouldn't," I say. "I just assumed. No major cloud cover."

Right now I need to make sure Aza doesn't go out hunting for her enemy in a panic. Panic breeds mistakes. If Heyward's down here, Aza's not safe.

"I think someone was probably imagining things, when

they said they saw Heyward." I attempt this line of reasoning to see if she lets me.

"Maybe," she says.

If Heyward's here, I have about forty things to do. Emergency prep. I have to—

What if Aza wants to go with her?

I swallow hard.

"What if . . . ?" comes out of my mouth. For one second, I think I might tell her everything I know, everything I've learned. I don't.

"What if what?"

"Nothing," I say. She looks at me hard, but I'm not saying anything else.

Okay, then.

It's not like I don't plan for things I can't achieve. I've only been planning Aza's future since she didn't have one. I don't let her see my face. I look out at the street. You have to be careful who you let see the deepest worries, the darkest fears. Your secrets.

"I've got you," I say, not looking at her. She'll see what I'm thinking. I hold her freezing hand instead. "I'm with you. It's going to be okay."

"How do you know?"

"This isn't nothing, you and me, here together. If we can be here, other miracles can happen too."

Aza swallows. I turn my head and she's looking at me, really looking.

I add, "You're still my favorite thing about being alive."

"Really?"

"Really." I take a second, because . . . why is she asking me that? I bring it back to our own version of discussion. As much as I don't want to ask this—"Do I hold horrors for you?"

She takes a second.

"No," she says. "You're my favorite thing about being alive too, and that's mostly because you're going to make me some kind of amazing cake. Yes?"

She gives me a look that's one part attempt at reasonably fine, no one here is stressed about anything, people are thinking only of celebration. The rest is silently pleading with me not to make her talk about any of this anymore. I know this look. It's the look she used to give to people who asked her what it felt like to be sick.

I provide her with what she wants.

I pretend it's fine.

She's up and going through the door before I even realize it. There's something about her that tells me she's lying to me, and there's something about me that tells me I'm also lying to her.

I know what *I'm* lying about, because before I follow Aza inside, I pull out the second phone she doesn't know I have.

And I send a text.

CHAPTER 7

{AZA}

When I get into the house, my mom's rocking out in the living room to something she's playing for my dad, and my dad's cracking himself up by making terrible jokes at her. I feel like I'm on the other side of thick glass.

All I want to do is hide from the people I love.

To spare them the thing I know is coming. I feel it. Both from outside, and inside of me.

Then, my mom: "Did you know that mice sing?"

Me (with effort): "Is that what you're playing? Mouse song?"

It sounds like electronic music, but apparently it's rodent in origin. It has a beat. Someone's added something to the little trills and whistles, and I don't even know what to do with that.

My mom: "This is like the mouse equivalent of . . . Barry White."

Me: *raises eyebrows*

My mom: "It's true. Mouse seduction. The mice in the kitchen? Are probably getting it on right now."

If she starts talking about mouse condoms—

No. My mom mimics the mouse song at my dad, who mimics it back at her, and the two of them dissolve into the snorting laughter of people who've cracked each other up since the Jurassic.

Okay, then, unrelated Henry and Greta parental hijinks.

I've been MIA all afternoon, prowling for Heyward. Giving her a chance to show herself. Nothing. Not a trace, not a sign, no one. No Breath ships above.

Am I uneasy? Yes. Hair standing up on the back of my neck? Absolutely. But no Heyward, so I'm just here, full of foreboding.

The mouse wooing song sounds like Magonia to me, like a flock of tiny strange birds.

I think about my childhood, sitting on the roof looking at constellations, hearing . . . something. And the reality, the crazy, crazy reality, that I was looking at my home, and that people from up there were trying to look back. Searching for me.

Maybe that's how everything is. Maybe everyone is looking for everyone.

That 52-hertz whale song Jason found online a few months ago at first made me way too sad. It made me think of injured squallwhales and acid rain.

Now though, I wonder—what if that whale, the "loneliest whale in the world," is just, like, a really good singer? Maybe it's a soloist, and so no one interrupts it. Maybe it sings an incredible, spellbinding song that no one else can sing.

I mean, maybe it's like me, a weirdo in the world.

Maybe the lonely whale is flying through a dark ocean, making things out of water and salt, singing shipwrecks into statues. Maybe it's changing matter around, rather than singing in sorrow. Maybe it's something Magonian dropped down, fallen into the ocean, singing alone because the sky is out of reach.

My poor parents. I did the reverse of that whale, if it's

Magonian, anyway. I rose up into the sky.

I think my dad never believed I died. He's the one who spent most of my childhood with me in the hospital. Maybe he had to be a dreamer in order to manage being next to me in ambulances all the time. Otherwise, it would have been too terrible.

"What do you think it'd be like to ride a whale?" he asked me once, when I was still Aza the dying girl and he was my dad holding my hand in an emergency room, waiting for someone to help me stop coughing.

"I don't know," I said.

"I think it would be like riding a zeppelin," he said.

"It wouldn't be like that at all," I said, coaxed. "I think it would be like hopping a fast train, but underwater."

"So, like hopping a submarine?"

"Yes," I said.

"What if we took off out of this hospital and became rail-riding submarine hobos?" my dad asked.

"We'd drown," I said.

"Never," he said. "You have no idea what we'd do. We'd wear diving suits, and the whole time we were under, I'd be the envy of every other creature in the ocean."

"Why?"

"Because I'd be traveling with the whale-hitchhiking submarine queen of the depths."

"And who would that would be?"

"My daughter. Obviously. I mean, if that daughter was willing to take me with her. I've got no experience whale-hopping."

I rolled my eyes, but I was obsessed with my dad's stories, anytime, every time, falling out of his mouth like he was basically just one long string of yarn. It's no surprise that when I came back from Magonia, my dad took almost no time at all to believe in me.

My mom, on the other hand, is the science in our house.

She took blood samples when I returned from Magonia, and all the oddities of previous Aza Ray were still in my blood. Different skin, same freak. All the weirdnesses of previous Aza Ray, the tilted wishbone of a solar plexus, the heart sideways—

The things everyone categorized in my last body as Azaray Syndrome? X-ray Beth Marchon and she looks exactly the same. That didn't stop my mom from doing some research.

My mom spent the past fifteen years developing this mouse thing, trying to cure asthma, but also giving the drug she'd developed to me. Completely illegal, my mom's activities, and when we finally talked about it, she looked at me for a long time, and then she said, "If you ever had a kid and she was sick, nothing would keep you from trying to keep her safe. I would do it again. And much, much more."

Did I mention that my mom is a badass? Did I mention that her team looks likely to get nominated for the Nobel Prize for the breath-holding mice? They might actually be curing asthma, and along with that, they might be making something that protects humans from inhaling toxins, enabling lungs to retain oxygen for long periods of time. Some of the drugs my mom's team has been working on deal especially with inherited diseases, but they have side effects for everyone else too, and who knows? A lot of the things on earth that could go wrong aren't immunological now, but warfare. My mom's team is making it so people's immune systems can be better able to respond to threats.

My parents. They've always believed in miracles, and I'm

not sure why. I've actually *seen* the impossible. They haven't. Or if they have, I don't know about it.

If Heyward is down here, I'm worried about them too. She'd kill them, if she was assigned to do that—

Uneasiness twitches around my back brain. Every kind. But what am I supposed to do? Be paranoid all the time?

Here's my completely warranted other fear: my parents want Heyward back. I can tell. That's why I don't want them to know anything about her maybe being down here. Magonia poisoned her against humankind. She wants nothing to do with drowners. Even the ones who are her biological parents.

Sometimes I catch my mom standing out in the yard, looking up. I can't blame her. I feel like the Aza she's wanted has always been, for one reason or another, just out of reach.

My dad has this feeling too, but he's calm about it. He thinks his other daughter is coming home. He has a feeling. Won't say why, won't say how, but he has a feeling. That's my dad for you.

Said dad is currently standing on a ladder, hanging streamers he made in my honor. He's been obsessed with sailors' knots ever since I returned, but he can't quite get the hang of them. He made a long garland of net out of gold glitter yarn, so it's not exactly supposed to catch anything, but my dad sees me walk past and throws an anchor over my shoulder.

As he throws it, I get an unexpected FLASH of Caru. There's a whirring sound, a hum from far off in the sky, and I feel Caru's curiosity, his interest.

There's something about the whirr that sounds familiar to me. I try to focus, but Caru isn't having it. My heartbird's looking at a Magonian naval ship in the far-off distance, the bat-sail stretched wide, and he's singing to it. There's strangeness in the batsail's song. Is it fear? It's intense, almost a painful sound to the song, something that grates against my ears, just for a second. But I can't figure out what it is, what kind of voice that might be.

Caru jets in the direction of this ship, and I see something just on the edge of my view, a fast black something, diving at the batsail.

The batsail shrieks in fury, and Caru is in pursuit—

"Aza," says my dad.

"What?"

"Are you listening to me?"

"No," I say, but that's done it, the connection's gone. I wrest myself out of the sky and pick up the "anchor" off my shoulder. It's made of chocolate, with a folded paper chain.

"Seriously?" I tell him, trying to sound normal.

"I took a class," he tells me. "What am I supposed to do with this knowledge except make terrible things for my daughters' birthdays?"

My dad used to be the worst cook in creation. In the last year, maybe because I ate a whole lot of birdseed-ish granola stuff aboard *Amina Pennarum*, my dad's cooking has either gotten better, or I've gotten more inclined.

Eli's hanging up a banner that says AZA RAY VERSION 2.0.

We look like a perfect family.

If you don't know about any of the things that make us Other.

I move to the kitchen and lurk there with Jason. That

vision from Caru—I try to get back in touch with him, but he's sending nothing.

I stare at the mice in their terrarium, watching them dive and hold their breath. Watching them run around in little mouse circles, all of them mutants.

You're experiments, I think. *Someone's experimenting on you.* I feel like someone's experimenting on me too. Like there's a large someone up there, moving my heart around, seeing how far it can stretch.

Jason sits down opposite me, cake spatula in his hand.

"Going to say any words at all?" he asks me.

"Words." I bite the insides of my cheeks.

I sing a Caru note again, but he doesn't respond.

With a flick of Jason's wrist my cake's painted with a ridiculously gorgeous version of the sky. The bottom, just above where it touches the plate, is full of constellations. The center of the cake already has a ship and a stormshark, surprising given Jason's experience with stormsharks. I wouldn't have thought he'd want to think about them again.

"I know it's selfish to be weird about my birthday when you had to actually plan my funeral," I say. "But my birthday has always been weird. And now, Heyward. And . . . Caru keeps seeing something strange out in the sky somewhere. What if—"

Jason makes a squallwhale with a few scriggles of frosting. It's pretty good. It has a nicely articulated storm spine.

"I think I'm gonna go out later and just . . . see."

Jason looks up and his eyes flash something I've never seen before.

"You're not going anywhere," he says.

Then he's looking at the cake again and I'm not sure I even

heard that. He draws a wicked line of lightning down the center of the cake. It's like Van Gogh doing pastry. He leans over, kisses me, and lifts my cake. . . .

But—did he just kiss me and dismiss me?!

Did he just *order* me not to go looking for Heyward? Did that really just come out of his mouth? I feel something rising up in me, something about how he doesn't know, doesn't understand—

And then my parents and Eli walk in, my dad blowing a noisemaker.

Here we all are, around the table in the dark, this glowing circle, and my family's singing "Happy Birthday." The candles are lit, and there're seventeen of them.

For the first time in years, my wish doesn't have to be *please, let me live*.

I close my eyes, grit my teeth, and blow the candles out. When I open them, Jason's watching me. I can't read the look on his face.

I cut the cake, slicing through the ship in the center, and giving him the piece with the squallwhale. I give each of my parents some clouds and Eli a stormshark. I give myself a piece of sky with nothing in it, so I can imagine Aza Ray Quel on my piece, and Caru singing with her.

So I can imagine everything I can't have.

Later, I walk Jason to his car, and we look out at the sky together, thinking our own thoughts, maybe the same, maybe not. I can see Magonia, because Magonia's everywhere. No Caru, but also no visible badness. A catamaran moving dozily across the clouds. A small pod of squallwhales, too far away to hear their songs. The moon's full and yellow, and I almost cry, but I don't.

"Shooting star," Jason says abruptly, and points. We both watch it arc across the sky, shockingly bright. It could be a message from one Magonian captain to another, or maybe it's just a piece of rock hurtling through the atmosphere. Sound and fury signifying zilch.

"What's going on with you? Really. What aren't you telling me?" Jason says, his left eyebrow so on point that I can't evade it. I feel like his brain has bored a hole in mine, and now he's wandering through all the skull passageways that, for anyone else, would only be accessible with six sets of keys and a series of increasingly arcane lock combinations.

Okay, then. Look at my soul if you want to look at it. It's a pissed-off soul.

I let loose. "Are you ordering me around on purpose?"

"What do you mean?"

"*You're not going anywhere*, I quote. Let me just say, if I was going anywhere, it'd be my business. Even if I *was* going to see if I could find Heyward."

I don't know why I'm so irritated. Jason can be obnoxious. This is a thing I know. I can also be obnoxious. But there's something in the way he's been lately, something about how he's like . . .

So convinced he knows what's good for me. How does *he* know? I don't even know. But the more he acts like he knows everything about my future happiness, the more I'm like, THERE MAY BE DEVELOPMENTS.

"You don't know what Heyward's like," he says.

"I don't? You mean I didn't have a giant battle with her last year? On a ship? Apparently it wasn't me who did that. Wait, was it you?"

"I spent more time with her than you did," he says. "She tried to KILL *me*."

Yeah, I want to say. She tried to kill me too. But I nearly turned her to stone *using only my voice*. If anyone's got the skills to fight her, it's me. I compromise.

"Maybe I want to find her because I'm worried she might try that again, on you, on Eli, on my parents. Did you think of that, or did you just think I wanted a random adventure?"

Jason relents.

"Please," he says. "Just . . . don't go looking for her tonight."

I feel prickly all over. "Should I just sit here and wait for her to show up and hurt someone I love?"

"Maybe we should tell someone?"

"What *someone* would that be?"

"The authorities. There must be someone who could help."

I stare at Jason. "WHAT *authorities*? Which ones? The ones in charge of Magonia? No one down here knows there's anything up there! Seriously? You want us to get hauled into some psych ward? Because that's what'd happen. Or they'd just think we were hoaxing again. We've hoaxed before, Kerwin."

"Maybe things are changing up there," he says. "The world's shifting, Aza Ray, all the time."

And, oh, *OH*, that just pisses me off. Boysplaining.

"You're such a cynic," he says, and touches my cheek. I barely keep myself from biting his finger. "You have too many factoids, too many details, too much wiki."

I sing furiously out to Caru. More nothing.

"He's probably just flying out of range," Jason tells me. He knew exactly what I was doing. I feel a snarled kind of despair.

Jason takes my hand. "It's going to be okay."

"It's already not okay," I say, and I shudder, because my own words remind me of dying in an ambulance, Eli crying to my mom, that same sentence coming out of Eli's mouth, me in the middle of leaving.

Déjà vu all over again.

Happy birthday, Aza Ray.

Am I mad at him? I can't tell. Is he mad at me? I can't tell. We're not looking at each other. We stare out at the sky.

"Don't go looking for her tonight," Jason says. "Promise?"

"What if she's down here? Do you think I can just let her—"

"Aza," he says.

"What?"

"Don't do it. Promise me."

"You're not in charge of me," I say, and my voice gets a little out of control. "I'm not a project you're running. I'm not an experiment!"

Jason looks at me, and his face is exhausted. "Please," he says. "I can't lose you again. I'd die. Okay? I'd die."

I wonder about everything.

"Fine," I say, after a minute.

I pull out my compass as he's driving away. It points north despite him driving east. I almost text him to say something about that, but I don't, because that suddenly pisses me off too. I just wait for his taillights to go, thinking *we've never done this before, pretended it was fine when it wasn't.*

I go back into my quiet house, with my sleeping family, my flight suit still on.

I'm curled up in a nervous, angry, fully dressed ball in the middle of my bed a few hours later, when FLASH!

Caru shrieks into my heart, into my lungs, and I gasp. Ropes, whipping out, things that are birds and aren't, black wings. Caru's screaming. Tangled.

NO, NETTED.

Caru's caught, twisted into a harsh, thorny net, and he's terrified. I'm off the bed in agony, unable to do anything. I look through Caru's eyes and I see—

OH NO, NO, NO.

It's Dai. His face is contorted. Indigo skin, new tattoos. White ones, lightning strikes up and down each of his arms, the rigging of a ghost ship on his back as he spins to reel Caru in.

Dai looks back at me, through Caru, and I swear, I swear he can feel me here. He knows he has my heartbird. He has my heart.

Blackness. Caru's nightmare, being caged in the dark again. He's been hooded.

He screams something at me, to me. *Where the air is mad! Where the wild birds are!*

Then the vision ends. I'm in the dark too, in my room, shaking, and I don't know what Caru meant.

I'm panting, gasping, tears streaming down my face.

All that *zugunruhe* meant something. I was at the top of my cage, and the world was spinning out there. My body could feel something. Magonia is calling me back.

I have to get to Caru, NOW. I'm up and stuffing things

frantically into the pockets of my flight suit, compass, little knife—

A sound from outside my window jolts me.

I turn, but I'm not fast enough. Someone's here. All in black. Face covered. More than one someone.

Heyward? A team of Breath? That's who it has to be.

One sound is all I get. There's a hand over my mouth, and I bite, but there's nothing but glove between my teeth as someone gags me with tape.

I get my fists up, try to get my knee up and stamp my foot backward.

Whoever has me makes a sound of pain, but still heaves me over their shoulder.

The tape tugs at the skin around my mouth and I wonder if it's ripping off my skin, if they'll yank off the tape and reveal half my Magonian face. My wrists are jammed together. I'm bent like a broken bird, and we're out and down the back stairs.

Frozen crunching footfalls, a car door, open, a car trunk, open.

They put me inside the trunk, shove my knees painfully up to my chest, put a cloth over my nose and press it hard to my face. I don't inhale. I don't inhale, I don't inhale—

But they cover my mouth, and I choke on bitterness, gasp, breathe it in. I feel myself tilt suddenly, like I'm shrinking down into the smallest version of me, a version that's voiceless, screamless, Aza-less.

They slam the trunk down as the world swims around my eyes. They start the engine.

I don't know where I'm going. I don't know why.

I'm in the dark again, this time without a song to save me, and then the dark is everything I see, everything I know, the inside of my skull a room I'm trapped inside.

I'm seventeen and I'm missing.

CHAPTER 8

{JASON}

I'm as miserable as Aza is when I leave her house. I bring my other pair of glasses out of my pocket. Just glass. No prescription.

Well, not *just* glass. These are special. Just like the other phone, Aza has no idea I have these. I can see Magonian vessels through them, squallwhales, and more. Nothing crazy up there. Nothing I can *see*, but that doesn't change my suspicion. I send another emergency text. If Heyward's here, I don't have much time.

I'm frenzy-clicking buttons on my phone, working my way through coordinates and patterns, making things make sense, possible trajectories. By the time I get home I'm nearly flat with exhaustion and confusion. It's not even that far between our houses, but getting through twenty-four hours of birthday has left me messed up. Fighting with Aza has left me wrecked.

We never fight.

Does she think she's the only one here who's in charge of anything? Does she think she's the only one with responsibilities?

I stumble up the stairs, pausing only to greet my moms, who are curled on the couch watching a documentary about black holes. Of course they are.

"Condoms," says Carol.

"Condoms," says Eve.

This is exactly the wrong moment to say that to me.

"You do know it's Aza's birthday, right?" I say, and both of them flinch.

"Of course," says Eve.

"It's only been a year," I say. "A year isn't very long."

They come to me on the stairs, their faces full of niceness, full of grief.

I don't know why I do this. They don't know anything about what I know, Aza-wise. I'm just making them feel bad. I want someone to feel bad for me. It's perverse, but it's true. I feel miserable, and like no one even notices, because Aza won't let me tell her anything about anything.

"We were talking about Aza tonight," says Carol.

"About how when you took off to her birthday party, that first year, and we thought you'd been kidnapped—" says Eve.

"Not your best moment," says Carol. "But then again, not your worst. Early warning for the kind of kid you were going to be."

"I remember seeing you at the roller rink, in your alligator suit, and thinking, oh no, this one's got his own dreams," says Eve. "There'll be no controlling him."

"What dream did you think I had?" I ask, curious in spite of myself.

"At the time I thought maybe you were going to be an Olympic ice-skater or something," she says. "But that's what's weird about having kids."

"What?"

"They're themselves from the beginning. You think you

know what they'll do, but you don't. You think you can predict everything based on your own self, but then they're weird in their own ways."

"Not that you're at all weird," says Carol, and gives me a particular look that says *ha!*

"I came from weird stock," I say.

"You did," says Eve, and laughs. "This is a house of weird people who love you."

"We loved Aza too," says Carol, putting her hand over mine. "We did a toast to her tonight."

"If she was your dream, she was a good one," says Eve. "But I promise, baby, you'll find love again. There's lots of love in the world."

Which makes me cry, because even if I can't tell them what's going on, they get me, at least.

My moms both hug me. For a second, I feel like nothing can drop out of the sky and make a disaster in the middle of my life. There are no skyships and no Breath climbing down anchor chains. There's only me, and my parents, and we're totally safe here in our living room.

For now.

The second I get upstairs, I turn on my tablet, open about nine apps, and wait.

I'm years behind on sleep. I get like three hours a night, which is not enough, but what else am I supposed to do when I'm keeping track of everything that's happening everywhere in every time zone? Not just on the earth, but in the sky?

I turn on the video feed to Aza's house.

Video feed. Secretly placed cameras. All kinds of dishonest.

There are things no one knows but me. And then there are the things a few other people know too.

Facts I never told Aza, volume one. Three nights after we got back from Svalbard I walked out of Aza's house and saw a black car.

"Get in," said the guy I'd met at the airport in Longyearbyen.

I jumped a fence, crashed into a mailbox, and ran. The car pulled alongside me. When I tried to dial 911 I discovered my signals were jammed.

"What do you want?"

"I'm picking you up. You've been summoned," said the guy at the wheel.

Summoned. Like this was a world of kings. Like I was going to be a knight. Turned out, it wasn't so different. Knights never had a lot of power either. Swords for hire.

SkyWatch Assessment Bureau, SWAB for short. Government agencies, for all that they're completely unfunny in myriad ways, tend to have a warped sense of humor, the secret super-nerd kind.

It's an agency in charge of watching skyships. *Swab the decks, matey.* Therefore, SWAB.

SWAB has been looking upward for a very long time. They were looking other places too, all over the internet, at people accessing information, and the way I was searching for Magonia-related topics, the particular groupings I was using, meant—

Well, it meant I knew things I wasn't supposed to know.

SWAB had video of what Aza did in Svalbard: singing a flood that began to turn the island into the ocean, that cracked the seed repository open, that could've ended everything.

The agency saw all the things I thought no one saw.

I was terrified they were going to take Aza, and if not them, that Magonia was going to take her instead.

And so SWAB knew exactly how to get me to do what they wanted me to do.

They offered me her safety in exchange for her secrets. *Tell us everything, listen to everything, report everything, and we'll protect her.* Devil's bargain. Fine, I'll burn.

They installed small and fancy security cameras at Aza's house, and that was a whole thing, but it was mostly okay. I have the monitors. So do they.

Since then, I've been spending weekends learning languages, nights memorizing coordinates. In the mornings, she'd wake up from nightmares about Magonia, and I'd pretend I hadn't been beside her all along, recording every word she said in her sleep. The daily reports I've given SWAB aren't much. Basically: school, me, home, stare at sky, communicate with Caru, communicate with me. What Aza and Caru talk about, as far as the deep details are concerned, is unknown to all of us, no matter how much I've tried to find out. They talk silently, and she's never really told me.

I shared her secrets with the enemies I could most easily imagine, in exchange for what I could buy of her safety from the ones I couldn't.

Aza's secrets should belong only to her and to people she's chosen to tell them to. Instead, I'm technically, no matter how I shake it, one of her betrayers.

I watch on my screen as three guys in black climb the wall

of Aza's house, the same way she climbed the wall of my house last night.

I switch over to the monitor in her room as they climb in her window.

She fights hard, but they get her gagged quickly enough that she can't sing any trouble into the air. I watch them tie her, and take her straight back out and into the trunk of the car.

If anyone sees it, they're kidnappers, not SWAB.

This is what I did to keep her safe. There was no way she wasn't going out looking for Heyward. I don't care what she promised.

I know who she is. I've known her since we were five. So I took it out of her hands. The thought of Heyward getting to her? I couldn't.

My phone buzzes. "There's a car waiting for you."

I walk out of my house and get in.

"Kerwin," says the agent behind the wheel.

"Let's go," I say.

Headquarters is an hour later, in a garage deep underneath a shopping mall. Above us, people are going about their T-shirt buying and shoe attempts. In a bunker below America, we're watching the sky.

I scan my thumbprint, and then I scan my eyeball—thumbprints aren't enough in a world where Magonians might be wearing skins to disguise themselves as human.

If you want to discuss how someone seventeen years old has ended up here, discuss it with the top, not me. For all I know, they're watching me every moment of every day, and

I'm merely a tool. For all *they* know, I'm just their informant, and not someone who's been spending his own every moment at headquarters learning anything he can about how SWAB is working. All that pi committed to memory? I have more than just pi in there. The whole time I've been working here, I've been stuffing the contents of SWAB's archives into my skull.

When I first learned about Magonia I thought it was impossible that no one else knew anything about it. Turns out, I was right.

Yeah, I know how this sounds. This isn't me in a tinfoil hat, though.

Governments know the secrets. They're in charge of making sure normal people don't find out about them and—and this is a scientific term—freak the fuck out.

But come on. There are always leaks. Aliens and conspiracy theories. There are always suspicions in the public. Things get seen. Secrets slip.

I pass the portrait of Amelia Earhart up on the wall. Speaking of secrets. When she disappeared, she was on a mission for SWAB. Official version is that she was captured by Magonia. There are photos of her plane, pictures of talon marks in it. SWAB buried it at sea.

Mystery of brave American hero? Solved.

I look at the picture and know I've done the right thing. If Magonia got to Aza, what would they do to *her*?

They'd use her. Or kill her. I had to keep her safe. I repeat that to myself. I had to. I had to.

I'm right, aren't I?

This isn't how I normally feel about things. Usually, I feel like everything I'm doing, I'm doing for definite reasons. Justifiable reasons.

This time . . .

This time I'm worried. There's something about it—everything about it, seeing Aza grabbed, taken from her house—that feels like I've just done something totally wrong.

But I had to.

She accused me of trying to run her life, and I—we've never fought like that before.

Since Aza came back down, though, Magonia's gotten steadily more desperate. No one up there is going to look kindly on a chosen one who wouldn't choose them. The sky is full of her enemies. Heyward would drop her in front of Zal, or Dai, or anyone else who wants to kill her.

I had to keep her safe. She'll forgive me. She has to.

Forty people work here. If you saw us, you'd think we were a paper supply company with astonishingly good tech. If you looked closer, you'd see that there are screens on every desk showing ALL the air traffic. Color-coded and tagged so SWAB can follow progress across the skies of the world by nation. And by more than nation.

All around those airplanes and helicopters, there are Magonian ships. SWAB has a monitor that tracks stormsharks, squallwhales, and a bunch of other things too. They tag them with weather balloons, which the stormsharks eat. As for the squallwhales, SWAB seeds clouds for rain, using a mixture of silver iodine and dry ice. The squallwhale perceive it as some kind of skykrill. Voilà, tracking devices in every pod.

SWAB has the premium version of everything I tried to

create last year when I had no access to data or real tools: small-craft monitors, and single-vessel monitors, a crop theft reports section, a board with renderings of known agitators, politicos and pirates alike. There's a portrait of Zal up there, and one of Dai, which I've studied more than I really want to admit. For an alien guy, he's appallingly and objectively good-looking, even to me.

There are other things here too. This agency has a whole roomful of artifacts from Magonia, knives and swords made of a light Magonian metal that feels like tin, but cuts like steel. Some of them don't look like anything you've ever seen before. Their hilts are shaped like birds, and their blades like gleaming feathers. They're sharp enough to cut through a table in a single stroke. There's a flute that's thirty-five thousand years old and made of vulture bone. You can play five notes on it, the five notes that most human voices can encompass. When you play it—I've never heard it, but this is the rumor—despite this being a scale of human notes, there's something about them that's not—glass cracks for a quarter mile in all directions. There are other things, Magonian bows and arrows, Magonian axes, things gotten I don't know how, over I don't know how many years.

Director Armstrong is sitting calmly at his desk, in front of about five monitors showing Aza's face in various versions. Some of them are Magonian, some of them Aza Original, the earth girl I knew for years before all this, and some are Beth Marchon.

"Kerwin," says the director. "Take a seat."

He's in his late forties, balding, desk job physique, stubble, a crumpled suit, bad squint. A spy, I've learned in the past year, looks like a spy. Which makes me wonder if I'm starting to look like a spy too. Armstrong isn't a field agent anymore. He started at NASA before NASA got publicly shrunk. SWAB was always part of the shadow identity of the space program anyway. Now what was NASA is SWAB, and the tech they developed for fifty years is entwined with our Magonian program.

I sit. Well, I kind of sit.

"Your girl's in custody," he says. "She's safe. And don't worry about Heyward Boyle. We got the tip, and we're on it."

"Okay," I say cautiously.

"But you didn't think to tell us about the escape?"

"About *what*?"

"Captain Quel."

I take another moment. Because this is . . . this is huge.

Aza's mother? Escaped?

"I—I didn't know." Shit. What else don't I know?

Armstrong gestures to a monitor and it clicks on. Surveillance footage. Not earthbound.

"This footage is from yesterday."

It's showing Caru, flying. I know Caru. I've seen Aza's heart-bird in the flesh. He looks like a normal bird, if you don't know what he is. A falcon, yes, but a bird.

Here he's flying with another bird I don't know. Little, yellow, twisting in the air in front of him, and crying a distress call. Caru flies closer.

Oh no. Oh, SHIT. Because I DO know who that bird is. There's no other canwr it could be. Milekt.

Aza's former canwr flits frantically away into the dark, leading Caru on, and Caru's following, until they get to a ship, on the deck of which is—

Dai.

The imprinted. The intended.

I feel my heart shift in my chest, because he's as good and as bad as reported. Trouble. Worse than trouble.

This isn't live. It's already happened, whatever I'm about to see, and I have about ten terrible possibilities in my head. Did they kill Caru? I want to shut my eyes, but I have to watch. Aza's going to—

I can't even think about what Aza's going to do.

Milekt lands on one of Dai's shoulders. He has two canwr now, one Milekt, the other—I assume—Svilken, and they look as hungry as he does.

And then. Dai twirls a rope and nets Caru.

SHIT. He's reeling Caru out of the sky, and Aza's heartbird fights furiously, screaming, panicking.

Dai gets Caru within reach, and I see into his eyes. He's angry, and focused, singing a furious song with Svilken.

My stomach drops. My heart lurches. Everything in me knows I did the wrong thing, because I just got Aza put into custody, her heartbird's been captured, and she can't do anything about it. She's going to be—

The director pauses the video.

"What the hell?" I ask Armstrong.

"You tell me," he says. "We had no warning. It gets worse."

"How'd we even get this footage?"

"Stay calm," says Armstrong, and he suddenly looks more in charge than he looked a minute ago. "We sent up some surveillance drones in recent weeks, and we have a few contacts in Magonia."

He shows a different video, again, an aerial point of view.

And what I'm seeing is unbelievable. I saw her once before,

but she was on a ship, and at that point, I knew almost nothing about Magonia.

Aza's mother, Zal, paces a gray cell, her wild black hair cropped, her hands cuffed. She's dressed in a night-dark uniform, nothing like her *Amina Pennarum* regalia. Milekt flies into her cell, wings flat against his body, snatching a key from off a hook as he goes.

Milekt drops the key into Zal's hand. There are burns on her palm. Cuts all over her fingers. But her hand closes around the key, and her face changes.

Zal takes off the jumpsuit, her back turned. I see the tattoo on her back, white lines, thousands of them.

She's etched with Aza's face, like a blueprint. Her skin is covered in marks, whip scars, lashes, deep and angry. Aza's face looks out from her shoulders, set into an expression I've never seen on it before.

She looks full of rage.

Zal puts on a new uniform. Neutral gray, like a storm cloud that's not going to rain. No insignia. She wraps a scarf around her head, covering everything but her eyes. She reaches her arm around the bars, and unlocks her cell. A long dark hallway. Dead Rostrae guards. Feathers in blood underfoot.

Zal runs down an alley, and leaps off the edge—the edge? Onto the deck of a ship. I see Caru, chained to the mast.

Dai's managed to break Aza's mother out of prison.

The footage ends. I'm back in my seat, in shock.

"If we have that, how is Zal Quel still alive? Why did no one take her out?"

"Surveillance isn't the same as conflict," says the director. He's gnawing a pen like it's going to morph into a breadstick.

"We're not in this war. At least, not officially."

I hesitate. "Zal's going to come after Aza's family, her parents, I don't even know who else. Me? Aza won't stand for it. We have to tell her."

"You're here, therefore you're safe," says Armstrong. "Aza's in custody too. Quel has no access to her."

"That's not going to matter to Aza," I say. "*Zal and Dai have Caru*. That alone would be enough. Now that Zal's escaped? There are probably already Breath on the way to Aza's house. Heyward was already sighted. Aza's going to go insane if we don't—"

"It's not my job to keep your girlfriend happy," the director says dismissively.

I want to leap across the desk and strangle him.

"She's the only reason you have me. Where is Aza?"

"We'll keep you informed, Kerwin," he says. "But right now, your job is to stay here and shut up."

"You got all your information from ME," I say.

The director puts his pen down.

"We thank you for that intelligence. It was very helpful in assessing a terrorist risk."

Every hair on my skin stands up. *Terrorist.*

Nonononononononono. That's all I've got in my head, a string of negatives. If they think Magonia's a terrorist state then Aza is . . . a terrorist. That classification is something you don't ever come back from. It follows you till you're at the business end of a drone strike.

"Your girl isn't human, Kerwin. You're not considering the implications of what this could mean in war. She's a weapon. Zal Quel can deploy her."

I take a second to keep from screaming with rage.

"I know what she is, sir." I manage the "sir" because it finally occurs to me that I'd better pretend as hard as I can that all is well, or I'm never getting back into the world where I can actually DO something about the thousand ways I've fucked up. "I know *who* she is too. Love runs Aza. If she was working with Zal Quel, she'd be betraying earth, and betraying me. She already proved she wouldn't do either."

A voice in my head reminds me that this time I betrayed *her*.

I stand up, but Armstrong grips my shoulder and propels me to a seat. Stronger than he looks.

"What about Heyward?" I ask. "What about her?"

"Don't worry about that."

I'm writhing with guilt and shame. I have a mental flipbook of eleven months' worth of Aza curled up on my bed beside me, telling me she loved me. I have texts from her. I have notes in her handwriting that are diagrams of bat bones, and little twists of rope, love notes in Magonian sailing language.

Jesus Christ, I've failed her. Failed her in so many ways. Seduced by the idea that I could get access to all this information, all this classified, all this wrongness. Seduced by maps and tech. By being *special*.

Because I wanted to be special, like she is. I wanted to be noticed. I wanted to be what I am, a spying, lying secretkeeper.

One of the monitors with Aza's face on it shifts before my eyes, and as I get ushered into a conference room, I see her smile go from bright, to darkness. It's like watching a total eclipse.

I hear the lock click on the conference room door, throw myself at it, but nothing's moving. I'm inside a glass room, looking out at SWAB, and they can all look in at me.

If her family's in danger, it's . . .

3.14159265358979323846264338327950288419716939937
5105820974944592307

My fault. If she's in danger, it's

81640628620899862803482534211706798214808 6
513282306647093844609550582231725359408128481 1
1745028410270193852110555964 4

My fault.

SWAB knows what she did in Svalbard because *I* told them. They know *how* she did it, the song she sang, because *I* recorded it and handed it over. Because I thought I could protect her from Magonia that way. Because I thought I was keeping her safe.

I'm the sun being reorganized into a pea, collapsing all of the things I thought I knew into the one thing I *really* know.

I'm the one who's supposed to be protecting Aza from Magonia. Not only from Magonia, but from *earth*.

If she's in mortal danger, if she's without her heartbird, and she's being held captive somewhere, if she's being seen as a *terrorist—*

I'm the one who did it to her.

Aza's imprisoned, and so am I.

But I'm the reason we're both in cells. I'm the one who got this wrong.

I wake up nauseated. Head spinning. Whatever they made me inhale, it caused me to sleep. I don't know for how long.

My stomach is twisted now, and my body hurts. My throat feels stopped up and thick.

I try to make a noise, and I—

NO.

There's something stopping me, a dampening, something around my notes, clutching them like a tight scarf.

My song is . . . strangled. They've done something to it. I can't feel it with my hands, but it's there. Like I swallowed a stopper. My VOICE is frozen. I can't speak.

I choke and try to spit it out, but nothing. It's in there too securely, whatever it is. I can feel it vibrating a tiny bit, and whatever it's doing, it's silencing me. When I bark out a noise, it hurts, like a shock, but I don't make a sound. A jolt of pain zinging into my vocal cords. My internal song, the one I use with Caru, is somehow dampened too, wrapped in wet towels and made into nothing.

I choke and cough and gasp, and nothing happens. I curl up in the corner of my cell with my knees to my chest, freaking out. I try to whisper, and find I can make a tiny sound that way, the barest rasp of words. No song, but a murmur.

There's hissing and spitting, humming, muttering all around me. I can hear growls and moans. I'm not the only prisoner here.

I never thought about prison before. Never imagined what it might actually feel like. What it feels like is *tension*. The air is crackling with want, and everyone here wants OUT. Out doesn't mean anything about safety. It doesn't mean anything about good or bad. It means everyone living wants to be free.

"Is this the one?" It's the kind of accent that sounds good amplified but in private sounds fake. "Doesn't look like much. Looks like a normal girl."

"I AM normal," I whisper. My voice is almost nothing, no words that carry. Just pain.

"Did you think you were going to get away after you attacked the repository? Did you think no one noticed?"

Jason and I escaped from Svalbard very smoothly, calmly, in disguise as normal people. It was almost a year ago, and no one's said anything. I was dumb enough to imagine no one knew it was an *un*natural disaster.

"Whoever said I attacked anything is wrong," I choke out, automatically, though Aza? If they're saying it, they already know.

A screen in the upper corner of my cell goes on and I see myself on a security camera video, suited up in my Magonian uniform. Jason walks up to me and I watch us kiss. All of this is my major memory of that day, and from this angle, it looks like exactly what it is.

Boy meets alien.

Renewed pangs of panic. If I'm in this prison, being

questioned about things Jason was involved in too? That means something bad must also be happening to him. I think of him driving away from my house.

Mid-fight. Fuck.

"Who are you?" I whisper or don't. "Where's Jason? Is he here?"

"You have a job to do," the voice says. "You didn't get taken back into Magonia. There were reasons for that. You owe someone your life. Now tell us, who have you been working for? Are you working for *them*?"

The voice echoes and rattles around my cage.

"Who?"

"For Magonia."

"No!" I manage, before things get high-pitched, screaling sounds, shrieking, rattling. My ears burn with something that isn't song. I can see the occupants of the other cages hurting too, doubling over, holding their hands over their ears. It's like a flute, but . . . not.

"We want the Flock," says the voice.

"Which flock?" I whisper. "Rostrae? Canwr?"

I have no idea what they're talking about.

The screaling sounds give one more loud, high-decibel blast that makes me dizzy and queasy before it's done. I'm left in ear-ringing silence again. In the dark. In the not-silent silence. Whispers and churrs all around me. My eyes adjust and I start to see the blurry things that are captive in other cells.

Not Magonian, and not things I know from earth either.

There are gills on a woman. A tail on another. Something rolling and twisting in a tank, like a cat made of smoke. I catch sight of an eye, pale green and enormous, but nothing else. The smoke flips over. For just a second I see a mouth, a hiss, red tongue, fangs. A giant man made of what looks like roots, kneeling in his cage, too large to stand upright. There's something swimming in a dark green, algae-encrusted tank, and the way that tail flips . . .

No. I'm not going to say mermaid. I can't.

Other things I have no words for. There's a cell full of fire, and shapes are in there, moving, flashing tails and whipping limbs.

I'm in a prison full of monsters. Some of them are looking back at me. I hear a gravelly voice coming from behind me. One of the prisoners.

"They took us," it says. "From our homes. They took us from our families."

I spin, trying to see who's talking to me, but I can't tell. Other voices come in. A twisting babel of lament.

"They hold us here," hisses something else.

Anything can happen, Aza Ray, Jason says inside my head, and I have a flashing memory of myself singing notes to make rain into rocks. *Anything can happen, and if it doesn't, it's because something else happened instead.*

Oh god, Jason. Oh god, everything.

I feel exhausted. I have no song. I only have terrifying, echoing flashes of the things Caru showed me, just before I got grabbed.

What's happening to Caru while I'm here? Does Dai really have him?

Time passes. Someone yanks me out of my cell, injects me with anesthetic that doesn't stop the pain, and peels a slice of my human skin back with a Magonian knife. A human knife would just show normal human flesh, while a Magonian one slices through the camouflage. Enough wound to show the Magonian flesh beneath it, blue and shiftingly tattooed with things that, in Magonian terms, explain everything about me. I bleed first red, then indigo, and then they're satisfied and bandage me up.

Maybe it's to scare me. It works.

Pain and the possibility of death. They were nothing to me before.

When you're no longer used to them, they're terrifying.

I sleep in fits and starts, trying to calm myself enough to be strong when something changes. I don't know how long I try to sleep, but long enough that when it comes, the voice jolts me awake.

"We have someone for you to see," the voice says.

My cell opens and people drag me down a dark hall, past dark cells that hiss and spit at me. Fire twisting in them, and smoke, tentacles and whipping mermaid tail.

Then I'm looking out across steel-gray, aircraft-carrier-sized decks. We're on a ship. The ocean around us is steel gray too. Where are we?

It's hot. There's a wind, and up above us, seagulls, which mean maybe land isn't SO far away, but I have no idea how far.

I want the birds to be Rostrae or canwr so much I feel like crying. I want them to be Caru. I open my mouth and start to sing a trill—but the guard grabs me and twists my arms.

Open deck. On it, small planes and helicopters, parked. I must have come in on one of these. There are two chairs and a table.

"You can speak," the guard tells me as they handcuff me

to a chair. "Your voice will return, but only enough for the minimum."

I feel something loosen around my throat, and I gag and close my eyes for a moment.

When I open them, there she is.

Across the table from me, also cuffed. Skinny body, her muscles smaller than I remember, her hair cut off. It used to be long, in a ponytail. Now it's hacked, like she did it herself. She looks exhausted. She looks broken.

The last time I saw her, she was fighting me on the deck of a ship, commanding an entire team of soldiers. She stares at me, her eyes reminding me so much of Eli's that for a second I feel like that's what's happening.

She looks human. She IS human. It's me who isn't.

Heyward Boyle.

CHAPTER 10

{JASON}

My brain's clattering against my skull, trying to map likely trajectories of Aza, likely emotional paths of Aza, and the rest of my head is insisting on a loop in which everything is broken forever and I have to find a way to save a girl who loved me a few days ago, but who maybe doesn't love me anymore.

Or, at least won't, the moment she learns what I did.

Other parts of my brain are mapping my own betrayals, and I don't know if she knows I don't know what she knows I don't know what might be about to happen, and—

678925903600113305305488204665213841469519415116094330572703657—

A monitor goes on outside the glass of the conference room, showing a huge ship, an aircraft carrier, really, in the middle of which ocean? No indication.

I see helicopters, small launch boats—

And in the middle of all of it is Aza Ray, in handcuffs. I jolt against the glass like I can get to her, but she's *there*, wherever *there* is, and I'm in a locked room underneath a shopping mall.

Someone else comes into the frame. Aza the way I first knew her, Aza the way I first fell for her. As in, not Aza. Black hair. Pale skin. Ice-blue eyes, the only difference from the version I used to know.

SHIT.

"Get her off that boat! NOW!" I'm shouting and pounding the door, but the SWAB people on the other side are working. Everyone's making lists and scanning data, and watching the monitors calmly.

Aza, and Heyward, opposite each other at a table.

I'm making sounds I didn't know I was about to make. I try to calm my adrenaline rush. I feel lightning struck all over again. The version of me that thought I was ahead of SWAB suddenly feels like a fucking fool.

Jason. Kerwin. You. Idiot.

The audio goes on in my conference room, and I hear Aza losing her shit in exactly the same way I am.

"AM I HERE BECAUSE OF *YOU*?" she shouts. "Are you working with them?"

Aza's gasping in a way I haven't heard her gasping in a year. She can't get enough air. I'm scared for her. I'm leaning forward, praying her off the ledge, but I'm too far away to do anything. She dissolves into coughing. Her voice sounds wrong. It sounds bruised. She holds her throat and winces.

"What did you do to my voice?"

No one answers her. I want to know that answer too.

"They want the Flock," says Heyward. The way she says it is chilling. She looks hard at Aza, and says it again. "They think you can give it to them. If you can, you'd better do it. Zal Quel has escaped from prison, and she's on the move. She's assembling her forces. Things have changed in Magonia."

The hair on the back of my neck is up, and I have goose

bumps all over. The doors are still locked. No one's looking at me. Everyone's glued to their monitors.

"What do you mean, escaped?" Aza asks.

"She has a ship. She's recruiting Magonians to her side. And she has one more thing—"

"Caru," says Aza, and her face contorts in pain. "She has Caru, doesn't she? I felt it. Who sent YOU?! Was it Zal?"

She sounds hysterical, and she also sounds like she's about to fall over choking.

"They want the Flock. If you're not working with Zal, you'll give it to them."

"Who's *them*? And how could I be working with Zal?"

I hear things from outside the conference room.

"Shut her down," says my boss. "Raise the levels. Slowly."

Aza suddenly chokes again, her hands around her throat, and then something changes. Her eyes widen. I see her mouth open, but no sound comes out. Pain all over her face. What's happening?

"Use the balance tones," says Armstrong. "Go."

There's a sound in SWAB's offices. A sound I recognize. It's Aza's song, the song that makes rocks out of rain.

It's the song I recorded. Oh god.

THIS WAS ME.

Those are files I gave SWAB for "research" in trade for security on Aza's house—a bargain for getting SWAB to guard her from Zal. Or so I thought.

Instead? I gave them everything they needed to control her. I've never had a feeling this bad before, never felt my whole soul orbiting a drain this way, but I'm on my way down.

"Convert it," says someone outside this room. The song

shifts into a whining keen, and on-screen, Aza looks horrified. I see her double over in pain, silenced.

I pound on the door of the conference room, and no one pays any attention. They're all out there, and on every monitor, on every screen, I still see Aza.

Aza's silently, furiously fighting as she is removed from the deck, and Heyward's watching her go.

The images shift, new cameras, following Aza and her guards below deck, past glass cells.

Full of creatures.

Smoke coheres into a green-eyed leopard, a blur. A man who seems to be made of lava has hands full of molten red-orange. It's pouring out of his fingers. There's a cage full of wings, rising, rising, and the wings are made of something like knives, not soft. Stiff and sharp.

I'm freaking out. This isn't anything I know about. This is something else entirely. One cell is all lightning. A stormshark? Shit shit shit.

The feed follows Aza and her guards as she descends through the ship. There's a huge glass tank two stories tall, and I see something in it I recognize.

At SWAB, there are the bones of an archaeopteryx found in Germany, not the ancient one everyone knows about, the one on display in London, but a much more recent version, its beak lined with teeth, its name translating back to *ancient wing*. It's the size of a blackbird. And SWAB has the bones of another recent specimen of something that should have been dead millions of years, an *Argentavis magnificens*, or *magnificent silver bird*, with a twenty-three-foot wingspan. Birds so big and heavy that some of them apparently had to jump off cliffs in order to take flight.

There's one there in the cell. A living one.

It's right there. Now. This tremendous extinct bird, this flyer. That's what it is. I know it.

I don't have words for what's reverberating through me, shaking everything I thought I knew about my life.

I can hear SWAB agents on the other side of the glass talking about the other prisoners, talking about how this is a maximum security zone for the most dangerous things in the world.

I see flashes of something in another cell, a thing made of dirt, shifting, piling itself back up from dust and into a form, the face of a man, hands and eyes, a thing full of worms and moles and earth tunnels, which then collapses, builds itself back again. Water pours from the ceiling to wash it away, and as it does, the creature made of dust opens its mouth against the glass to scream.

I'm being turned inside out, a sweater tugged over a head and unraveled into yarn. I'm as paralyzed by wonder as I am with horror. This exists.

Oh my god.

SWAB has a prison full of monsters, which I knew exactly nothing about, never mind my research, never mind my connections, never mind my allegedly capable brain.

Are they all "terrorists"?

How did I not have any version of this in my head? I know things about prisons. I know things about possibilities, and yet, I just thought, safe facility, safe house—

Oh my god, I'm an idiot.

SWAB knows WAY more than I know. And Aza's in their clutches.

Aza struggles past a lab containing a little boat, which levitates inside its confines. It looks to be made of silvery wood, but it bobs in the air. It's tied to a table, and a team of people are around it, sawing into its wood, taking samples. I see Aza turn her head to look at it, and the look on her face is yearning.

A Magonian boat, it must be. Aza looks more like herself than she's looked in a year when she sees it. She looks like she's seen something from home.

I've been missing memos on every front. I've been in the dark.

Pi appears in the air around my head, digits crawling up the walls and twisting before my eyes. The entirety of the universe feels covered in fog. There are too many unknowns. I shouldn't ever have trusted anyone but Aza.

The conference room door opens at last.

"Kerwin," Director Armstrong says.

"What's happening?" I ask him. I keep my voice calm.

"Quel's on the move. Your girlfriend, she's safe shipboard. But we need her to give us the Flock. What can we use? We know you've got something that'll make her bend. It's for her own good."

"What's the Flock, exactly?"

"The Flock's the way to take Quel out without officially getting involved," Armstrong says. "Thanks to your intel, we turned Heyward Boyle. You can be proud. She's agreed to work with us to get the location of the Flock out of Aza."

Never, not once in the past year, have I heard Aza reference anything called the Flock.

"You don't have to get it from her. *I* can get it for you," I tell Armstrong.

Armstrong's face changes. "*You* know where it is?"

I stare him down.

"But I can't do it from in here," I say.

Finally, he nods.

I get the agents to take me to my house. The SWAB car speeds down the highway, me in the backseat.

I'm not supposed to be the guy who can barely keep himself from shouting numbers, who wants to obsessively touch the lock over and over again, who is looping like no one has ever looped before in the history of the world. I'd put that Jason behind me. Or so I thought. Do you ever put yourself behind you?

There's an owl flying near us, surrounded by a bunch of other birds, nothing I can identify from here. I'm instantly on alert.

But, that might just be an owl.

The owl looks into the car window. I get a chill like I'm its prey. The bird, I swear, flexes its talons. They're as long as my fingers. Its face is round and its eyes are huge and it shouldn't be out in daylight, but it is. How long was I underground? The drive to headquarters is an hour and now it's . . . afternoon of the next day, the day after? I don't know.

I'm not going to clue the people in this vehicle into the fact that there might be a flock of Rostrae following us. I see a blue jay beside the owl. And then, above the whole thing, a golden eagle. They're flying fast.

Outside the window, the owl banks and rises up again, with the rest of the flock of random birds. Out of range.

Okay. Okay.

Jesus Christ, get it together.

I shut my eyes and visit my number. A loop of a number that could contain everything, could contain me and Aza. I imagine us in the center of this twisting circle of trillions of digits. I imagine a circle that could contain every possibility for the rest of our lives together and separately, that could keep us both on the same continuum, even if we were far apart.

Aza at one end of pi, and me at the other endless end, getting pushed and pushed away from each other every time a new digit is discovered. But we'd still be tied to each other.

We *ARE* still tied to each other.

What will I do with the rest of my life if it has no Aza in it?

I feel like I could take off on the open wind, not caring if I make it. There are certain kinds of swallows that rise up yearly and make their way across the straits of Gibraltar, across the Sahara. Those birds are British to begin with, and they make their way to South Africa every year to spend their summer vacationing feasting on insects. At this time of year, this moment when I'm sitting in this car in America, looking out at ice and snow, they've migrated to sun.

If I couldn't find Aza, I'd like to think I'd be like one of those birds. I'd get up one night and just start flying. I'd fly until I found her.

But I can't fly.

I can't sing.

I can't sail.

My house. My front door. We pull up a half block away, and I see no cars in the driveway. I don't want to deal with my moms. I've been gone too long, and—

I don't have enough brain for questions. Not right now. I feel like I've had about ninety cups of coffee.

"We'll wait," the agent behind the wheel says.

There are birds everywhere when I get out of the car. They're all around the trees and all over the front lawn. I ignore them, even as one flies almost into the house with me. I have pi in my head and Aza is everywhere pi isn't.

I run up the walk to my front door, up the stairs, open my bedside drawer, and search frantically until I find another compass, the twin to the one I gave Aza.

My only hope is she wasn't so mad at me that she took it out of her flight suit and left it in her room. I saw what she was wearing when she was kidnapped. She was still dressed. It was in her pocket, or at least that's where she put it on the morning of her birthday.

Is the compass more than meets the eye? Yes.

Epic? Yes.

Hacked? Obviously.

I press a button on the back of the case and my compass hums and shows me a screen, a flat black space on the inner face of the cover.

"Aza, can you hear me?" I say. "AZA RAY."

CHAPTER 11

{AZA}

Guards haul me back to my cell and draw the curtains. I'm like Caru when I met him in Zal's cabin, hooded in a cage. It's dark. When I press my hands to the glass, it now vibrates with some kind of current.

I'm not willing to die by electrocution, trying to smash my way out of here.

What can I do without my song? Without Caru? There was no sign of him up there, no pang in my heart of him trying to connect.

I hardly feel anything except despair. Zal, free. Caru probably with her. Dai, clearly plotting along.

What do they want with Caru? Zal can't bond to him. He's my heartbird now, not hers. So what's she looking for? Why's she using him?

To get to me? She's not wrong.

Except that I'm imprisoned and I don't even know who has me, or why.

Something hums inside my flight suit pocket. I fumble and find the compass I forgot I had. It's pointing north, ferociously, and I look at it for a moment, wondering.

I open it and Jason's face appears inside the cover, a tiny screen I didn't even know was there. He looks panicked.

THANK GOD. I don't care if he's panicked, at least he's okay, oh thank god. He's alive. Zal doesn't have him. He's in his room. I choke on relief, on my heart rising up and pounding in my throat, on the possibility of the rest of my life without him, and on just how much I don't think I could do that.

"AZA," he says. His voice breaks. "Oh my god, Aza, I'm so sorry."

I'm instantly talking as fast as I can, whispering, my voice still muted.

"I don't know where I am. Heyward's here too, and Zal's escaped and so has Dai, and they have Caru, oh my god, and I'm here, I can't get out, I can't help him, you have to help him—"

"You're on a prison ship," he says. "I'm tracking your location now. I'm downloading coordinates. I'm going to get you out. I don't know how, but Aza . . ."

"What?"

He takes a deep breath. "I'm so sorry, I—"

I interrupt.

"—No, *I'm* sorry! I shouldn't have said you were trying to run my life. You were just worried about me, because you love me. And I'm an idiot. It was a bad moment, okay, and I lost control of my mouth, because I love you too and—"

"No. NO! I have to tell you something. You have to let me tell you. Aza, it's—"

What's he going to say? Is he crying?

Oh my god. Has Zal come for my family? My parents, Eli—

I can't survive that, I can't take it, I—

Jason breathes out raggedly. He shakes his head and then he

blurts, "Az, there's something you don't know about me."

I stare at him through the tiny screen.

"Not true. I know everything there is to know about you," I tell him. "I've known you since the beginning, and I'm planning to know you until the end."

He swallows.

This is totally freaking me out. "Just tell me; whatever it is, we'll deal with it, okay. Tell me."

"I'm the one who made them arrest you."

"Right after we got back from Norway . . . they didn't give me a choice. I joined an agency. I've been reporting to them for the past year. They said they'd help me keep you safe—but now they . . . we have to get you out of there." He pauses. "They think you're a terrorist, Az."

WHAT.

WHAT?!

The way he stopped sleeping, the way he seemed like he had more information about Magonia than he should, all the questions he asked me—

It starts to make sense. In the worst, most miserable way.

I want to scream. I want to cry. I want to be sick.

"You lied to me," I whisper. "You've been lying to me for . . . what? A YEAR?"

"I wasn't lying! I was just . . . not telling you some things. I had to protect you from the Magonians—"

He says it like he might say *aliens*. Or *monsters*.

"I'M MAGONIAN." My eyes are hot. My skin is burning.

"You know what I mean! From Zal, from Dai, from people who'd use you!"

"*Use me?* What do you think I am? Do you think I'm not a

person? Do you think I don't have any choice about anything?! You think I'm just something to be *used*?"

"I saw what almost happened in Svalbard—"

"YOU SAW ME FIGHT THEM. YOU SAW ME WIN."

He breaks, sobs. "I was trying to keep you safe—"

Tears are running down my face. My throat hurts. It feels like I'm about to choke.

"I love you so much," he protests frantically. "That's why I did all this—"

I'm breathing too fast, thinking about all the things we did together. Was he lying the whole time?

Nights sleeping in his arms, feeling like we were sharing a language more real than any other language anyone else ever shared—was it all fake?

What am I supposed to do if the person I trust most in the world lies to me? If he can look right into my eyes, wrap his arms around me, and lie?

I feel like I can't breathe. I feel like a dying girl all over again, dying Aza Ray, all those years beside him, all these years, almost my whole life beside him.

I think about {{{{   }}}}.

Oh my god.

If I can't trust Jason, who can I trust? He acted like he was always on my side, every moment, every day, every time I messed everything up. He was next to me in hospital rooms. He was next to me in my bed. He was holding my hand. He was telling me he loved—

"I'm gonna fix it!" he insists. "Aza, I'm getting you out. There has to be someone there I can talk to. Don't trust Heyward—"

I stare at him. Is he actually telling ME who to trust now?

Rage surfaces like a shark in my sea of disbelief. Rage feels better. Rage, at least I understand.

"Who should I trust, then?"

There's a sound on his side of the compass. A banging on the door, and someone bursting in. Carol calling his name.

"Jason? JASON! Oh my god, we thought you were gone."

She's hysterical. I've never heard her sound this way before. She's weeping.

Then Eve. "We called the police! We thought they took you too—"

Jason looks stunned.

"*Who* took me too?"

"Whoever took Eli and Beth," Carol says.

I freeze. I'm in this cell a million miles from anywhere. What did she just say? Took ELI??

"We thought you were with them. What happened? Do you know where they are?"

"I'm calling the Boyles," I hear Eve saying. "Maybe Beth and Eli came home too." She's dialing.

Jason's eyes tilt toward me on the screen, frantic.

Because we know. Both of us. Who else would it be?

Zal.

If I'd been there—

If I'd been home, she'd have taken me instead.

Jason's been lying to me for a year, and *this* is what his lies have done.

Zal has my sister. I wasn't there to protect her. She probably came for me, and she got Eli instead. Eli, grabbed by Breath. Eli snatched, Eli breathless, terrified, and all because of Jason.

Everything's wrong.

My heart is pounding. My heart is breaking.

I look at Jason, the love of my life.

I've loved him since we were five.

I can't love him anymore. He's crossed the line I didn't know was there.

I see him try to speak as I close the compass, but whatever he says, I'm not listening.

The thing buzzes in my pocket. It buzzes and buzzes and I don't open it. I put my hands to my chest and try to feel where my heart is. My heartbird is gone. My sister is gone. Jason's gone.

I throw up in the corner of my cell, because there's not another response. I'm a _____ instead of { }. I'm a flat line.

And I am all alone.

CHAPTER 12

{JASON}

I never deserved her to begin with, and now she knows it. I try again on the compass and nothing. I try again. Again.

"What are you doing?" Eve asks, leaning over me. I'm not even hiding the compass. I'm not bothering to hide anything. I don't have it in me to lie anymore, to pretend I'm not who I am. Who I am is Jason Kerwin, who's been in love with Aza Ray Boyle since he was five; Jason Kerwin, who just betrayed the girl he loves. Jason Kerwin the monster, the failure, the abyss of idiocy, the creature made entirely of shame.

Eli gone? I can't even—

"I lost her," I say to my moms. I can barely get the words out.

Eve looks at me, worried. "Who, baby?"

"Beth, he means," says Carol, glancing quickly at Eve. "Did you break up? What happened? Where is she? Where's Eli? Are she and Beth together? Tell us."

"AZA. I LOST AZA!" I say, and now I'm sobbing, now I'm shaking, now I'm losing everything.

I can't stop. It all comes pouring out of my mouth, all of my secrets, all of Aza's secret's, all the world's secrets. Magonia and SWAB, Aza and Beth, Zal and Dai. Everything.

I open my computer to show them proof, but all that's there is video of Aza's house.

I try to log into SWAB, but I get an access denied. I try to show them the SWAB car out the window, but it's gone. My moms are looking at each other, and still, I can't stop talking.

"No one's really looked up, not since what, *War of the Worlds*, Orson Welles on the radio scaring listeners half to death with his report of ships from the sky. Different kind of ships. Same kind of thing!"

"Baby," says Eve. "Okay, hang on for a second. Jase."

I can't, I don't have time, there's no time, I have to explain.

"No! You don't get it! This could be *War of the Worlds* any day now. Over our heads there's an armada. Aza's mother wasn't even put in prison for owning slaves but for trying to war against earth, trying to drown us, and take back the Magonian airplants. Did they even ever work? They exist, but I think their capabilities are seriously in question. Mom? Would they work?"

"Honey," says Eve, and her hand is on my back. "Just slow down for a second. We're listening, but slow down. You're talking really fast, okay?"

I can tell they don't believe me. I bring out books. I open websites. I try to prove it to them.

"Magonians sometimes fall off ships. That's been true for centuries—these things from medieval histories are all the result of Magonians falling overboard and landing among humans. There's a database at SWAB filled with Magonian sequencing. And there's a case at SWAB full of samples. Hair. Skin cells. The oldest date to the late 1800s!"

I keep going. Now it's out there. Now I can't keep from telling them everything all at once. I know how it sounds, but

I can't stop. It's a relief to tell all the things I've memorized, all the things I've hunted down.

"And last year! The helicopter after Aza died, the medical helicopter that crashed. It was attacked by Aza's mother's ship! There's a recording, the black box, and the pilot, the medic, they saw the ship—"

My moms look at each other.

"How long has it been since you slept?" Carol asks me.

"I've *been* sleeping," I say. I'm not even here. I'm hurtling through space.

Because I lost her.

I lost her.

I lost her.

"They have Eli," I tell Carol, and even my voice sounds wrong to me. "Zal Quel has Eli. MAGONIA HAS HER."

"I know," she says. "It'll be okay. We're going to get you some help. You'll be okay. I promise. We're going to help you so you're okay. Trust me."

"Just call Aza's parents! They know! They'll tell you!"

And I stop, because Eve's choking back a sob.

Then Eve's getting my coat. Carol's packing a bag.

I get my backpack myself. It's just full of paper, but it comforts me to have it. I need it. I drop the compass in. I drop my phone in. I wish I could drop myself into it too.

Carol puts her arm around me, and Eve takes the other side. We go down the stairs in a sea of pi, a whirling mass of past and numbers. I'm a catastrophe. How did this happen? I thought I had this.

Carol's opening the car door. I see Eve smudge a tear off her cheek, but she turns to me and smiles.

"We've got you," she says. "We've got this. This isn't beyond us, okay? You're safe. No one's leaving you to do this alone. Love is permanent. We're right here."

We drive. My mom is holding my hand and telling me I'm going to be okay.

I don't feel okay.

I've been this route a million times before, with Aza coughing and choking. I've been driving in opposition to this route for the last year. Literally around the other side of town to avoid it.

We turn the corner and there it is, all white and tall, pretty trees and nice picket fencing to distract you from the fact that this is the children's hospital.

I have sway with some of the people from Aza's department, but no one in psychiatric. I feel slow. Like my brain's locked, and I'm on the outside. All the places I keep to store my memories, all the rooms, closed. I'm just walking down hallways, looking at doorknobs.

Is this real? Are we really here?

Birds are quietly landing on the dried-up winter lawn. One by one, owl and eagle, hummingbird, blue jay. More.

There are people coming out of the hospital, and toward us. I let go of Eve and Carol and take off running as fast as I can, stumbling, leaping over some kind of decorative this-isn't-a-hospital icy pond.

I have no idea where I'm going except for directly at the huge flock of birds landing in the center of the hospital grounds.

"HELP!" I'm shouting, like I can talk to Rostrae, like I can talk to birds at all. They look at me, but nothing happens. Maybe they're not Rostrae. Maybe no one can help me.

"HELP!!!!"

And then someone tackles me and they're putting my wrists in restraints. I look up from the ground, and at the birds. Eye level. Are they birds? Are they not?

Am I lost? Losing?

"It's okay," says Carol. "Don't panic. You're just having a little—"

A little what?

"Episode," she says, like I've ever had an episode like this before. This isn't anything like my memorizing chunks of the OED, or like pi. This is a disaster, everywhere, all over the world, and Aza's in the middle of it. This is the beginning of the end.

"Aza got taken! They're going to kill her! She's on a ship! She's in prison! It's my fault, it's my fault, everything is my fault, make them take me instead—"

Someone jabs a needle into my thigh, and I feel myself twisting out of my skin, trying to fight whatever it is, my brain full of dark, my body limp.

"He'll sleep now," someone says.

I see Carol's face, and then her head tilts and she's an owl. I see Eve, her face close to mine, looking into my pupils, and then she's an eagle, and then I can't keep my eyes open.

My skin and my brain aren't affiliated with each other. I'm separate from myself, separate from anything that makes sense.

I catch a glimpse of that tiny green hummingbird flying up, up, a twisting whirl of feathers, and then the dark covers the edges of my eyes, and I live in it for a moment.

I know I'm a liar. Maybe I lied to myself too.

What if the last year has been some kind of wish that I hallucinated into being? What if Aza's funeral was real, and that was the last thing that actually was?

What if I'm just a guy who lost his shit?

What if there's no Magonia? What if there's no any of this?

Maybe there's no country in the sky. Maybe this is Jason Kerwin, seventeen-year-old shit-loser, and maybe my brain has secretly revised itself.

It's preferable to the other idea—that I'm the worst person on earth, who sold out the girl I love, and everything horrible is my fault—

I fall, tearing myself apart as I land. I'm here, on the ground, not in the sky. I don't even know where the sky is.

Or if there is a sky.

Or if there is a me.

Or if there's anything but nothingness.

I'm on my back in the grass, looking up at a darkening flock of birds, the sky covered, coursing over the rest like an oil spill, a rushing tide of wings.

Doesn't anyone understand what's happening?

That's Magonia. Everything up there is wrong.

And Aza. And Eli. And

Oh god

What did I do?

My heart is origamied into a flat packet full of everything Jason and I ever said to each other, everything we ever whispered.

Every lie he ever told me.

I'm cataloguing every moment of the last year, every time he was probably full of shit, every time he was telling me he loved me when what he really meant was *I'm not who you think I am—*

I thought I was strong enough for anything, but I'm not strong enough for this.

Footsteps are coming down the hall. The curtains drop, and fluorescent lights blind me. My cell is open, but open so fast I can't do anything.

Then Heyward's pushed in, and they lock it up again.

"You're not going anywhere unless you talk to me," she says. "I don't like this either, but we're in here for as long as they feel like keeping you."

I don't know why she isn't ending me right now. I can't believe she'd ever want to do anything with me but get her revenge.

Imagine the life she would've had on earth.

Imagine the life she's had in Magonia. Her mind poisoned like mine was. Filled with lies about righteous wars, about justifiable annihilation.

Zal and I would've flooded the world.

I am not the Captain's Daughter.

I'm the dictator's.

The zealot's.

The terrorist's daughter.

Which means I belong here. If we're talking about biological inheritance, Heyward's the clean one. I'm the one who's made of danger.

"You have to talk to me," she says.

I can't be sure if the tightness in my throat is betrayal, or manipulation. I can still only whisper. I point.

"They'll fix that," she informs me, and signals to a camera I hadn't noticed before, up high in the corner of my cell. Someone up there's been watching me.

Jason's people. Spying on me. I don't even know for how long. Rage. And grief.

After a second I feel the bonds around my voice loosen. Not enough to sing. My song is still pinned like a butterfly in a case. But I can whisper stronger than before.

"Whose side are you on?"

"The side that keeps me alive. Zal, your mother, I was on her side. In the end, her plan was . . . unsustainable. And now? Now it's insane. I left Magonia." She pauses. "I want to go home."

"Home?"

"To the life I was supposed to have."

Her whole body trembles for a second.

"You mean *my* life," I say.

"Your life," she replies. "Yes. The one I missed."

Her face looks like she's telling the truth. Other faces have looked that way.

"This is a place for monsters," says Heyward. "That's why you're here. It's a place for things SWAB want to use as weaponry against human enemies, and against enemies elsewhere. Do you want to be their weapon? You've done that once before and you refused Zal at the last moment. Will you work for them instead?"

No. It's too much. I've had enough.

"Get away from me," I tell her.

"You missed the last year in the sky. You missed what happened up there. This is the beginning of a war. Zal's escaped. She's going to make it happen with or without you. They're trying to stop her, but they need the Flock."

She's scared too, I realize. Which is the strangest thing I've seen today.

"Why?" I ask. "Why would you come back to earth? You had power. You were a captain."

"It's a slave kingdom," she says. "Even for the Breath. We thought we were free, but we were working for Magonia, and we couldn't leave. If you attempt to quit they put a bounty on your head, hunt you down, and kill you. I risked my life coming here, but I did it anyway. Because I wanted to feel . . . what I felt . . . when I was here before. I couldn't let earth get taken away without trying to save it."

What she *felt*? When? When she met Jason? When she tried to kill him? My heart contracts.

"You don't have to believe me," she says. "But it's true. You had this beautiful life, and you didn't ever appreciate it. You had people who loved you. You felt safe. I've never felt that way. I've been learning to fight since I can remember. Now we're all about to be fighting. No one is safe. Unless you help me."

"Help you?"

"Help them," she says. She looks up at the camera. "Footage."

The television in the corner of my cell goes on, and I see the deck of a ship, and then closer in, the ship's wheel. At the wheel is—

I step back involuntarily, queasy, press my back against the wall.

I haven't seen her in a year. I'm already off guard, too open, heart too shaky, and then. My mother.

Her body is covered with more tattoos than she had the last time I saw her, hauled up from the ice in Svalbard, dragged screaming into Maganwetar, a city of whirlwinds and storms.

Magonian tattoos are part of the way our skin is, our loves and hates written on us, visible to everyone. My mother's a criminal. She's a murderer. She's a monster. Her tattoos show it. She has the most violent, brilliant scars.

The footage shows her from behind first, her shoulders, as she steers the ship. And on her back, I see my own face. My whole body rejects the image. I shake.

She has *my face* tattooed on her skin.

Is it love? Hate?

Probably both. I'm part of what made her a monster. Maybe she was already terrible, but then I was kidnapped. She spent fifteen years hunting the sky for me, and I don't know what happened to her in those years. I can't imagine them, and I don't want to. Whatever she is, we're here.

I refocus, forcing myself to look at what the images on the screen are telling me. Dai's beside her, and he's navigating. Caru is there too, tied to the ship. He's screaming, fighting the bonds around his wings, flying out into the sky, and then yanked back in. As he screams, I watch something getting closer, approaching like it was called to the ship, another dark twirling object. Blades. Wings. There are things out there that . . . aren't birds. I don't know what they are.

Zal's sailing her ship through a sky full of Rostrae screaming battle cries, diving against her. I can see her purposefully plowing into the Rostrae closest, running them down, but they're fighting. They're flying at her, even as her ship's cannons shoot into their midst.

Rostrae are falling dead out of the clouds. I gasp, feeling their flight broken, feeling their bones crackling. I don't know these Rostrae, but I'm watching them die.

The video pauses on Zal, her face frozen.

Another film comes onto the screen. This time it's wobbly footage, half-degraded, of more of those things flying; black, birdlike, twisting. There are Magonian ships in this footage, and I watch the black things flying into the sails, watch smoke and flames shoot out of the ship's holds, out off the decks, crew panicking, jumping out into the abyss, batsails burning—

I'm crying when the footage stops. I was already broken.

I remember what I heard Carol say. Is Eli missing? If she is, she can only be up there with Zal, right?

"What's Zal done with my sister? Where is she?"

"Your sister?"

"Eli," I manage. "Someone took her. It has to be Zal. Who else would it be?" Something occurs to me. "That's why you were down there, isn't it? That's why her friends saw you. You were sent for Eli?"

"No." She shakes her head. "It's you. I came . . . *they* came . . . for you. I changed my mind and deflected. No one was sent for Eli."

I choke on that, and then swallow and keep myself together. I have to stay together. I can't lose it. I have to be strong enough, even if—

Even if anything.

This is what *chosen* really means.

People choose you. People tell you, this is your job forever. You have no choice. You have no say. Running, hiding is useless.

Heyward just looks at me, weirdly patient.

"I don't know anything about Eli being taken. Zal Quel was in prison until a few days ago. Dai was released a few months ago, I don't know why or how. Those black things, Nightingales, they call them. They're some kind of new weapon. And they're deadly."

These other birds, these Nightingales, are the things Caru saw on the edge of the sky, on my birthday. The visions he sent showed me that.

The Nightingales are singing Magonian song. I play it back in my head. No, not just Magonian, more precise than that. They're singing *Caru's* song, but twisted somehow.

How is that possible? Each heartbird's song is different. None more so than Caru's.

How are they singing *my* heartbird's song?

Zal didn't get what she wanted. I broke her plans for drowning the earth. What does she want now?

"She wants *you*," says Heyward. "Why do you think she

took *your* bird? Just for fun? She can't sing with Caru. She wants Caru because *you* want Caru. She's drawing you out. Otherwise, she'd kill him."

On the screen, lightning flashing, dark clouds full of stormsharks. Dai's face, covered in rain, and then Zal's face, wet with both rain and blood. Not her own blood.

"How do you have this? How am I seeing it?"

"They have airborne spy cameras up there," Heyward says. "*They*, as in the people in charge of this ship."

Where is Eli? Where is she?

"Audio," says Heyward. The screens go dark and something crackles on in the cell. Zal's voice. I'd know it anywhere. She's speaking to a crowd.

"Magonians," she says. "Your leaders are liars. Your slaves have rebelled. Your children starve, and your songs shrivel. The food you take from the drowners is poisoned, and their crops kill your families. We must take Maganwetar, and once they can no longer oppose us, we must destroy the drowners."

I hear the Nightingales screaming a tormented, twisted Caru song. I hear the shrieks that call for flood, for death, for the sky raining rocks. I hear a cheering crowd speaking Magonian.

My stomach twists as I listen. I ran back to my family on earth, and I left Zal and Dai alive. Maybe if I'd stayed in Magonia—

"ZAL QUEL! HAIL!"

Heyward grabs my face and turns it so I look at her.

"Old stories are tempting to a starving sky," she says. "She's whipping them up, preying on their honor and hunger, to get them to war against the ground. There are singers up there in her service, and weather she has control over."

I lurch back so she's not touching me.

"Did she send you to kill me?" I sputter.

Heyward looks at me. "No. I told you the truth. I left Magonia. I thought I could just—"

"What?"

"Change my life," she says, and her face is rueful. "What was I thinking? Now Zal Quel is loose. There is no more home."

A shiver racks my exhausted body. "Someone has to sing her into silence," I say. "I don't think I can do it alone."

Heyward nods. "We need to find the Flock."

Frustration level to ten. "The Flock. Again. What is it?!"

"All I know is that it's strong enough to kill her. They've been watching Zal a long time. The Flock is the only thing she fears. I thought you'd know more."

I don't know what she's talking about, and it makes me angry. The camera above me makes me angry. And in my rage I have a tiny capacity for song. I force sounds out and shriek a high and damaging note, things starting to twist in the air around us.

I feel the cell starting to bend to my tones, but Heyward gives me a look.

It's a look that says *wait*.

I blink.

Then she's leaping toward me, flipping backward, her leg up in the air and kicking. She hits me in the throat, and I'm gagging, choking, bent over double, trying to scream, and no one's coming to help me, no one's opening the cell. There are soldiers outside watching her as she grabs my arms and twists them, as she puts her hands around my neck.

I wait for her to break it like a bird's throat, but instead I find—

The thing they've done to my voice—it's broken instead. Heyward's mouth is just over my ear and she whispers, "We're getting out of here. I don't work for them. I work for myself."

I feel Heyward's hands around my throat, prying at something, and I feel my song opening up again, more and more, until I know I have the whole thing, my voice back. She unlatches something I can't see from around my neck, and I'm free.

"NOW!" Heyward shouts.

And I sing.

I sing the walls of the cell into shattering, like that, sand from glass, sand to water. The floor of the prison is suddenly covered with ice. I sing a haywire song, something that isn't anything I know, all the elements at once, no Caru, but I can sing it anyway.

The corners of the prison light up, and the guards each find themselves surrounded by fire. I sing softness into the walls, mire into the floors, and they're up to their ankles, their boots caught as they shout for help. Heyward is with me as we jump the barrier that used to be a cell wall, and we run as I sing other cells into collapse.

My song is full of grief and rage. I don't know what I'm doing.

My song is Jason's betrayal and Eli's absence and Caru, trapped. My song is the nightmare of being my mother's daughter.

An empty center to my heart, and the song echoes inside it.

The notes course through my bloodstream, like the cold of an IV when it's just inserted, when all of a sudden your blood turns to ice and saline. Soldier-sailors run through the prison, wearing body armor and flotation gear, trying to cover their ears.

I sing the glass of the cells into oblivion. I sing a prison break, because even though I don't know what these prisoners did, I can't leave them to be tortured.

The ship is all monsters now, running, flying, leaping, and I sprint with Heyward up the stairs. She's yelling at me, telling me which way to go, and I'm still singing. We burst out into the open air, onto the upper deck.

I see the winged monster take off into the sky, feathers rotating and turning, the creature inside them sleek and smooth as a fish. Gone, shooting across the blue.

The leopard made of smoke arcs backward and flips above the deck, a plume of burning air. The smoke hurts my eyes. I turn my head away from it as fast as I can, only to see the man with the lava in his hands start throwing molten rock at soldiers, none of whom know what to do.

"DOWN!" Heyward yells.

A movement over my head, and I drop to the deck. Close to me. A sound. A hum like a hive of bees. Something dark flashes past, close enough to touch my hair.

One of the soldiers turns to look at me and I see his expression, like the faces of kids I used to see in the hospital, the ones who weren't gonna make it and knew it.

The song gets louder and louder. It's coming from outside me, from the air. The soldiers are still running and they're all tearing at their armor and dropping their weapons.

I see soldiers starting to fall, unable to breathe, and I remember something, a thing about what sound can do. It can collapse your lungs, if it's the right tone.

I'm *Magonian*. That's something *I* can do, if I sing the right way, but this isn't me. This is coming out of the sky.

The birdsong is higher still, and louder, amplified, and they're humming. The sounds they make aren't from the natural world. They're recorded and altered. They're . . . mechanized.

It's the song I'd sing with Caru, made poisonous. Electrified, turned into something nonliving and made of spikes.

KILL, the song sings, from a hundred birds at once. *Die. Break now. Deathsong, killsong, screamsong.*

The soldiers are all leaping off the ship.

Heyward grabs me and yanks me out of the way, just as a cloud of smoke covers the deck where I was. She lets go of me and leaps out, running. Do I follow her? My semi-sister, the lost child.

She almost killed Jason. She almost killed *me*.

But the sky is attacking us both.

There's a huge lurch and waves higher than they were a second ago explode over the deck. Small detonations, fire dropping through the decks, and this ship has got to be powered by something. Fuel tanks? Where are they?

Shitshitshit.

I sing a path, shifting parts of the wet on deck—seawater and, oh god, blood—to stone, to steps, to a place for us to run. There's violence everywhere. Confusion. People are screaming, dying.

A red dot appears in the shine of Heyward's black hair. I throw myself at her knees, knocking her out of the range of whatever's aiming at her.

And then, a gift from nowhere: I see the Magonian launch

that sat in a lab earlier, being experimented on. It was far enough from me that I thought I'd never see it again, but I melted all the walls. The launch is still here, floating above the deck.

I grab the edge of the little wooden boat and heave myself up into it, reaching out my hand to get Heyward too. I wonder what I'm doing, but then it's done.

This is a Magonian vessel. It wants the clouds. It rises. I stand up and SING.

We sway, but it's okay. The song is supporting us. I've braided the hull of the boat to the wind. I know some things, and others are coming back to me. I learned them all on my mother's ship and now I need them.

Heyward is beside me, and we're rising up.

The last thing I see as I look out from this launch is the team of soldiers screaming at me from a hundred feet down. Then a thousand. Then ten thousand.

I sing us faster, move us harder across the sky, away from those things on the ship, away from whatever Zal sent to attack us. To seize us? Faster. Faster. As far away as I can get us. I sing so hard my lungs feel broken, until I'm panting, gasping. I look down again.

Blue earth, blue water, blue sky.

I spin, searching. It's a Magonian boat. That means there are Magonian materials on it. That's all I need. Something sharp. Finally, I find a small nail made of Magonian metal, jabbed halfway into a plank and pointed enough for my purposes.

I take off my flight suit, and put the tip of the nail to my arm.

I'm not supposed to do this, my mind's screaming at me, but

we're all in bodies that are dying, from the moment we open our eyes.

I cut.

It hurts, but it doesn't take much to shed a Magonian skin, once you start. It's like a zipper. The kind of zipper every part of you is programmed not to open.

This body, this body that's been kissed and held and danced with on earth, this body that's been mine for a year? It was never mine. Just like the last body, the one everyone called Aza Ray, was never mine. Both things were fake.

Was *everything* fake?

I wasn't faking.

I reveal an entire blue arm. I'm used to brown skin now, not this flesh tattooed with constellations, not this gleaming Magonian skin, this utterly not-human skin.

Let go of the body you loved him with.

Let go of the skin he touched. Let go of the fingers that touched him. Let go of the mouth he kissed. Let go of the body that slept beside his, the body that curled into his arms in the middle of the night when he was the only one who could comfort you after you lost your home in the sky.

Let go of love.

Let go of who you were when he was lying to you.

Let go of all of it, earth and the world below.

You're Magonian, Aza Ray. Quit denying it. This is who you are.

You need this body, this strength, this fight. You need to be all the way again. You need to be exactly, entirely what you are.

It's time to grow up. It's time to go back.

I tug Beth Marchon over my head, and roll her off my body, feeling the skin surrender, the bond that attached everything to everything ebbing. Feeling my Magonian hair unfurling, my skin taking in the high air, even alongside the grief of losing yet another human self, another chance at happiness.

I loved him.

Loved? Oh god, do I past tense it now?

Does my heart live inside my chest, broken? Does it just stay there? Do you die of this feeling?

I'm naked for a moment and then I put my flight suit back on. *Carpe omnia.* ELI. That's why I'm doing this. My sister. My heart.

I stretch my Magonian arms, feel my Magonian song, the vocal cords unbinding from their human covering.

In a movie version of my life, I'd be whole now. I'd feel complete. As we rise to the country I came from, I'd heal the crack in the center of my heart as easily as I shed the skin.

But I don't.

{I—}

{&,&,&}

I can't crack now.

There's a clock some people made that's supposed to keep perfect time for ten thousand years, a system of weights and pulleys, of gears and hope, and ten thousand years from now, it will still be telling us what time it is, so we can keep track of the seconds we have with the people we love.

I didn't know I'd have so few of them with Jason. I thought we'd be forever. Nothing could take us away from each other besides dying, yet here I am, alive, and there he is, alive—

I'm sailing as fast as I can back to the country I came from.

I let myself cry for what I've lost. I don't even care that Heyward's watching.

I can't stop.

I cry over the edge of the launch, my tears mixing with the rain.

CHAPTER 14

{JASON}

No pictures, no phone. No internet. Unplugged.

Long hallways, locked doors, and each room full of prisoners. People who fell apart. People whose nearest and dearest took one look at them and went, "Nope, you're done."

I'm sent to group therapy and I say, "I never tried to kill myself," and everyone looks at me like *yeah right*, and I shift my weight and try to look exactly like someone who really never tried to kill himself, which is exactly the person I am, but I can tell I look wrong anyway.

How can I not?

Aza Aza Aza

I'm broken.

A doctor informs me that I really am broken. She tells me that I had a psychotic break, except I swear I didn't. But maybe that's how everyone feels when something in their brain goes haywire. *No, no, I'm fine, really.* Except that you're wearing your shoes on your hands.

The brain is running the show. If the brain's got it wrong, everything else goes wrong too.

"I never tried to kill myself," says someone in the group, and then explains that instead, he swallowed three pairs of scissors, which were not to kill himself, but to kill the spirits of the dead that had possessed him.

I look at this person and feel very sad for him. Whatever happened, it happened in a major way, and now here he is, swallowing sharp things in an attempt to barter with the fates. Which I don't *think* I'm doing.

But . . .

You.

Never.

Know.

I'm in a locked ward full of people who are fucked up. We are all fucked up together.

I can't help but think of the place Aza's in. This isn't all that different. She's there, I'm here, and there's no normal. Maybe not for anyone.

"I hear you believe in aliens," says a kid.

And I say, because I'm momentarily foolish, "No, I believe in *one* alien."

"I hear you tried to blow up your high school," says another kid, and after the millionth time that comes up, I say, "Fine, sure."

"I heard you said you were a spy," and I say, "No, I never said that. I never said any of that," and I take my pills and sip my water, keep breathing despite the fact that every inhale is a struggle, knowing that if she never speaks to me again, I will deserve it.

Everything has a little border of yellow, of weird shine. I don't know what drugs I'm even taking. And honestly, I don't care.

Who am I to say what's true? Maybe everything is. Maybe falling apart is a normal response to the way the world looks, weirder and warmer every day, people starving and being consumed by cracks in the earth, by tidal waves, by drought and plague. All that sounds very biblical, but it's also very actual.

Very Magonian.

I watch the weather like I'm in charge of it. In group I say, conscientiously, "I know I'm not responsible for every horrible thing that has ever happened and will ever happen in the universe."

(In truth, I might be.)

"I know I have to forgive myself for my best friend dying."

(No, I don't, not for her dying the first time, not for her being taken prisoner now. I don't have to forgive myself.)

"Do you believe in people in the sky, Jason?" asks the group leader.

"No," I say.

"Ships that sail in the clouds?" she asks.

"No," I say.

"Do you believe your friend is still alive? Do you believe in aliens?"

"No, yes, no, YES," I say. "YES! YES, I DO. CAN WE STOP FUCKING TALKING ABOUT IT?"

If I hadn't lost it already, I'd be losing it now. I think I'm losing more of it. Whatever "it" is.

Single bed. No Magonia. No contact from SWAB, who are probably happy I'm here, stuck. Imprisoned. Out of their way now that they have no use for me. It's not like me talking about SWAB is a risk for them. I'm here, binned, and they're out there doing whatever they're doing.

No Aza Ray Boyle. No Aza Ray Quel. No Beth Marchon.

That means no Jason Kerwin. That's what I'm thinking

about. Even though I'm still here on earth. The world's too small, and though I've spent my whole life trying to memorize the entirety of it, and it should be a good thing that now there's less to memorize, I'm looking around at these rooms, and I know that there was a sky full of ships, and I also know that maybe I'll never see it that way again.

This is how it feels to fall out of the world.

I take a moment and look around the circle, at all of the fucked-up kids in it, who may or may not be reasonable refugees from civilization like myself. We are the bandaged and the beaten up. We are the drugged and the despairing. We are the ones who looked in the mirror and didn't know our own faces, the ones who crashed our cars when speeding away in the middle of the night, the ones who got so sad that it looked like there was only saltwater out our windows.

Maybe we're brokenhearted, but why isn't it rational to have a broken heart? It is utter shit out there, the things you can't control. The world is full of wrongs, and mess and distress and horror. Who can really be blamed for wanting to dig their way down and live in a hole, or disappear into a cave and never be around humans again? If all people do is hurt each other? If all *I* managed to do, loving Aza as much as I'm ever going to love anyone, was injure her?

There is a case to be made that I should totally be here, locked away, because the only thing I can do to the people I love is wound their hearts. My moms. Aza. Eli? Maybe not *just* their hearts. Maybe things I did have resulted in the people I love being captured, kidnapped, pulled out of their lives and into other versions. Even dying.

I want to disappear.

I'm made of guilt. Made of shame. Made of fail.

And suddenly I get all of it, the last fifteen years, all the things Aza was trying to get through in order to live her life. *I'm* the patient now, and I have no patience. I'm the invalid, the one without validity. No one hears me or believes me.

She spent fifteen years like this. No wonder she got furious with me for trying to dictate her life.

I've been loving her all wrong.

I call a nurse.

"What if I wanted to get out of here?" I ask out of the side of my mouth. He looks at me like I'm exactly what I am. A seventeen-year-old patient, not a super-connected hacking machine with the capacity to memorize the universe.

"It takes time," he says.

I sag, and watch the snow. I take my pills. I drink my water. I look at the locks. I stare at the windows.

Gray sky full of everything.

And I think some thoughts I've never thought before. I think thoughts about places in this hospital I might be able to go to hide myself long enough to be gone. Forever.

I'm half gone already. The part of me that is Jason Kerwin is no one without her.

CHAPTER 15

{AZA}

A plane passes us, a passenger jet with a tropical paradise logo. There are people's heads in the windows, and I can see them reading books, watching movies.

But a little kid is looking out, and for a second I wonder if she sees our boat, traveling across the blue. Then the plane's gone, and we're out here alone again, rocking perilously in the wake of its passage.

A year absent from Magonia and what's changed?

Everything. Nothing. Everything. The sky's suddenly rose-colored.

Compass in my pocket. North.

I can't go north.

"Tell me there's a ship for us up here somewhere," I say to Heyward. "Tell me you have a plan."

"There isn't," Heyward says. She has a gaspy sound to her voice, a sound I find very familiar. Because, like a Magonian on earth, like *me* for most of my life, she can't breathe. "I wasn't lying when I said I was rogue. I was down there alone, and now I'm up here alone, except that I'm wanted by Magonian authorities. As are you. Maybe you noticed."

"Can you breathe?"

She nods. "Enough. Breath train for this in case we're with-out our equipment. But we need to move. The whole sky is going to be after us soon, not just Magonians, but Nightingales. I think we got away from them with that song, but I don't know how long that's going to last."

The black birds. The . . . the *machines.* Yes, that's what they were.

"You saw what they do. If they attack us in *this*? We need to find something better than this launch."

We're no match for anything. We don't have cannons, nor any crew of Magonian war singers. It's just us in a little boat, exposed to the elements. No supplies. No nothing.

"How are you at celestial navigation?" I force myself to say. "If we're going on alone from here, I want to know where 'here' is. I spent half the time I was on the ship passed out. I don't even know how many days have passed."

"Five days, since Zal escaped."

Five days. I think of my parents. They're insane with worry. They must be. Me, Eli—both of us gone? Unless . . . What did Jason tell them? That I left on purpose? That I decided not to stay on earth? And what could he have said about Eli? That she came with me? There's no Eli here. I so wish there was. I can't even think about her with Zal and Dai.

I have to get to her.

"We're in the Tangle, above the Atlantic," Heyward says. "Magonia recruited Breath from airplanes and ships here in the early days. They messed with navigation. Downed a whole bunch of people, then just took them. Programmed them. Brain-washed them. Like me, but the adult version. It's not just babies

Magonia takes. This is a strange piece of the sky. Compasses point to true north here, not to magnetic north."

The Tangle. She means the Bermuda Triangle. It makes perfect sense that this would be a Magonian territory. All those legends of ships disappearing in this area, and planes too. That should have occurred to me before.

Against my instincts, I pull the compass out of my pocket. I want to throw it overboard, but instead I open it and look at the screen. Blank.

My compass wouldn't point to true north. Mine would point to the opposite of true. I put it back in my pocket, feeling like crying all over again. It can't help me.

"Now the area is less trafficked, by humans and Magonians alike. There's been a rumor for years of something far to the south of here, an old weapon, well guarded."

She points.

"Breath don't sail that deep into the cold but that, apparently, is where it is." She pauses. "Three guesses on *what* it is."

"The Flock," I say.

"That's my thought. And according to the drowners, it's strong enough to defeat a Zal Quel who has much more power than she did when you last saw her."

"I'm not chasing after a rumor," I tell Heyward. "We need to get to Eli. She's probably in Zal's ship. There'll be a brig there, and whatever Zal wants with her, it's going to hurt Eli. She'd only take Eli to get to me."

"And when you find her? Then what, Aza? Give yourself to Zal in exchange for your sister? Is that your plan? Because fighting Zal's not going to end well. She's had a year to figure out how to work on you, and she made use of it. While you were sleeping with your boyfriend, she was planning the end of drowners—"

I bristle instantly. Not only is he not my—

He's— I can't.

"Don't talk about him."

"Wasn't Jason why you went back down? You don't belong there. You know that now, don't you?"

I wince. No. Yes.

My family. My world. My sister. My life. Did any of it really belong to me? I push it all away. I need my brain to think about other things. My murderous mother, for example.

"We have to do *something* about Zal."

"She won't relinquish her new power easily, and you can hardly sing. You have to practice and strengthen. That was desperation you were singing on the ship, not skill. I heard you. That was a panic song."

She's right, but what else can I do? "The longer Zal has Eli and Caru, the worse it will be."

Something moves far out on the edge of the sky, and I feel a pang of misery that shakes me from my head all the way down. An airkraken, silver and brilliant, its tentacles undulating, curling, rolling in the atmosphere. Those cause tropical cyclones, I remember from the last time I saw one. The tentacles twist the air and blast cold down from above. They're rare, and even Magonian ships tend to move quickly away when one is sighted. No one wants to be caught in a long tentacle of icy wind, twisted and flung up into the sky, higher than anyone has prepared themselves to be flung.

But all I can think of when I see this airkraken is Jason and the giant squid video. It was last year's birthday present. Stolen from the deep web. My couch downstairs, our hands touching for the first time. We almost kissed, the last moments of my old life.

It feels like a thousand years ago, but it was only last year. Everything hurts, my whole body, my whole soul. Everything I thought I had is gone.

Everything except Magonia.

Airkraken are predators. I don't care that they're beautiful. Giant squid too. All they want to do is eat things that are weaker than they are, things that don't know they're coming. They work by moving silently and surprising their victims. They wrap their arms around their prey and tear them apart with their razor beaks.

I glance at Heyward. There are plenty of creatures like that in the world.

"Why are you helping me?" I ask her.

"I don't want the world to end, do you?" Heyward says simply. She breathes in deeply, and for a long moment, she coughs. She looks like it hurt.

"I thought I hated drowners. But it was Breath teaching me to hate them. I stood outside your house for days after they brought you up here last year. I watched your family, your sister, and Jason, learning them. I watched how they grieved you. Breath have no families. No one's ever loved me like Jason loves you—"

"He doesn't love me," I interrupt.

She looks at me, and her face is sad.

"Zal is run by vengeance, not by logic. Dai's family died of the actions of drowners. He has no desire to let them live. Together they'll complete Zal's mission. Even if they have to sacrifice their own lives to do it."

The wind howls around us, a hollow, lonely wail.

I remember something, belatedly.

"Caru spoke to me, just after he was taken by Dai. I think he was telling me what to look for. *'Where the air is mad. Where the wild birds are.'*"

I don't know what makes me so sure of what Caru was saying, but I need to get Eli out and away from Zal, back on the ground where she's safe. Which means I need to make the ground safe, as safe as I can. Not all dangers are Magonian, obviously, but that's what I have power over, if I have any power at all. If Caru was telling me to find the Flock, then that's what we need to do.

Heyward bends over with another sad choking cough. Her lips are slightly blue. I imagine Eli up here, breathless, Zal watching her slowly suffocate.

If Zal took her to get to me?

Yeah. She's gotten to me.

My sister's a fighter. She won't stay calm and preserve her air and energy. She'll have been screaming at them since they took her. I have to get myself to wherever they are, as fast as I can.

But I also know Heyward's right. I need to be strong enough to fight them.

Where the air is mad. Where the wild birds are.

I stare at the compass and choose south, as far from any

northern anything as I can go. I sing a tiny hum into the ship, and we sail, clueless, through the Tangle.

I don't like needing help from anyone.

But I need help this time.

CHAPTER 16

{JASON}

"You have a visitor," the nurse tells me, interrupting my miserable thoughts. I move to the visiting room, darkly expecting my moms, who look at me with a mixture of love and guilt whenever they come. I don't want to see them. They love the hell out of me. It's a problem to be loved like that if you're in here considering the end.

But instead it's Mr. Grimm.

Last time I saw him, I was busted mapping flock deaths and saying "Aza" instead of "Beth."

Now I'm hospitalized for losing it, and Grimm is confirmed in his suspicion that I've been losing it for a while. Like, maybe since Lightning Strike Last Year.

I sit down, warily. Grimm looks at me, his eyes betraying nothing. Not the sympathy face. Not any face.

"Kerwin," he says. "Fancy meeting you here."

Fine, Grimm is not unfunny. I can fake normal. As normal as I ever am.

"You didn't bring me flowers?" I say. "Balloons? Dirigible?"

"Stuffed animal, actually," Grimm says, and pulls something out of his bag. He sets it on the table between us.

It's a little yellow bird with a black beak.

I look slowly up at him.

He leans in. "I don't have time to explain the history of the world. All I can tell you right now is, I know Aza Ray's alive."

I'm paralyzed. "What do you know about Aza?"

"Everything," he says.

Is he cooperating with someone in here? A doctor? Someone to prove that I continue to fall apart?

"Aza's dead," I say carefully. "She died a year ago."

"Kerwin," Grimm says. "You want to call a girl hopping onto a Magonian launch accompanied by a key Breath operative dead, that's up to you. But she's in the Tangle, and currently on the move."

I'm out of my chair now.

"She escaped?"

"Aza escaped," he confirms. "She's in the air, hunting for Eli. You're the one who got her taken by SWAB in the first place, aren't you?"

I look around to see who might be listening. No one's listening. No one's even watching. I wonder, for a little longer than I wish, if Grimm is real.

"Don't pretend you don't know what I'm talking about. You joined them."

"They blackmailed me," I protest.

"You think you're not at fault?"

"I KNOW I'm at fault." I slump back into the chair, broken by the whole thing. "I'm wearing pajamas. I have no real clothes. And *that* is the only thing I know. The guy who broke everything. That's me."

"Then it's your job to make it right, Kerwin," Grimm says.

A very slow, and very startled, and very stupid realization bubbles to the surface of my drug-fuzzed brain. "You're Breath," I say. "Aren't you? You're not just a weird English teacher. You work for Magonia."

I want to put my head in my hands, I've been so blind.

"You're supposed to be a genius, Kerwin. Did it never occur to you?"

Grimm rolls up his sleeve and shows me the tattoo of a whirlwind on his wrist. Aza always said he had tattoos covered with makeup. She thought maybe he had some kind of embarrassing something, a pot leaf or a pinup girl. Nope.

"I *was* Breath. I left. Now I'm rogue. Protecting Aza."

"But you weren't protecting Aza," I say. "As I recall, she died."

Grimm looks at me contemptuously.

"I was watching her for two years," Grimm says. "When she started to fail, I was in the process of acquiring a new skin for her, keeping them from finding her. Magonia got to her before I could save her."

"Why would you be 'protecting her' anyway? Why would you care?"

"Some things are bigger than caring, Kerwin," says Grimm. "Some things are about saving the world. Not to put too fine a point on it. You have a lethal weapon, even if you're not the one who created it, you do your best to keep it away from someone who'd use it."

"So generous of you," I say, because I have suspicions about every part of this. "And Heyward?"

"She's my asset now," Grimm says. "She came to me. She

was trying to reintegrate into earth."

"She was lying," I say automatically. "She's not reformed. If anything, she's taking Aza to Zal. She's loyal to Magonia."

Grimm shakes his head. "Things are becoming even more unstable. The sky's starving, and there's unrest everywhere. Many are questioning everything they thought they knew. Not just Heyward.

"I think Eli Boyle's been taken by someone other than Magonia. There's no indication Zal has her. She was grabbed from down here, early in the morning, same day Aza was taken by SWAB. There weren't any storms nearby the night Eli went missing. I tracked weather patterns for the entire area. That means it's not Magonia, and it's not Breath. They'd need cover, and there was none."

Something occurs to me, idiotically late. In all my certainty that Zal had Eli, it didn't occur to me that one of the things Eli does early in the morning is *practice*.

That tree out by the cemetery. That field.

I look down at my pajamas. I was about to do something I couldn't come back from. And now everything's different.

I look up at Grimm. "Get me out of here."

At three in the morning, I slink through the hallways and down to the office. I pick the lock. Yes, I know how to pick a lock. I have to do *something* with my brain in the quieter moments.

I open the filing cabinet, find my file, and pull it out, along with the Ziploc of my possessions. My phone with its solar charger. My compass. My ship-viewing glasses. I open a cabinet and find my backpack, intact. Good.

I look at my file. Lot of pages. It says I've been working up to this break for years, that I have an active imaginary world, that *blah blah blah* various diagnoses, and though some of them are valid, Magonia isn't anything but Magonia. It also says I have a savior complex regarding the late Aza Ray Boyle.

That part is uncomfortable reading.

I put the file back. I replace my things with things scavenged from other files, other people's phones, other people's eyeglasses not allowed because of glass. I don't want SWAB having an easy time knowing where I am, knowing immediately that I busted out with gear they gave me.

An hour later, I'm in Grimm's car. We pull away like we're headed for an early morning coffee rather than escaping a locked ward and looking for a girl stolen by—maybe—a country in the sky.

It's so easy to escape, I think to my shame, the only thing that was keeping me in there was the lingering suspicion that I might actually need to stay in.

Which is still lingering.

Savior complex.

Yeah. It's not like I'm your usual.

Grimm's silent. I look behind us, expecting to see SWAB, police, but there's no one on the highway. We're alone. The whole horizon is black, lightning moving like strobes. My SWAB glasses are showing me ships all over the sky.

I open my backpack and bring out the information I swiped from SWAB on my way out the door the last time around.

"SWAB's been trying to source images of Maganwetar for years," I say.

"They still haven't put eyes on it?" Grimm asks.

"No. And it's pissing them off. They're using drone

surveillance, and a couple of small planes taking unusual paths. It looks like they want to overtake it. Use it to bring weather to some places on earth and . . ."

"And deny it to others. If you control the weather, you control drought, for yourself, and for your enemies."

"SWAB wants to control the weather. Whatever they want with Aza, they want to use her."

Grimm looks over at me, assessing.

"Not bad," he says grudgingly, and drives.

I can see the field, a big wide expanse of nothing. There should be a giant skeletal tree right there at the edge of it, a black, perfectly straight-lined tree bigger than any tree for miles.

But there isn't.

We pull over and get out of the car. Just a field. Nothing in it. Windblown, trampled cornstalks. A crater where the tree used to be.

There's a print on the smooth clay of one side of the crater. I look more closely. A small human handprint.

A shining object on the ground. Eli's phone, in its distinctive constellation case, dark blue enamel, silver stars in the positions they were in the moment Eli was born. A gift from Aza with a manufacturing assist from me.

Grimm's instantly mobilized, shoveling away at the edge of the pit, banging a stake into the ground. Attaching ropes to it.

"What happened?" I ask.

"A bounty hunter," says Grimm. "This is worse than I thought. It will have taken Eli on a Magonian contract."

"*Who?*"

"Not who. What. A mandrake."

I . . . what? "A mandrake."

A mandrake isn't a sentient creature. It's a *root*. A root that people used to think could scream and kill people with the sound of its voice. Folklore. Plants that walked and talked, old-school witchery, that kind of thing, and even as I think that, I think, yeah, skyships, *that* kind of thing.

Who am I to decide on what's possible? I should know that by now, if I know nothing else. Who am I to decide if there's such a thing as a mandrake bounty hunter?

An old Aza phrase, coined in a moment of total indecision. "Analysis equals paralysis, Jason, let's just go!"

Is this good advice? No one said it was. But it's the only advice I have in my head right now.

"Everyone up there is looking for Aza, and the mandrakes are high-end hunters, no surprise one of them would come looking here," Grimm says. "They just misjudged the fact that SWAB—"

He gives me a look of disdain—

"—got to Aza before they could. I'm guessing they didn't realize they'd gotten the wrong sister. Otherwise, Aza and Eli would both be captive, to be sold to Zal for the highest price they could get. Mind you, I'm just as wanted as she is. Breath is a permanent job. If you leave, you're a fugitive—"

Something catches my eye on the cemetery cliff. Something on the edge.

That tree. It shouldn't be there.

"Grimm—" I say.

But Grimm's looking too, and his face changes.

"RUN!" he shouts. "NOW! GO!"

The tree on the edge of the cliff disappears before my eyes. Like that. GONE. Like it's been sucked away, or taken by a sinkhole.

The sky starts screaming, and it's suddenly full of birds. I'm hearing shrieking and wings, and I'm standing here, in the middle of this cornfield, with feathers falling all around me.

There's a ripple in the surface of the earth, in the crater. The field starts to roll up, right next to my feet, like a carpet unfurling backward, the whole field shuddering and shaking. An earthquake?

"Go, Kerwin!" Grimm shouts. He has rope and some sort of torch, and he's looping the rope frantically into a knot.

I can't keep my balance. I'm running over the ruts in the field, and the whole of the ground is moving, and in the sky, birds everywhere, still screaming, a flock of them spinning hard above me.

My foot gets stuck in a hole I swear wasn't there before, and I'm yanking at my ankle, trying to get it loose, when something lurches up out of the earth, fast-moving with tons of spiky branches, and even as my brain identifies it as "tree," I know it's not.

It has arms and legs. It's made of roots, or wood, pale and twisted. It has a *face*. A face that is gnarled and set in a howl. It rises up out of the ground with a wailing moan.

My foot's stuck. I can't move. I'm still not moving when Grimm steps in front of me, and the thing that isn't a tree, that isn't a person, snatches him up in one fist.

It must be thirty feet tall.

Things go into slow motion. I can't absorb what I'm hearing, Grimm screaming, fighting, and then his spine making a noise a spine shouldn't make, a broken crack like the sound of something being trampled.

The mandrake bends over and picks me up too, claw hands, splintered fingers, crushing me in its fist. I'm shouting and my body is in agony, my lungs bursting, my brain a morass of numbers, thousands of numbers, shaken out of sequence, a collapse of decimals, data—

Then birds screaming—

Birds screaming—

Feathers falling—

Birds are diving at the mandrake, bombing it from above—

It's crushing me, turning me to pulp, ribs cracking, body breaking—

When it looks up at the birds and howls. It dives into the crater.

The cries of birds and then nothing.

Darkness and the screal of wind through my ears, as we

F

    A

        L

      L

through the earth.

CHAPTER 17

{AZA}

We travel silently through the night, deeper into the Tangle, and then out the southern corner, and across the sky, moving past the equator. I realize I've been so, SO missing this—the wind around me, the tossing of ships on clouds and storms. This last year of land legs makes me understand why sailors in earth's oceans often refuse to come in from the sea, and when they do, just keep leaving again, no matter what happiness they have at home. Or that's the story anyway.

Maybe they don't actually have happiness at home.

Maybe someone's lying to them, someone they trusted, and maybe that's why everything you've ever read about sailors is them searching for some mythic mermaid to fall for, some manatee in the shape of a girl-delusion, some white whale out in the middle of the waves. Maybe there's no reason to come in from the sea once you're out. Maybe the world is better in solitude.

Maybe you should just stay away from love. Lonely whales. Maybe that's a better version. Maybe that's how it's supposed to be if you're the only one like you. No one else around you. Out there in the dark, singing your song alone.

I smell thunder. The sky shakes when we move through it, invisible waves of wind and rain.

It's both exactly the same and vastly more beautiful than it ever was. In this little boat, with my not-sister, I can see it all more clearly than I did the last time I was up.

I can see the way pods of squallwhales are everywhere, not just escorting Magonian ships, but roving wild on their own. I can see other things too, scars on the squallwhales' skin, but at least these are free. Not tied to any vessel, not making storms for anyone but themselves.

A surging pod of white-speckled whales stops beside the boat and sings to me.

I put my hand out to touch one of them, and it comes closer, so I put my leg over the edge of the boat and climb onto its back.

I'm thinking of my dad. *What would it be like to ride a whale? Like a zeppelin. Like a submarine. Like a train.*

Like riding a whale, is what it's like.

Its skin is rougher than I'd have thought it would be, like the texture of ice over sand, and there's nothing vaporous about it. It feels real. It IS real, I remind myself. It's a squallwhale, not something I made up.

I touch the ridge over the squallwhale's eye, and it's hard and tough, like touching a dinosaur.

This isn't a matter of skill, but of trust between the squall-whale and the passenger. Heyward watches from the boat, her skin going bluer by the minute.

She's human. I'm from up here. We're from different species, practically.

Is that what matters, in the end?

That's not how I want to see things, but maybe I should

try to keep my brain from imagining utopia—everyone holding hands and sharing their food, a giant potluck attended by both Magonians and humans. It's not like I ever felt comfortable in those situations. It's not like I was ever a person who held the hands of her whole town. And it's not like there's perfection down there. It's not like everyone is kind, not like everyone is generous, not like everyone is even remotely *good*.

Maybe differences matter more than I want them to. Maybe I belong in the sky, and ONLY in the sky.

I cling to the squallwhale's back as it navigates, a huge thing moving gracefully, not drifting but swimming. It's rapturous in its lightness, in the cold, in its task. It sings a frozen song, and I sing too, the notes coming from my throat and chest like icicles. Part of me wonders what we're doing to the world down there, if we're bringing snow that we shouldn't, in a place that makes no sense.

But we're over the ocean. It has to be okay.

These things about the sky could break anyone's heart, the sapphire of the heavens, the way the world is around and beneath us, the chilly solidity of the whale, the grace and power in its movements. I sing with the whale's particular sonar, our voices mingling into a soft snowfall that covers everything below us with flakes.

Only a few creatures sing. Whales and bats, humans, birds. Magonians. Mice, according to my mother anyway.

It's a special thing to be one of the world's singers. I should be grateful to be this. I should be grateful to be out here, alive, whatever else is wrong.

Some people never get to have anyone who understands them. Some people are lonely forever. Heyward. I haven't been lonely. I've had people who love me. If I'm lonely from here on out, I can live with that.

There's an unwelcome memory in my brain, of me and Jason in bed together, him rolling toward me and putting his hand on the part of my chest that feels like a wishbone, him touching me over the place in my lung where my canwr door is.

It makes me sad, angry, and confused.

So I sing ice with the squallwhale that won't melt for a while. I wonder what people will think of it, below us. Frozen blue weather that doesn't turn to water, in the middle of a place that should be warm. A tiny berg, newborn in the sea. Maybe if we sang hard enough we could reverse the things that are happening on earth. Save humans from the wrong things they've done to the climate. Save Magonians from the wrong things Zal's doing to the sky. Maybe I could sing balance, and that's my job, not to live, but to fix the weather as everyone else breaks it.

Maybe that's why I'm here.

Maybe love doesn't actually matter, not for me. Maybe I'm just supposed to do this alone. Would that be the worst thing, to have a job like that? Am I being selfish, wanting more? Maybe I can't have everything.

Maybe no one gets to have everything.

Come, the squallwhale sings, and swims me to a piece of the sky where at first, I can't figure out what I'm looking at, and then I can see. It's a nursery. There are tiny squallwhales all over, little storming whales, each creating tiny rainstorms.

It's trite to feel safe with whales, but I guess I'm trite. I hear a series of pings and chirrups, the whales conversing in a language I don't share with them.

I look over at Heyward, patiently piloting our boat through the squallwhale nursery. Her face is expressionless.

Who is she? What does she love? What would make her risk her life?

I think maybe Heyward fell in love with the ground somewhere along the line. Or someone on it. We move away from the squallwhale nursery and back into open sky, and for a while, I drift, trying not to think about any of the things that hurt, trying to focus on what I just saw and let it make me stronger. There are plenty of hard things, but there are still squallwhales being born. That has to be a good thing.

Suddenly Heyward motions me urgently to get back into the boat.

There's a sizzling sound. Birds are circling us out of nowhere, black birds and red birds, huge winged things, all of them on fire. The edge of the sky is smoke and the birds are flame. They look like . . .

A flock of phoenixes?

"SING!" Heyward shouts.

If we had sails, they'd be on fire by now. Our pod of squallwhales are being hit by falling embers, and they're singing rain ferociously, screaming in pain as the birds burn their skin.

I bend a note from out of the sky, a note that says *RAIN*, and heavy drops start to form above us, condensation in the clouds to put the living candles out. They sizzle and hiss as the water falls, and I sing harder. I can't even see them, really, they're moving so fast.

TURN BACK! they sing. *LEAVE THIS SKY!*

Golden beaks and feathers in blue, red, orange, and black. They smell like a wildfire and their voices are hisses and crackles.

Heyward is urging us on, and I can see a sea of red flaming mouths wide open and full of fire, and wings spread wide, and then they're all in a line before us.

Is this the Flock the agency wanted, back there on the ship? It makes sense. They're weapons. They're a flock of something violent. . . .

But they're not going to work with me to take Zal down. They're wild. Firebirds with their own rules.

I sing harder and the rain comes in torrents, the kind of rain the world could drown in, and inside my heart I'm remembering last year, the water rising up out of stone, me trying to unbalance everything. But in my throat I'm singing a different song. *Drench, simmer, sizzle.*

Firedie, I sing. *Firefade. Smokefall.* Some of the birds turn from red to orange, and from orange to steel gray. Some of the birds turn from blue to black, and their wings are like torches, still dully glowing, but dimmer. Coals in the furnace, only waiting to be stoked.

Are you the Flock? I sing at one of them.

TURN BACK! it sings in answer.

I glance over at Heyward, who's bent, pushing the ship hard into the dark, gasping and coughing as waves of rainwater pour over her.

One of the birds comes close enough to burn me, and I feel the edge of its wing. At first it's soft as silk and then it hisses in, a slice like a hot knife through butter.

No more! screams one of the firebirds. *Turn back!*

I cry out. It opens its beak. It's a dragon, a snake-bird, and all of it is made of glory.

I'm drawn toward it. I want to press my body to it and hold

it. I know that if I do, I'll die, but I feel myself leaning in, feel myself singing into it, and now my song is something else.

Not rain, but un-rain. Air, and a fanning of flames, a new wind made of song, and I'm singing fire, and the phoenixes are getting brighter, all around us. I'm singing with them, and I'm making them stronger. They want my anger and fear, and I'm filling them with it.

With my desire to start everything over from birth to seventeen.

With my broken heart and fearful mind.

Right in front of me, this beautiful creature speaks in a brittle bright tone, a bell of light, a cracking whip of sound.

Breathe in, it says. It opens its brilliant beak, and flares its shining feathers, and pours fire out in a song. It scorches the air coming into my lungs.

And then there's Heyward. She screams a Breath battle cry and uses our rain bucket to drench the bird that's right in my face. Its wings spread out, and all of it is on fire for a moment, and then it dims, black feathers, black beak, dead song. It flicks away, ashes.

There's a hiss that hurts my ears, and one by one the phoenixes blink out like an electric fence with a short circuit in it, leaving a space for the boat to pass through, and onward; the edges of the smoke a path leading us forward into forever.

One phoenix remains, a bright trail across the sky ahead of us. It looks back.

That way is death, it sings in bleak, fragmented Magonian. *For your kind.*

I feel like I'm half dead already.

Still, I sing us forward, my voice a current of heat in the

now-cooling sky. The bird's glow is orange and brilliant, and from below it must look like a comet. It flits and smokes a pattern, until we see what it's lit up for us.

She was here, the phoenix sings. *Magonia was here, destroying.*

It's like a reflection seen on fog. Or a *fata morgana*, a mirage in the sky. It's an image of a ship. Not *Amina Pennarum*. That ship, the only skyship I ever REALLY knew, was destroyed, a wreck on the shore of Svalbard.

No, this ship is another pirate ship, a gigantic thundercloud made of black, and its sails are not bats, but manta rays, their wings bending and maneuvering the winds, their bodies tense against the sky. They're huge. Each one is as large as a house. These rays are flying too fast. Their wings are bending more than they should, pushed by the wind, buffeted by forces they can't control.

I can see Heyward looking up at the clouds, watching the images the phoenix has made.

My heart sinks.

My mother's standing at the helm of the ship, next to Dai. She's dressed in a new uniform, and this one has insignia all over it. It's indigo blue, and the insignia's gold. This is a new ship. A bigger and better one, stolen from who knows where.

Zal looks strong and ferocious. Nothing like the woman I watched being taken up to prison a year ago, dangling from a rope, helpless, half-suffocated, and broken. Nothing like the woman who escaped from prison just a few days ago. This woman's the captain of a warship, and more than that.

She's gained a lot of power. Because now the image shows me that she's surrounded by tethered ships, all in a circle.

She's at the front of the fleet.

Chained to her shoulder is Caru. I feel my heart lurch, and I gasp in pain. My heartbird. Chained not to a mast anymore, but to the monster herself. My whole body rebels against it, but I don't have time to fall apart.

Where is ELI??

The Magonians on Zal's ship are uniformed like she is. White-haired men and twilight-haired women. Everyone looks angry, and I don't know any of them. What I do know is that they're strong. I can see their voices from here, even without hearing them. There are songs all over that ship, and the songs are pulling at tendrils of the sky, tugging gravity into their own desires.

I can see their songs moving the ship, fast, too fast, and the manta wings make the fleet of ships appear and disappear, one moment darkness, the next an assembly of faces and singers, each bending things.

What I'm looking at seems clear. We thought we'd defeated her, but we only made her stronger. Through her imprisonment she's netted herself sympathy, knowledge, and an army.

Another ship comes into view opposite my mother's ship, and the people on it, Magonians but not uniformed, are covering their ears in pain. My mother's ship pulls up to them and takes their supplies.

That would be normal for Zal, I think. It's a provisioning ship and my mother is, after all, a pirate, even if she's never acknowledged that. But the people onboard look very hungry, and the ship is in severe disrepair. Its batsail is missing one wing. It hurts to look at. She isn't coming to help them.

No, she makes them kneel. Some of them refuse.

What is she doing? Isn't she supposed to be *stopping* the famine? *Helping* her people? Her goal is feeding the hungry, not helping to starve them out of the sky.

My mother's crew brings out their swords. I can hardly watch as they slaughter a ship's worth of innocents for refusing to submit to Zal's will.

Zal herself cuts the one-winged batsail off its mast and lets it fall. The carrion birds swoop after it.

The lightning in the *fata morgana* flashes and then the image recedes. It's like it's the ghost of something that happened here, projected by the phoenix's song.

I don't need to see any more. I know Zal. She wants to look down from that ship and see no lights, no earth, nothing but empty water. My mother's a destroyer and I'm a—

What am I?

Now that the image is gone, in the place where it was I see the actual shipwreck Zal left here, this time real, tangible. It's right here, the aftermath. We're sailing through a graveyard.

The air wreck Zal created is ruined and bobbing in the air, smashed to planks and splinters. The squallwhales around us sing out in horror, and I notice that hanging from the ship's hull are several dead whales, the escort of the ship Zal raided. Also, the rigging's full of bright feathers, and as we get closer, I see that they're canwr.

Dead, all of them, brilliantly plumaged skeletons. I see no crew, only massive holes in the wrecked ship's deck. The sails are tattered and the masts are splintered.

Nightingales, hisses the phoenix. It flies closer to us. *They came from Magonia. With her. Nightingales. Singing death.*

Then it's gone, a bright star twisting away through the night.

I know what Zal wants now. I know that she doesn't care about life. She only cares about destruction. It was never about hunger, or if it was, it hasn't been for a long time. She's broken and seeking revenge on earth and Magonia both.

I look at Heyward, and I look at the squallwhales.

"Do we keep going?"

A squallwhale answers me instead.

Glowgone it sings, looking at one of the mutilated squallwhale corpses. Petrichor is the smell, not decay. Rain and stone. But the whale is dead, and the canwr are dead, their necks broken, maybe a hundred of them. The deck of the ship is covered with feathers and bones.

Deeper sky, sings the whale. *Brighter song. To the pearl clouds and the ice.*

Heyward nods. "Keep going," she says. "South."

CHAPTER 18

{JASON}

A flock of bats flies around my face, twitchy things with glider wings and little fox faces. I'm—

In a cage? A moving cage. I can't see the mandrake. I'm being carried, heading down, on a steep, slippery slant.

I hurt all over, and my vision is weird. I feel like maybe I have a concussion, but I'm whole. Grimm, it comes back to me, is dead. I can't even think about what happened to him.

Why didn't the mandrake kill me too?

It's a *bounty hunter*, my brain informs me. That means the mandrake wants to sell me to someone. That means it thinks I might be valuable.

I jostle and slide from end to end of my cage, and all around me there are high-pitched creaks. The knowledge of how I'm being transported finally rolls over me like nausea. These are bars made of the mandrake's rib cage, and I'm inside them.

There's a staircase going down into the dark, and far below us I can hear water splashing. We're going deeper into the center of the earth.

I have no GPS. No Google. No Wikipedia. No maps of anything underground. I spent the past year memorizing the sky, itemizing constellations, plotting charts, learning languages, but not *under* the earth. Not this.

This is becoming a pattern. Cluelessness over and over again.

Far in the distance I can hear a ghastly sound, a shrieky howling.

The roots in the ceiling rustle and stretch. They make a sound that isn't makeable by humans, or at least I don't think I could make it. Maybe Aza could.

We walk, and as we walk, roots listen and consider us, moving in the earth above our heads, guiding us down one of the tunnels.

Far off down the river I hear a long, wavering scream.

My vision goes in and out, twitching, and I'm not sure which direction we're going. My compass, still on my person, is pointing west, but I have no idea if that's true.

Not just one scream. A bunch of other voices, shouts, chanting noises. High- and low-pitched, something that sounds like a drum. Something that sounds like a waterfall.

The mandrake stops, growls, and I feel it quiver, somehow taking root.

We drop through the dirt.

We tunnel downward and sideways, really, really fast, like the kind of vines that strangle trees and pull down houses. Kudzu. That's the word I'm thinking as we twist around rocks. I gasp when I can, when we move through caverns and empty places in the damp ground.

At last, we're skidding along a slippery black path with a stream alongside it, and the increasing smell of something burning. The walls are made of pumice now, and they're hot.

There's a tunnel, and glowing light and sound. The screaming's stopped and now all I hear are a million languages at once, howls and whistles, whispers and barks.

The mandrake moves through the tunnel, slow and sure. There's light down here.

It's bright as a volcano, because it IS a volcano.

It's a giant hollow space. Large animals—animals I don't recognize—are spitted and roasting, and I don't want to look at them too closely. One of the creatures being cooked looks to be a giant tortoise, roasting in its shell. Everywhere, there are monsters, some tall and slender, others low to the ground, and everything's speaking at once, cacophony.

There're vats of orange lava spilling out and bubbling on the floor. I watch a giant, stony creature put his hands in, and pour some down his throat. Some kind of earth elemental, some kind of lava monster, which—

This isn't my specialty. A *cherufe*, is all I can think, something from Chilean mythology, an eater of lava and humans. Who knows what a cherufe might look like? This thing? They're supposed to cause earthquakes and landslides. And to be imaginary. Of course. Like everything is imaginary.

Like apparently *nothing* is imaginary.

This is like a theme park, the kind of ride where things jump out at you. It's dusty, with clouds of grit rising up whenever anything moves, fine black sand on the ground and red sand on the walls.

It occurs to me to be scared.

It occurs to me that I might not make it out of here, that I might end up over one of the fires. I don't see any other humans. This is no place for humans, clearly. It's a kiln.

But I can't access scared from this place in my soul. I can't access why I should care if I die or not. I'm here, and Aza's there, and Grimm's dead, and Eli? I have no idea where Eli is.

I feel detached from grief, concussed and done with wonder. This is what's underground? Fine, this is what's underground.

There are other mandrakes here too, and I see their long twisted limbs and strange faces.

They're talking very slowly, and they sound like trees in a storm, moving, scratching against one another. They have holes in their trunks, and inside each of their chests I can see open space surrounded by root bars, like a birdcage. Like the space in Aza's chest, except the mandrake version is not covered by skin.

The mandrake strides into the center of the caldera like it belongs here. Maybe it does.

Everyone's in a circle suddenly. The creatures start to stamp their feet, shaking the ground. How many times have the things like this moving below the surface of the earth caused buildings to fall up there? It's like football tackling, or like a bunch of fans in the stands, full of grunts and groans and beer. If enough fans stamp their feet, an entire stadium can shake. Could this be an earthquake happening above us?

And maybe I'm thinking about that to avoid thinking about THIS. I look up from inside the mandrake's chest. Way, way WAY above us, I can see sky. In front of us, though, I see something else.

Eli.

Alive. Caged in the chest of another mandrake. She looks hurt. Her hair is a tangle, but her face? There's a ferocity to it, like she's been through everything, but also like she's angry. I hope that's true. Anger is useful. She's not limp. She's on her feet.

"LET ME OUT!" Eli yells. "I'M NOT YOUR PRISONER!" She shakes the bars, and they tremble, but don't come close to giving.

Her mandrake spins for the benefit of the caldera, showing them the captive.

"Witness the transaction! The Singer," the mandrake yells, and the voice hurts my head. But it's a voice. It's not a sound like wind. There are words.

"How much will the sky pay for their chosen one?" says something else, not a mandrake, but a circling twist of smoke.

"For her life, or for her secrets?" says another creature, this one the man who seems to be made of rocks and dripping lava.

"Enough," says the mandrake that has Eli. "They will pay enough. They come." I feel the mandrake I'm with tensing, and in the cage, Eli tenses too.

There's a humming noise and we all look out through the mouth of the volcano, to see something descending. It looks like a small submersible, connected by a cord to something high above us, extending up into the sky.

Chained to the front of the submersible is a bird with fiery feathers and a dragonish look. It smokes and hisses.

It's a phoenix. No other possibility. I don't have time to assess it. I'm just sort of . . . floored.

The vehicle lands and out of it comes a figure in a diving suit.

I can see his face through his mask. Even if I didn't recognize him from SWAB wanted posters, from the many images of him up on the walls there, and from the surveillance footage I watched from the conference room, Aza sang his likeness once, into an image for me to see, and the tenderness with which she did it nearly killed me.

Dai.

He's here to buy Eli. What the hell can I do about it?

The mandrake that has Eli starts to open the bars of the cage in its chest, bending them to get her out.

"Your prisoner," the mandrake whistles at Dai.

Dai shakes his head. "*This* is a human, not Aza Ray Quel."

He doesn't know who she is. He doesn't know she's Aza's sister—shut up, Eli! Don't say anything to them.

"Take me to Aza!" Eli shouts, deaf to my psychic attempts to stop her. "Where's Aza? Where's my sister?!"

Damn it. Dai's face changes. He stares at Eli for a moment, assessing her.

"Eli Boyle?" he says slowly. His face changes. He looks completely uncertain. And also torn. I wonder what he's thinking.

"That'll do, I suppose," he says at last. "I'll take her."

"The payment," says the mandrake.

This is the moment that Eli sees ME, and yells some more. I don't blame her. She looks at the edge.

"JASON!" she screams. My mandrake is spinning and so is hers.

Dai turns. "YOU!" he shouts.

He manages one step toward me, when there's a glint of green and red, a fast-moving dart, and then a flash of spotted wings, another flash of bright blue feathers—

And then there's an explosion of birds, diving through the volcano's opening, and into the chamber with us. There's screaming and chaos, and for a moment I'm face-to-face with Eli, who is clinging to her bars.

Eli's cage fills with birds, and the birds transform. An owl woman bites through one of the wooden bars with her beak, and the mandrake the bar belongs to screams.

There are flames rising all around the caldera, and I start shaking the bars in my own cage, but then the blue jay's in with me, and she transforms too. A girl with a bright blue mohawk, dressed in armor, muscles very visible. Her arms are lined in blue and black feathers and her face is unholy beautiful. I can't even think about what this means, before she passes me an ax from her shoulder and shouts:

"Get to it, fool!"

She's hacking away at the other bars, and my mandrake is screeching, and staggering, and I catch a glimpse of Dai, doing something with the phoenix attached to his submersible.

My mandrake shrieks as a jet of fire hits just beside me. I'm smelling a smoke that could suffocate anyone, and I see Eli cover her face.

"It'll make you see things," she shouts. "You'll hallucinate. Hold your breath, Kerwin."

We lurch, and suddenly, my mandrake is crouching and leaping, and I'm bashing against the wood like I'm being beaten with two-by-fours. Eli's twisting inside her cage, like she did on the tree before, flipping up and around, kicking from the inside, and I see she's trying to kick the bars out.

I feel a shudder in the body of the creature I'm in, like a tree considering which direction to fall when sawed down. The mandrake is gushing sap, which pours down, stinging me, burning my skin. It's wet and mud and fire and blood.

Eli's kicking at the bars in her cage, swinging from the top of them and pushing her heels against the part of the mandrake's chest that's weakened, and her mandrake screams in fury and pain as she does it.

The blue jay girl takes one more swing of the ax, and my bars give. There's fire everywhere now.

I leap out, and the blue jay girl comes with me. There are Rostrae everywhere, fighting the creatures from underground, and the mandrake are being stabbed in the eyes by flying birds, beaks, talons.

Eli's an inch away from freedom. I tug at the bars that are caging her, and she pushes. I feel them starting to splinter.

I turn my head, and Dai's there, his hands clutching the phoenix's wings. The phoenix is tremendous. He's barely holding on to it, but he looks straight into my eyes and then he pins the bird's wings back, screaming as he does. They're burning him. It screams too, and phoenix fire streaks across the cavern, a meteor of orange and blue flames, directly at us.

I don't even think about it. I throw myself between Eli and the fire.

It hits me in the chest, a blastbomb of light and sparks, and the phoenix is still screaming, a flood of fire pouring from its mouth.

The mandrake holding Eli bursts into flame and carbonizes, a black smoke cloud, a flaming echo around the screaming face.

I'm on fire, I realize, slowly, and Eli's shouting, and I can't hear anything, and then I start to feel the flames, the pain—

Eli twists upside down, her arms clinging to the bars of the cage. She kicks one foot, and then the other, until she's vertical, and as she does it, she kicks through the remaining charred head of her mandrake, and flips upward through her cage.

Dai's hands are tangled in phoenix feathers. He turns just as Eli high-kicks him in the chin, knocking him flat.

Then Eli's rolling me in the dirt, yelling, "You're not going to die on me! Roll! ROLL!"

Real death isn't like something from a movie. It smells like cooked skin and cloth, and a forest burning too. Breathing too hard, lungs scalded. Worse than lightning. Worse than hospital. Worse than being lost in pi.

Something grabs me by the straps of my backpack, and then another something grabs me, and I'm dizzy, but the flames are out. I rise.

I turn my head and Eli's beside me, rising too, both of us dangling from—

Talons.

Rising up and out of the volcano. Far below me. Tree-tops, buildings, fields. I pass through a cloud and feel myself shivering.

I can hear nothing but birds, screaming, shrilling, and I'm not in any kind of state to assess anything. *Analysis/paralysis*, says my brain, and laughs hysterically.

Birds have me by the neck, the back, the ankles, the arms. My head's pounding. There's no room for pi in there anymore, and that at least is a relief, though there's no room for logic either.

"Wait," I croak. I start struggling. "Drop me! Leave me! I have to fight him!"

"He's hurt," says Eli, her voice strangely calm for the voice of someone flying. I feel like I'm far away from myself, far away from the sound of voices. "He's delirious."

I'm gasping, my lungs fried, my skin feeling crisped. I feel cold and hot at once.

I look down and see, what seems like a million miles below us, my own feet dangling in midair. Take me to a hospital. Take me to the graveyard. I'm dying.

My future is flight, says my brain as we rise.

I'm a hoax, a dying boy who's grown wings.

CHAPTER 19

{AZA}

We sail for days. We're starving and freezing. There's no food, nowhere to stop, and the boat has no provisions. We're wet, and an empty sky stretches around us for thousands of miles.

Neither of us has said it yet, but we're lost. What destination did we have to begin with? Not enough of one.

Will we die out here?

I'm missing Jason. Missing Eli. Missing Caru. Missing everything. Missing even Heyward, who is with me, but increasingly silent, trying to conserve her breath. I'm familiar with this kind of silence. She's blue-lipped, and every once in a while she chokes out a ragged, rasping cough. She's barely talking, barely moving. She keeps a hand at the center of her chest, and periodically a trickle of blood drips from her nose. Altitude sickness, combined with lack of oxygen. Her head hurts.

She doesn't complain, but I can see it on her face. The studied blankness of Breath has been replaced by a line between her eyebrows, and a dark blue circle under each eye. She looks so much like the Aza I used to see in the mirror, the sickest version of myself, that I can hardly stand to look at her. I know how she feels. I know *exactly* how she feels.

"We could stop," I say.

"Where?" she asks. "There's no land, not up here, and not below us."

I worry. About everything, myself included. Hunger twists around my spine, and into my guts.

The sky around us is dark and heavy, as confusing as it's ever been, and everything is a sea of shadows, twisting parts of air wrapping around our boat. It's much colder as we move south, which makes me think I've never properly understood anything about geography. Could we be heading toward Antarctica? The clouds are strange colors, marbled like the endpapers of fancy books.

I close my eyes and try to feel Caru with Zal, on her ship, but all I can feel are the points of a thousand stars, my focus divided all over the sky, and a terror that he's mad and panicked.

Caru. What if he's the way he was when I found him on *Amina Pennarum*, caged, trapped, damaged, terrified?

Or dead.

There's that possibility too.

The door in my lung hurts, like nothing will ever sing from there again, and my heart aches.

My Magonian tattoos are a hurried rush of pictures, Caru all over my skin, like a flock of birds flying, but it's the same falcon, flying across my arm in a stuttering image, calling for help, trying to find me, trying to keep ME safe.

I look at my arms, despairing, and watch the Caru tattoo move in agony, screaming across my bicep. Worse than that, I see Jason suddenly, a tattoo of him assembling itself on my palm. Eli next, beside him. A flashing motion of my sister's face.

I close my fist.

That's just my head and heart talking. Misery appears on my skin. It's not real. It has no prediction power. It's only my thoughts made visible. And my thoughts are sad and stupid. What ever happened to the Aza who could imagine good things? I swear she used to exist.

Heyward coughs again, choking at the depths of her lungs. She's getting worse.

"Aza," she whispers.

"Yeah?"

"If I die out here—"

"You're very much, a hundred percent NOT going to die," I tell her.

"If I *do*," she says.

I relent. "If you do, what?"

"Tell me what my life would've been like down below. I don't want to be out here for no reason. I wasn't ever a drowner. Maybe Breath was the best thing that ever happened. Maybe it was . . . better than what you had. Look at it down there. It's not so good on the ground either, is it? It's not what I thought it was."

I think about my life. I think about how my life would have been if I hadn't been sick and Magonian. I can't lie to her.

"Your life would have been incredible. You have amazing parents," I say.

She smiles. "Really amazing, or just good at their jobs?"

"Really . . . amazing. Mom . . . our mom can sing mouse songs," I say. "Our dad can do a backflip on a trampoline."

"What's a trampoline?"

"It's a . . . thing you jump up and down on?"

"Why would you do that?"

"For fun," I say.

She looks at me.

"Strange," she says.

"Don't you have fun up here?" I ask her.

"We have work," she says. "We learn to fight. We learn to be good at it. But we don't play."

Then she coughs again, and I feel like I should explain everything about why earth is beautiful, about why seeing a sunset can make you believe in happiness, and why a birthday surrounded by people who've known you since you were born is important. Why any of this matters. Why it should be saved.

Why people are loving, and why it's worth it to be loved by them—even if they hurt you.

"You would've had a sister," I say. "She's brave and tough, and acts like everyone else should be just like her. She's strong like you. You have that in common. And she's the best person I've ever met. She's been like that since she was tiny. She was born after you . . . left."

Heyward looks at me. "It might have been nice to have a sister."

"Yeah," I say.

"Is it like this?"

"You mean is it like being castaways together?" I say, and smile at her. "Basically, exactly the same."

I think about all the things I've read about rafts lost at sea, about stowaways dropped off ships, and ships running out of fuel in the middle of the ocean. I think about Zal and her plank.

I think for a dark moment about worse ways to die. I've thought of plenty of bad ways over the years. I never imagined there were still more to think about.

A gust of wind blows through, and water whips around us. There's a clap of thunder. Rain starts falling from nowhere. No squallwhales overhead. In the thunder, I'm hearing song, but it's an echoing, aching song from far away.

The air feels strange suddenly. A prickling electricity runs through it. And then the sky starts to shake.

I don't even look, I just tense, and inhale, ready to sing.

When the sound begins, it's not what I'm expecting. There's a high hum, and I'm instantly flat to the bottom of the boat, Heyward dropping beside me.

She rolls hard toward me just as something zings through the air. She grabs me and yanks me out of the way, putting herself on top of me.

"Nightingales!" she shouts. Another dart flies and she rolls, still protecting me as another dart flies past us—

"Are you okay?"

She doesn't answer. She just points up.

There's a warship above us. Magonian. A capital ship. There are Magonian soldiers onboard, and the masts swarm with hundreds of the black bird things that flew at us before, when we were on the prison ship.

"AZA RAY AND HEYWARD BOYLE!" the ship's broadcast shouts. "SURRENDER ON ORDERS OF MAGANWETAR."

The capital. The only thing Zal despised more than drowners down on earth. The ship begins to let down lines, ropes for our capture, and I wait in the bottom of the boat, preparing my song.

I'm weak. I don't know if I have enough strength, but I have some, a moment, and I feel Heyward beside me. She makes a sound of pain, but then she's crouching too, ready to fight—

There's another note, not from the ship, a sound like nothing I've ever heard before.

"LEAVE THESE SKIES!" something sings, a ferocious howl, and out of nowhere, the sky's—

FULL.

Exploding with song. Birds, maybe a hundred thousand, spinning out of thin air, a rush of wings, and all of them are singing, singing in unison with someone, flying from everywhere. They're like a swarm of bees, or like a veil crossing the blue, and they're everywhere.

We're in the center of it, and they twist around us like a tornado, then around the Magonian warship. I watch the ship tossing in the wind, losing control of first its sails, then its steering.

A crane is up in the air shrilling a note at the top of her pitch, and a small silver bat is up in the air too, voice high and fierce, singing rage.

The bat sings crisp notes, each one pinging on my ears, and as she sings, I start singing with her, a sonar song, inaudible to anyone but Magonians. It throbs my lungs and twists my vocal cords, but it's mine, a strange song that grabs at the edges of the sky and tries to fold them up. I've sung with bats before, back on Zal's ship last year. I remember how to do it.

The whole sky is glowing and screaming and slow motion. REALLY slow motion. The sky stops moving at its normal rate and drops down to a half-speed strangeness, a strangled pace. Almost out of nowhere, the warship turns on end, pushed by song like a ship hitting an iceberg. It cracks in half. Its crew leaps into the sky, falls into thin air, dying.

I swallow hard, because the wake of that song is coming for us, I can feel it, a rushing roar of noise, a tsunami of voice and wind.

Heyward's pale and sweaty, her hair twisting in the wind as our boat flips in the echo of the other ship sinking. I don't have enough breath left to do anything about it. Even if I did, it's bigger than I am.

We fall. We're dropping through the atmosphere.

I grab Heyward's cold hand. She holds on to me, too, and it's a small comfort, her weak fingers in mine, her body beside me as the earth speeds closer.

This is the end of our story.

I see Heyward's face and it's like I'm watching myself in a mirror. She looks at me, and I know she's seeing the same thing, but the Magonian version, my body turning to un-body, an ashen drifting nothing, someone who'll blow away like sea foam.

But we smack against something, hit hard, and slide. Below us there's still only open air, but we've stopped falling.

I turn to look at Heyward.

She's unconscious. I bend over her, frantically, checking her breath, her heartbeat, and she has both, but they're faint. She's pale and hardly breathing.

I look at her chest.

A dart. It's right there, and there's a spreading ring of red around it. Oh no, no no. I put my fingers on it, but I don't pull it out. I don't know what to do. Eli and Jason are the ones who know first aid.

I'm the one who was always needing it.

The surface we're on tilts, and we slide. I grab Heyward's wrist, and hold on to her, clinging with my other hand. I don't know where the edges are. At first I think it's definitely ice, but then, I can just feel the edges of slippery planks. We're on . . . a deck.

I sing a panicked note that turns the air frigid, just for a moment, and I can see the outlines of—

A ship. It could be made of glass, it's so transparent. A ghost ship, or a piece of reflected sun. It's prismatic. The edges blur and gleam. Its sails billow. There is a cabin on the deck. It looks like a glass house, but the walls are the color of cloud. Through the deck, I can see all the way down to earth, the sea, the outlines of land.

I can feel my compass thrumming against my heart, the arrow spinning, and we're nowhere and everywhere at once.

An old man appears, coming through the door that isn't visible, up out of a cabin that isn't visible. *He* is, though.

I'm on guard instantly, leaning over Heyward to shield her, but he's not attacking.

He's small. A gray figure with twisting hair, tattooed all over in white lines like a star map. His eyes are golden. Skin, pale gray, the color of early morning storm. The old man's chest isn't like mine. I see one door open, over his lung, and the crane flies to him and places a ring in his chest. Not a canwr, like Milekt. A heartbird, like Caru. The door closes and together, they sing a note that makes my hair stand on end, strange and piercing, perfectly balanced. I've never heard anything like it. It's beautiful, but it's the kind of sound that hurts everything, one degree away from fingernails on a chalkboard, and on the side of glory instead, but only barely.

This is the one who was singing. The one whose song sank the warship.

HOW did he do that?

He looks at me, and his eyes are the saddest thing I've ever seen. He stares at me, then shakes his head.

"You surely know you're trespassing," he says. His voice is sonorous, beautiful, and very quiet. "This is my sky."

"My friend is hurt," I tell him, and my voice cracks. There's a trickle of blood coming from Heyward's mouth. Her heartbeat feels fainter and the dart quivers with each beat. "I think she's dying. We need your help."

"You fell from the Magonian ship, did you not?"

"No! They—they were trying to capture us."

"Criminals, then?"

"Please help us," I say. "Please. She's not okay."

Heyward's eyes are flicking behind her lids. She's not seizing. But is she about to? I try to keep her head from falling backward.

"That is a drowner," the old man says. Contempt fills his voice.

"She was Breath," I say, and he grimaces. I lie slightly, on a hunch. He just sank a Magonian warship, after all. He's no ally of Zal's. "She left them. Now she's a fugitive. That's why we were being chased. Please. They shot her with something. She's dying."

I don't know if the dart was meant for me, or for Heyward, or just hit her at the perfect angle when it was meant only to hurt, not to kill, but this is where we are. I hold Heyward's hand tightly.

First I took her life on earth, and now—

Another door opens in the old man's chest. Another bird flies into it.

My jaw drops.

No. No, that's not how it works. No one has more than one door. No one has more than one canwr—

Not a bird, I realize. A bat. The tiny silver bat. Now they're *all* singing, this old man with two canwr at once, the silver bat rendering all the notes into vibrations, the crane singing peals, and the old man chanting the bass.

"What are you?" I ask him. "*Who* are you?"

"Something extinct," he says. "Or nearly. The last of my kind."

His bat shrieks something soundless. Out of nowhere, there are more birds, not just the silver bat and the crane with the orange beak, but a raven, and a white falcon—like Caru, but smaller. All these land on the old man's arms.

Heyward's lungs are making the sound mine did on earth. I hold her tighter. I can feel her heart working to keep her here.

"Please," I say. "Help us."

"The world is ending," he says. "Things are getting worse, not better. I left a sick country, and now the entire sky is infected with the same plague. You should let her die."

End of everything sings the old man. *End of songs*, and his bat joins in, then his crane. This is a griefsong and an angersong, but it's a helpless, giving-up kind of anger. Sung by all these voices at once. I've never heard anything so beautiful. Nor anything so dark.

Then, off the edge of his deck, I see a plank becoming visible. The air around us bends with his chorus.

"Please," I whisper. Heyward's blood is soaking my hands. My sister, even if she isn't. My family, even though we're not.

"She'll die if you don't help."

I don't know what to do.

So I—

I do something I don't know how to do.

I reach out my hand to the old man's crane. *Come*, I sing. *Help me.*

The bird looks at me, a black eye, voice loud and silken. She tilts her head. This isn't allowed, to call to someone else's canwr, but there's no choice.

The crane sings back to me, an eerie echo. Then we sing a note together, and though the crane isn't mine, we sing anyway. We sing like strangers who discover they know the same songs.

I'm running on faith. I don't have time to decide, to think, to plan.

I *sing*.

I remember with a blast of agony the first time I sang with Caru, the first time I sang with Dai, Svilken, and Milekt—

I sing *light, change, heal.* My voice feels tiny, full of the dead and of fear for Heyward. Full of loss. But his canwr is singing with me like she knows me. Like she's mine. Like we've done this before. We haven't. I've never seen her. But it still feels right, weirdly familiar.

The old man stares at me, stunned.

"What are you doing?" he says.

"Singing," I tell him.

He looks angry at first, then astonished, then angry again.

"Tell me your name."

"Aza Ray Quel," I say.

I don't break eye contact, no matter how panicked I am

about Heyward. I can't afford to. Heyward makes a tiny sound of pain, a little gasp, and I keep looking at him.

"Who are *YOU*?" I ask him again.

This time he tells me.

"I am the Flock."

*I come to my senses, surrounded by feathers and in scream-*ing pain. It's not quite light in here, not quite dark. My brain spins. All around me is—

Insanity.

Jumbled-up combinations of humanbirds that I *thought* I understood. That I *thought* I could picture from Aza's descriptions. I was wrong again. My brain couldn't ever conjure the things I'm seeing. But I know what they are. I try to sit up, but someone presses me back down. I try to move, but I can't. I'm pinned. My chest feels like—

Like it's been torn open.

I'm surrounded by something out of a crazy surrealist painting. Wings and faces, not cartoonish, not like anything I had imagined before, which was admittedly half puppet. This isn't like that at all. These Rostrae are ferocious, angelic, eerie, their arms muscled, the feathers on their shoulders and heads sharp as knives. They look like dreams.

Someone's cutting at my skin—

Someone's cutting my clothes away—

I look. Talons, claws, knives—

Someone is bending over me, cutting at my chest, snipping threads, opening my shirt, clipping, slicing, and it hurts so much I scream.

I scream. I can't help it.

A talon touches me in the center of my chest, and I light on fire all over again, burn with broken skin and blister. I wonder for a crazy second if something's going to happen. If my chest is going to fly open. If there is there a canwr in there I never knew about? Am I . . . could I be Magonian?

But nothing happens. No birds sing from out of my lung.

There's no magic reason, no alien reason I'm the way I am. There's no explanation for all the years of pi. I'm just human. I'm cracked with disappointment even though I swear I already knew this. There's a part of me that hoped.

"You're badly injured, boy, but you're not dead. We've been trying to cut the fibers of your clothing away from your skin since you arrived."

A female owl. Pale with dark speckles, a partially human face, giant feathered wings. I know this owl now, I realize. I know who this has to be.

"Wedda?" I croak.

She flicks her wings open and then shut again.

"Is Aza here?" I ask. "Did you come because of her?"

But Aza doesn't appear.

"Jik," I say to the blue jay girl beside my bed, because now I know exactly who she is.

"Jik," the girl who prodded my wounds confirms. "You should have come with us when we tried to get you the first time. We couldn't make ourselves visible at ground level, only below or above, but we were there. We waited at the hospital, but you didn't come out. We had to track you to the mandrake, and that was nothing any of us wished to do."

I think back to that car ride with the SWAB agents, I have no idea how long ago, the birds outside the window. The flock of birds surrounding me as I got out of the car at home. The birds I ignored.

The Rostrae just look at me.

"Where is she?" I ask. Last remnants of hope. "Please tell me she's here."

"Not here," Jik says. "You matter to her, so Zal wants you. She wants Eli too. There's been a contract out on both of you. We got to you first."

"Wait," I say. "Am I a hostage?"

I feel my lungs contract, and I cough, agonizingly. I have a plaster on my chest, and bandages, now. Everything hurts, but I'm in better shape than I have any right to be, all things considered.

Eli appears in my line of sight. She looks bruised, but intact. Her hair is twisted into complicated knots. She's wearing a uniform that matches those of the Rostrae.

"Jason," she says, and her face is made of relief. "Awake, finally. I wasn't sure you were ever going to be—"

I cough some more.

"—better than you were. You didn't think about breathing up here?"

I cough. "I wasn't trying to come *here*," I say. "I was trying to find you. Are we really . . . in Magonia?"

Eli nods. "I was about to be brokered to Zal. You arrived just in time to get added to the deal. Only one of us was ready for that possibility, though."

Eli shows me a pill. "Always be prepared. Isn't that your motto, Kerwin? Where's your go bag full of everything you could possibly need in any situation?"

"It's full of classified documents," I say. Miraculously, I still have my backpack. That's what they used when they picked me up. It doesn't have anything in the way of first aid in it, though, because I'm dumb. "What's this pill?"

"You're the one who's supposed to be some kind of genius," she says, poking at me like we're sitting at her parents' kitchen island instead of *here*. "What do you think it is?"

No idea. Not unusual for me right now. I feel like the world has turned inside out and everything I thought I knew is utterly irrelevant.

"The drugs my mom developed," she says. "The ones that helped Aza all this time. I've been carrying a supply for months, just in case. If they made a Magonian able to breathe on earth, I figured they'd make a human able to breathe in Magonia. At least, enough to get by."

"Mouse drugs," I realize.

"Mouse drugs," Eli confirms, and puts one in my mouth. "Swallow."

I choke it down. If this is how mice taste, I wouldn't be surprised.

"Stop making that face, Kerwin," Eli says, reading my mind. "You're lucky I have them to share."

"How long have we been here?" I manage to say.

"Four days," she says. "I couldn't do anything about the breathing until you were conscious. You kept spitting out the pills."

I inhale experimentally. The drugs haven't had any effect yet. I still feel like I'm on top of a mountain. I struggle with the restraints. I seem to be tied into my bed with ropes. Or . . . netted?

She looks at me. Her eyes, in spite of her attitude, are teary.

"You're not a prisoner. It's because you kept trying to tear off the bandages. You told us to let you die. And seriously, you almost did. Those burns—whatever kind of fire hit you, it was major. Dai was trying to kill you."

"Where is he? Did he—"

"Gone," she says. "I couldn't do anything. We got saved by Rostrae, but he's still alive. You were basically on fire when we left the ground."

"But he'll go after Aza, he'll—"

Eli looks at me patiently.

"You're hurt. You were hallucinating. Wedda made a poultice out of something. You kept saying you deserved to be punished, that you'd betrayed Aza completely. Did you? Tell me now."

I can't talk about it. I can't talk about this.

I stand up, feeling my skin stretching in pain, but at least I can move. No one stops me. I shuffle out onto the deck of the ship we're on. It's not quite a deck. We're on a huge raft made of branches and twigs. It looks for all the world like a nest.

I laugh bitterly. A nest. Of course. Rostrae. What else would they sail on?

The whole rest of the sky, as far as I can see, is filled with black smoke. The entire upper level of this vessel is full of Rostrae. Hundreds, maybe. And the rest of the sky immediately surrounding the ship is full of them too. None of them in chains. None of them wearing harnesses of any kind, or tied to ships. They're free.

I look at Jik and Eli.

"These are rebel ships," says Jik. "There was a price. Half of us are dead. Dai took command of the Nightingales, and once Zal Quel was free, she waged war in earnest, using them."

"We left our old lives," Wedda says. "We no longer thieve food for the Magonians, perhaps, but there is little forage here, and more danger than we needed to find. My friends are dead. Captain Zal Quel is marauding through the skies, but what she wants is Aza. Look out there—"

Wedda points with a talon, and shows me a part of the sky where black snow is falling.

"That's a ship burned by my former captain. That is another. Her Nightingales sing disaster. They attack Rostrae and other Magonians alike. Anyone who doesn't agree to serve with Zal is murdered. She kills canwr and their owners die with them. She's stilling songs, all over the sky."

"But where is Aza?"

"All we know is that she came off a drowner prison ship and flew into the Tangle with a Breath. Since then, nothing. The entire sky seeks her. Zal to use her, the rest of us to shield her, but she's vanished. We thought you'd know more than we do," says Jik.

Jik spins on her heel and walks away from me. Long blue feathery tails trail beneath her black coat.

I look at Eli. She looks at me, and she looks disappointed in everything. And by everything, I mean me. I AM supposed to know more than anyone else. That's my job. That's what I've spent my whole life doing. Learning to be ahead of everyone else. Learning facts, memorizing secrets. But I've got nothing.

"You told us you did something awful," Eli insists. "To Aza. You told us you betrayed her. What did you do?"

Pi is dancing around the edge of my brain, and I can feel things twisting like I've got an orrery in my skull spinning the planets.

I have to do something. I have to make it right.

"I worked for an agency called SWAB. A federal one. They're in charge of Magonia. I was spying for them."

"Spying on Aza?" Eli's eyes blaze.

"In exchange for protection for her."

"So that's who was parked outside our house for the past year. It's not like I didn't see them. There were like three cars trying to look like they were doing nothing. I figured you hired security and were keeping it to yourself."

I wish I had. I'm an idiot. Of course she noticed it.

"I got them to take her into custody, so she wouldn't go out hunting for Heyward. I thought I was keeping Zal from getting to her, and then—"

The look on Eli's face is pained and beyond pissed off.

"Why?"

"I thought I could save her."

"From *what*, Kerwin?"

"Her . . . destiny."

"That's bullshit," Eli says. "You don't believe in *destiny*. You thought you could keep her from making her own choices. The ones *you* were afraid of."

And she's right, of course. She's exactly right.

"It wasn't that I didn't want her to have freedom. It was that I didn't want her to—"

"Leave you," says Eli. "Which is pretty low. She's allowed to leave you. That's how love works. Have you never been a person, Jason?"

"I was scared," I manage.

"Welcome to being alive," says Eli. "Everyone's scared. Life is scary. Maybe you missed that memo. So?"

"What do you mean, *so*?"

"So you're going to make it right," she says. "It was your fault SWAB, is that their name? That's an embarrassing name, by the way. It was your fault they took Aza. But it was my fault too. I was sleeping, and I didn't wake up. I heard a noise, but I didn't get out of bed. In the morning, I saw that she was gone, her window open, tracks in the snow. And I took off, trying to get Magonia to take me too. I stood out there in my field yelling at the sky, and the mandrake grabbed me instead."

"I messed up more than you did," I say. "You don't know how sorry I am. I'm so, so sorry."

"It's not a competition," she says. "You can apologize to Aza, when we find her. For a few years, you're probably just going to have to repeat it, over and over again."

She relents slightly, her face kinder for a moment. "You told me more while you were delirious than you've said in twelve years of basically living at my house. Including some things I wish you'd never told me. I had no interest in learning how much you . . . *like*, love my sister. Pretty much epic, the level of screaming. It was TMI. Moving on. We can't change any of the things we already did. All we can do is find her.

Now, what's *the Flock*? You kept saying it."

"The Flock!" The words burst out of me before I even know they're there. "According to SWAB, the Flock is some kind of powerful weapon, something that can fight Zal. They were hunting for it. They wanted Aza's help. But I—I don't know what it is. I don't think she did either."

The Rostrae rustle and confer. There is a lot of startled rattling and trilling.

Wedda turns to us, at last.

"Not what. Who. The Flock is Zal's ethologidion. Her mate. Her match. Imprinted on her the way . . ." She trails off and I can feel the thing she's not saying. *The way Dai is on Aza. The way Aza is on Dai.*

"I was on *Amina Pennarum* when he still sang with Zal. Once Zal was convicted by Maganwetar, everything was broken, and the Flock fled. I thought he was dead. If he is not?"

"Aza's hunting him?"

"That would follow," says Jik.

If I could see Aza's face, I'd know what to do, and that's all that's real to me right now in a sea of pi and bird people, on a raft made of twigs in the sky.

I think about a night months ago, when I woke up from a rare hour of sleep, with Aza in my arms, curled up so tightly into a ball that she had no edges, no elbows, nothing but her Aza-ness, the scent she's always had, this thing that never made sense until I knew what she really was.

She's always smelled like a storm.

It makes sense. She IS a storm. No one who's ever known her would think she was sunshine. She's clouds and lightning and hail, and oh my god, she's the only one I want.

I woke up feeling like I'd won the world and didn't deserve it, but that I'd take it anyway. Her spine against my chest, the peculiar Magonian bones hidden inside her skin, the sound, deep in her lungs, of a very quiet song. I could tell that Caru was out somewhere singing with her in her sleep.

I almost told her about SWAB then. Almost told her everything. But I didn't. She woke up, turned her head, and kissed me without even opening her eyes. She trusted me totally.

There I was, untrustworthy.

I want her back. I want another chance. Will I get one? We all get our versions of heaven. Was this mine? Almost nothing makes any sense to me. But it doesn't matter if it makes sense. Doesn't matter if I have a plan. Doesn't matter if she ever forgives me.

I can't let her pay for my mistakes.

If she never loves me again, that doesn't matter either, not in the larger sense of the world. There are things I've got to do.

I hold the compass in my hand, an island of cool in my burned skin. It's intact, by some miracle.

I open it, but just as I do, there's a sound, a humming buzz coming directly at us out of the sky, and a song. I KNOW that song. It's a voice that is—

"Ghost bird!" shrills Wedda.

Jik jolts beside me. "NO, NIGHTINGALE!" she screams.

She twitches her arms, tosses her head back, and now she's all feathers, brilliant blue, black, and white. She springs off the deck, and instantly, she's flying right at the dark shape buzzing toward us, like she's something more than flesh and hollow bones.

She reminds me of Aza, who doesn't care, Aza who's always been looking at a horizon of darkness. Death was nothing to her until it was. Jik seems to be the same. Fearless. No wonder Aza liked her.

Jik taunts the thing, twisting in the air in front of it, singing a song of barks and high coughs, swooping around it like a trick pilot.

It rolls and twists, and then tries to twist again, too quickly. It leaves half of itself rolled over, while the other half is flipped to expose its underside.

Jik dives and snatches its feathers into her beak, and Wedda comes to grab the wing in her talons.

Jik and Wedda bend the bird's wings back and bring it down, triumphant. It's making a clattering sound, the sound of something frustrated against glass, a sound like I'd make if I got stuck in a revolving door and had to bash against it, no progress.

It's a sound I wouldn't mind making right now, because everything is making brand-new sense to me. Yeah, Jason. You know some things at least.

I kneel to look at it. It's light. Maybe it weighs two pounds. It's small too. Six inches long, extra significant wingspan of a couple feet, and the wings are totally articulated and flexible. It's supposed to be convincing.

It *is* convincing, from a distance at least. It has a beak, and a face, and it's made of something that's a mixture of metal and plastics.

I feel like half my brain—more than half—takes a moment to catch up, but I'm there in a second. The un-bird looks at me with its un-eyes.

It's a drone, in other words. A really good one. I've never seen one this close before. Most of them are just little robots with spinning helicopter wings. They don't usually look like birds. They look like what they are. This one is special.

"This would be a Nightingale," Jik, now a girl again, tells me.

Wedda is shaking off her bird-ness too, turning back into a part owl/part woman/part warrior in armor. "Where are the rest? Is it a scout?"

Wedda's scanning the sky. "It's alone."

"Do they know we're here?" Eli asks. "Is that why it came to attack?"

"They will soon enough. That one sings back to the rest," says Jik.

Or doesn't sing. It's a drone. That means it's connected to the rest of the drones by network. All the Nightingales know what this one knows. *Knows* being the nonscientific term. The Nightingales are sending everything to one network. No doubt owned by SWAB.

This Nightingale is focusing on me and its eyeballs click. Which galvanizes me. Hell no.

Its wings start to arc inward, toward my shoulders, and at the tip of each one there are blades. I scramble to find the panel on its abdomen. Two seconds later I have the thing open and I'm looking at its circuits. Two seconds after that I've disarmed it by yanking the battery pack.

I check out the little orb of camera that retracts inside its belly, and I cover its glass eyeball. I've seen the footage from these. It's intense. High def, with recommendations for dispersing payloads. It gives you a target and then it gives you a little *X* mark for blowing to smithereens whatever that target is.

I fumble as carefully as I can until I discover the tiny but effective explosive waiting for deployment in its central core.

My heart definitely stops for a second, then starts again as I disable the explosive.

I shut the Nightingale down completely, and all it gets out from its backup battery is one last note, a shrill trill that sounds like a love song.

It doesn't seduce me.

I pry out the little drive inside the bird and consider it, because it's not like I have the tools to do . . . anything.

Jik looks at me.

"We've killed dozens of them, boy. We know more about the Nightingales than you do. There's a huge flock of them, and they're canwr. Strange canwr, but canwr all the same."

"Don't call me boy," I say. "We're the same age."

"You *are* a boy, though. Human."

She stares at me, her eyes appalling blueness.

"The captain's Nightingales aren't birds," I say. "They're drones. They have motors, not hearts. They're using Caru's song, the one he sings with Aza."

"And you know that how?"

"They belong—or belonged—to SWAB. I didn't know what they had up here taking footage, but now I do. I'm an idiot. Spy drones disguised as birds. The song they're singing came from recordings I gave SWAB of Aza and Caru. That's why they sound like that. The rest, I don't know. They aren't supposed to be able to do this. They've been . . . reprogrammed."

They're full of strangeness, full of something more than

science, something more like magic. . . . That song isn't just a recording. It's linked to something living. I heard it shift as it sang. Which means that someone's singing with them.

And since it seems they now belong to Zal Quel . . .

I know who it must be.

CHAPTER 21

{AZA}

The Flock's birds take wing and lift Heyward off the deck, carefully gliding her into a cabin, their movements lighter than air.

The Flock sings hard, his little bat singing with him. After a moment, the crane joins him, and they sing together, the two canwr perched on Heyward's chest. I notice the texture of the air changing. It's denser.

The song is trying to save her.

But she's human.

She doesn't have a crooked heart leaning over on its side to make room for a song.

She's seizing. I'm holding her hand, and she's clenching her fingers, hard.

Her eyes open and she focuses on me. The corner of her mouth turns up and she gives me a look that is Eli, that is me, that is our parents, that is every moment of last year, the ambulance, and I see what she's telling me.

She's telling me she has to go.

I can't let her. I can't. She hasn't had a chance to know the things I have. To live the life that was hers, not mine—oh my god, my parents. Eli.

NO.

"You're not dying," I tell her. "You're coming with me!"

But she's looking at me like I'm a thousand miles from her. Her skin is paler and paler, her body is cooler, and her eyes are rolling back.

"NO!" I shout.

I can feel her going. I can feel her leaving like birds taking off from a lake. Like she's the water and everything in it is slowing, slowing, freezing—

Until there is nothing left but a ripple; peaceful, beautiful circles that move and widen and fade. One last breath, my fingers hard in hers, her clinging to me, me clinging to her, and then—

I feel her go.

I feel everything leave her.

The heartbird sings a high note.

The Flock is singing too, he and his birds, a strange twisting song. The dart is still in her chest, a bright red spot around a black spike.

She took that dart to keep it from taking me. I don't have a song for this.

The Nightingales killed her.

Zal killed her.

I'm on my knees on the floor without even knowing I'm falling. The birds are singing that song, a griefsong, a song of misery with me. They're making clouds around her, covering her in a bank of whiteness, and I can see outside the ship the same thing happening, all a blanket of grief and paleness, all for this.

I feel a hand on my shoulder.

He's not who I want. This stranger, this singer on the edge of the sky. I want my mother. I want Eli. I want . . . Jason.

But this is who I have. A hand on my shoulder. A girl dead in front of me, a girl who should be alive.

I lose control of my sobs. I cry for everything, everyone, for the life I took from her without even knowing I'd done it. I was loved in *her* life. Her family. Her house. I won sixteen years of love. She lost everything.

The Flock's many canwr perch all over my shoulders and hair, on both of us, and they sing, all except the two heart-birds, who stay with Heyward's body, singing a high, sweet song, trilling words.

"Caladrius and Vespers are singing the girl to the land of the dead," says the Flock.

I want that to be a place that's real. I want there to be something that makes this better.

No. Don't be stupid, Aza.

She was dying from the moment the dart pierced her skin. The Flock looks at me, and his face isn't as expressionless as it's been. He looks genuinely sorry. He should be. If he'd been faster—

I think of my mom standing in the backyard, looking up at the sky for her lost daughter. Here we are, lost together.

I'm the only one who can take revenge on the person who did this. It was Zal's Nightingale, and Zal's orders.

I stand over Heyward and look at her body. Still as a painting.

Look at her, Aza Ray, keep her in your memory. This girl with pale skin and black hair, this girl who is you and at the same time, the opposite. You're going to keep her in your heart as long as you're alive, so you'd better get it right.

Her eyes, shut, her body, not as thin as mine was when I had the body that pretended to be hers. She has curves inside that uniform. She has human bones.

She was always human. And me? I'm the alien standing at the deathbed of the person I was supposed to be.

I open my mouth and try to sing the song I know is due Heyward Boyle. I sing a star to light the night over her. A deathday rather than a birthday.

I sing a star ringed in blue and silver, a star that as the night passes spins into a black center. I sing a star that could be spotted in a thousand years, and I name it my sister's name.

But the whole time, my song is twisted with something ugly. I can't keep it out. I'm so angry. Why does it have to be *like this*? Why did Zal do this? Why does Zal even exist? And why is she my mother?

I want to find her.

I want to kill her.

I want nothing to do with her, no history, no future. I want to be myself again, someone who didn't inherit this rage, someone who isn't being moved by Zal even now. I want to be in charge of my own life. Instead, she's pulling strings from across the sky.

The Flock is watching me sing, and I feel like he can see it, the red border on the edge of the star, the note in my voice that sounds like a knife, but there's nothing I can do to make it go away.

In the morning, I wrap Heyward in a sail, and the Flock carries her to the edge of the deck. The clouds are light out here. The sun's never set. It's just circled the sky. Everything looks like mother-of-pearl, like we're at the bottom of some sea I've never heard of.

I haven't slept. The Flock's canwr are with me, on my arms, and they're comfort, but not enough. I thought I'd imagined everything that could ever happen. I thought I was the one who'd be dying. I think of all those years when my parents and Eli and Jason were watching me go, and of that day when I went, and I know, now, I know how everyone was broken by it. I know that everyone, for the past year, has been scraping the pieces of their hearts together. Hurting as hard as I was.

I know that Jason—

The thought itself is enough to strangle me. Both with fury and with sadness.

That Jason did what he did because he couldn't bear *this feeling* I'm feeling right now. He couldn't bear it if I died again.

The birds are singing a ritual.

Fuck rituals. They don't make it better. You do them because you're trying to manage the corners of existence, trying to make it okay to leave in the middle of the party.

But maybe that doesn't matter, when you go. Maybe you just fly out from yourself and you're relieved of all the things you carried.

Maybe you just walk into the dark.

Maybe.

I thought I knew, but I don't know.

I think of my dad jumping on the trampoline and flipping backward into the night. I think of my mom looking up at the sky, staring deep into the black behind the stars, looking for her lost daughter.

I think of Eli—

I can't think of Eli.

The Flock sings over Heyward, and his birds sing too. There are feathers in her shroud, feathers from each canwr. There's an apology list I wrote.

"Who was she to you?" the Flock asks.

"My sister," I say. "She was my sister."

He looks at me, and decides not to press it. Together, we roll her over the edge, and off into the sky, over and over through the icy silver morning light. Where will she land? I don't know. In the frozen ocean, and maybe in a thousand years someone will find her, wrapped in Magonian threads, my apologies next to her in an iceberg.

I'm sorry you didn't get to live your life.
I'm sorry you never had anyone who loved you.
I'm sorry you had to learn to fight.
I'm sorry I took your family.
I'm sorry you died.
Now I carry you with me.

The Flock sings with his canwr, moving them across the sky with a few notes, a wave of thousands of birds singing her into the sea. He has so many. Not only a couple of heartbirds, but all the birds in the sky sing with him. None of them seem trapped or forced. They all sing with their own voices. A sheet of small green birds rises in an arc, and circles the ship, spiraling up into the sky and down again. Next come other birds, his little hawks, hanging in the air and then diving as one, together a line of talons and hooked beaks. They all merge together, these canwr, and Caladrius, the heartbird crane, flies at their head, graceful, long and pale in the sky.

The Flock sings like nothing I've ever heard. His voice is bright and strange, and sounds not like music, but like birds in a storm.

The song he sings fills my mind with images, the images brought to it by the bat, who sings a cave in a cloud filled with a colony of silver bats, and by the crane, who sings a song of birds swooping across the sky, their beautiful feathers floating in the wind, and the rest of his flock, the falcons, an eagle, all singing at once, their memories of an unbroken world, a world in which the sky and sea and land are not divided, but one.

I see trees bending in sky winds and then, from the bat's song, the roots of the same trees, hanging in the darkness beneath the ground, silvered and trembling. I see insects twisting in the air, clouds of gnats and tiny moths, and then, a dive into the water, clouds of small fish to feed hatchling birds.

The Flock sings a song that is nature in her glory, in her balance, a song that is life and death, on either side of a long string of breaths. A song in which death is normal, not tragic, not horrible, nothing out of line with life. All in the same string.

Like pi, I think, like that. A string of numbers and at either side of them a beginning and an end, and we never know where they stop.

It's summer here, over Antarctica, which means it's never night, but a constant glittering pale, and the Flock's song divides the midnight sun into blinding sparks. All the birds fly in a circle around the sun as he sings, their colors merging into the light, so that they make a rainbow entirely of wings. A perihelion. I stare at it.

A deathsong. A funeral song.

Our funerals are their sunsets, Zal told me last year.

My own birthday, a glowing aurora borealis.

Heyward's burial, a rainbow around the sun.

I watch it. I watch it. Rainbows aren't enough. Beauty isn't enough.

"Teach me how you sing with so many canwr," I say.

"There's no teaching this," he says. "And it's not a song that can be sung by everyone."

Twinge of anger. "So it belongs only to you?"

"It is a song I can sing," he says, and shrugs his gray shoulders. "That's all. You have your own song, I am certain, and you will use it for your own purposes. I use mine for these."

He sings a note, and his flock of canwr echo it. I watch the air condense, harden, take shape. An iceberg forms in the sky as it drifts down into the waters below us. A green-blue hulk, a floating piece of thin air become tremendous and solid.

It shifts as it hits the water, and groans, but it's diamond sharp, bright, made of the sky rather than the sea. It's new ice beside old ice.

It's something much larger than I can do, something stronger than I've ever done, even in Svalbard, when I was at my strongest, singing destruction with Dai.

It's stronger than the song I sang after that, with Caru, my heart full of love for Jason, when I reversed the damage I'd done.

I haven't sung like that since. I don't know if I know how to sing like that anymore.

Love? I don't have enough. I'm too broken to use my voice that way, or to let my heart use *me* that way. Flat origami, all the folds crushed in on themselves, no room for anything to expand, no room for me to open myself up. I don't even know how to start.

But the Flock's doing something in the same category as me. I can shift the elements. He's much stronger than me, though, and all the canwr? They amplify him in ways I can't touch.

If I could sing like he's singing, I could sing new icebergs to replace the ones that are gone. I could unmelt parts of the sea. I could make things better.

But that's not why I want to learn this song, not right now. I want to use it for something darker, the way the Flock used it to wreck a Magonian ship, the way he sang a wave and a sinking.

I pause. There's only one thing to tell him. The truth.

"I need to kill Zal Quel."

He looks at me for a moment, his face unreadable.

"More death, then? You care nothing for life, the women of Magonia. All of you, fixated on power and war. All of you, killers."

I'm stunned. The women? This is, as ever, another world.

"I have no help for that," he says. "But I can offer a place for sleep, a place for calm. My ship is called *Glyampus*, and you are welcome here. It may seem transparent, but from the sky, none of Magonia's ships can find us. From below, we look like a wisp of iridescent cloud. My song hides us. When you are on my ship, you are safe, and you will sleep. There is more to sing than these bitter songs, and when you wake, perhaps you will try to sing some of those instead."

And that is all he'll say. He ignores me, and goes into his own cabin, while I sit staring at the frozen sky. There's nothing to hear or see out here.

It's a silent world made of ice and a slowly moving cold sun.

It's the middle of nowhere, and I'm in it.

CHAPTER 22

{JASON}

I open my compass and look at the screen. No one knows where she is, and I don't either.

I press the button that calls to her. The screen lights up on my end, and I hope for a moment, but nothing. No answer. No Aza. All I see is dark, which cues up even more panic, but I can't do anything about it. All I can do is be here. I try again. Again.

She's not speaking to me, or maybe she's—

She's out of range. That's all. She's out of range.

The burns feel like my heart has been taken out of my chest, and though I know that's not true, it's persuasive. Wedda keeps covering them with new damp bandages. I have a fever. I'm not right at all, and I think that's what I deserve. If I die of this, it's fair. But before that, I have things to do. I feel a chill and then a rush of heat, a shivering questionable thing inside my skin, like I'm collapsing. Pea/Sun. Sun/Pea. I feel like I contain a lot of things I never meant to contain.

You don't know how much you can lie until you find yourself in the middle of it, lying again to cover the lie you already gave out as truth. You don't know how much you can mess your own life up until you're looking out from the inside, and thinking you're not the person you set out to be.

It's possible to lie to such a degree that you start seeing yourself in the distance, coming over the horizon, because you've been lying to yourself too, telling yourself you're in charge of the narrative when really, you're just messing up someone else's story.

I was never the hero.

I try to let it go. No savior. No hero. Just a person. A person who's now in Magonia, looking at a sky full of planes. I know what kind of planes they are, because I used to look at the monitors, where these planes were being tracked. I was the below, and this was the above.

Now the worlds are one. We're entwined. The planes are casually moving, slowly circling. The Rostrae I'm with ignore them, as birds all ignore planes. They're used to air traffic.

But these are SWAB planes, surveilling, watching the Rostrae, watching Magonia.

If you're from earth, you know what unmarked police cars look like. This is the aerial version. I can see that SkyWatch has the area surrounded. What are they waiting for? Zal to start a war? Aza to show up? The Flock? Any of those things, so that they can be justified in moving in and doing something major?

What do they want? The sky unclaimed? Or someone up here working for them? It occurs to me that it's not beyond governmental policy to recruit a villain to do some dirty work on our behalf. There's plenty of history of that kind of thing. So . . . maybe SWAB has been using Zal to start something, just so it can get a better claim on a war-torn region, the sky.

We move faster than I thought we'd be able to. These barge ships, these nests, seemed unwieldy, and instead, they're agile.

The Rostrae raise a sail made of tightly woven feathers, and it fills with wind. I look up and see that it's actually a kind of wing with at least a forty-foot span. Something blue enough to match the sky.

We're still far from Maganwetar, as far as I can tell, but we're feinting and twisting with way more control than I'd expect. Then I notice that Rostrae are also guiding the raft, high above us, ropes in their talons. And Jik is commanding them all.

Periodically she takes flight and issues an order from above, her wings spread wide, her face ferocious.

Everything is heading for the same place—every rebel in the sky, according to Jik. We're all going to Maganwetar.

I suspect SWAB is following us because they can't see the city. They need a guide, and a fleet of vessels across the sky is enough for them.

At least I understand SWAB's tech. War is toxic science, payloads and gunpowder, jet speeds and pilot capabilities. I don't know how SWAB—or anyone for that matter—thinks they can take Zal and Maganwetar out without creating a giant catastrophe. What would happen if Maganwetar just fell out of the sky? The equivalent of a meteor?

I have dark weird thoughts about other meteors falling to earth. What if some of them were sky cities? What if some of them were civilizations crashing down out of the clouds?

Ice ages and planets tilted in their orbits. Who says life evolved the same way in Magonia as it did on earth? All Magonians need from the ground is food. There's been food longer than there have been humans.

Who is to say that the sky hasn't been warring for thousands and thousands of years, that Magonia wasn't around concurrent with the dinosaurs? I look at the Rostrae on this ship with me. There's a whole thing in the back of my head regarding birds and evolution. Maybe some Rostrae came from flying dinosaurs. Maybe, maybe, maybe. Maybe I will never understand any of this, and that's probably fine, but also a little bit something that my brain would historically have obsessed over.

Too much biology to analyze with no tools. No time. Middle of a war, Jason Kerwin, I remind myself, but I'm still me, what can I do?

We need a weapon, the kind of weapon that can fight against manmade weapons. What's SWAB doing up here? What is their plan? Think about it. I try.

They're hunting the Flock. A weapon powerful enough to attack Zal for them. To cancel Zal's song, to make her unable to sing it. Like they've done to Aza's song. A reversal of her own notes. Is that what the Flock can do as an ethologidion? Is that who he is?

If so, the thought of Dai getting anywhere near Aza again is a painful one. I thought he just amplified her song. What if he can silence her as well?

She's not here. I am. I only have myself to rely on right now, just my brain to use to try to find a means of dealing with this before it gets to her.

Jik points out into the distance.

"Maganwetar's orbit," she says. There are sparks of lightning—*stormsharks*, I think, and flinch involuntarily. I feel a fiery pain in my chest where I'm wounded. A lightning strike would take me out. I don't even know how I survived it last year, and this year, I'm already broken.

Otherwise, though, Maganwetar is eerily silent, an expanse

of quiet sky. I can't see ships, and I can't see any armada guarding anything. Just a still blueness surrounded by a wall of lightning.

"Where are the squallwhales?" I ask Wedda. I haven't seen any. It's all been Nightingales and Magonian song magic.

"Fled," she says. "They don't take sides. Unless—"

"Unless what?"

"Unless they find someone they'll sing with."

Which is no one. Not Zal. Not Jik and Wedda. The whales sing their own song. I imagine an entire population of them on the other side of the sky, far from this, and I wish I was with them. Nothing about this is going to end well.

A flash of thoughts about my moms. They think I escaped from a mental hospital. I wasn't okay. I'm still not okay. Really, *not okay* isn't even the right phrase. My face is frozen and my chest is burning. No. My brain is frozen and my heart is burning. That.

I'm full of darkness, and all the parts of my body orbit around an empty center. I feel like my heart is a black hole. I look at the disabled drone. It's the same as me. Nothing in the middle. I look into its flat black eyes. It's a replica of the bird from thousands of years ago. The archaeopteryx. Its beak is lined with teeth, but it's only the size of a magpie. Someone at SWAB having a joke, reinventing an extinct bird from the Jurassic and turning it into a spying weapon. It has a long, bony tail, which is one of its key traits. This one is made of metal covered in feathers like a fern frond.

What do I do? How can I use it?

Eli sits down beside me, takes the drone like it's nothing, and examines it, turning it around in her hands. It was a smart move SWAB made, sending these up here. It was a less smart move underestimating Zal's ambition. Of course she took them, or Dai did. It makes sense. Magonia has a long history of harvesting things from the sky, and these were up here in their airspace. But even I'm surprised she was able to repurpose them this way. When Aza described *Amina Pennarum*, when she described Magonia at all, it sounded like something out of the 1700s. I didn't think Magonian technology existed. I knew they used ropes to wrap around intruders, crashing helicopters, maybe planes. No part of me imagined Magonians might be able to use their songs to change earth technology into something they could use for themselves. Another flaw in my thinking, clearly, as it seems that's exactly what's happened here. And it's dumb, because I'm pretty sure Aza could do anything she wants with her song, technology be damned, and *she's* Magonian. I should've seen this coming.

"Send it to get Caru," Eli says.

"What do you mean?"

"Send it back to Zal's ship. Zal has Caru, yes? And Aza needs Caru so that she can sing the way she's meant to sing. So, get the drone to go in and release him. Unless you have some other crazy brilliant plan, in which case, I'll step back."

I stare at her. "We don't even know where Aza is."

Eli looks at me.

"Her heartbird does. Her heartbird can *feel* her. Am I wrong? Isn't that what a bond is? Isn't that what we've been talking about for the past year?"

Um.

I have the drone drive between my thumb and forefinger. I'd been thinking about snapping it half, but instead, finally, slowly, something occurs to me.

Jason Kerwin, you dumbass.

Eli's watching me. "How many remote-control items do you think you and Aza have made over the years?"

"A few," I say, and think about things ranging from a tiny flying dragon we brought to school in seventh grade to a remote-control floating lemon—don't ask—powered by self-made batteries, which we were pretty sure would be an awesome science project, and which was actually just moldy and messy and surprisingly splatter-ish.

I pull my phone out. No signal, of course, but it has a solar charger, because I wasn't as dumb a few months ago as I was just now. There've been times I was prepared for anything. Maybe let's remember that part of me again.

I charge my phone, then connect the drone to my cell.

My phone chirps. I have a signal connecting the drone to . . .

My phone opens a network, and asks for a password.

OperationAzaRay I type, on a hunch. I'm right on the first try. Yep. SWAB. Of course this is SWAB. But what I want to know is *why*.

And what they thought they were doing sending drones up here, drones that seem to have been taken over by Zal Quel, and by Dai. What was their plan? How do I counteract it?

When I get its drive on-screen, it's not what I thought it was. Things in it are altered. It's not just that these spy drones aren't supposed to be able to drop explosives. It's that they're now also set to broadcast song. Whatever SWAB did with Aza's song, I assume they did it because they were trying to have the option of canceling it out. But these drones are attacking Rostrae, and creating weather magic, or at least that's what it sounds like. What I'm looking at is that particular MP3 file, set inside each of them. But what I hear when they sing? It's not always the same song. It's twisted and changed. Zal has added something to it, and she seems to every time she sings.

She's controlling them. How's Zal singing with these? She's not supposed to be able to sing at all. That was supposed to be her punishment: no canwr, no song, no Caru, and no Aza.

Now she seems to have all those things but Aza, and I have no idea how it changed.

I don't need to know, though. I only need to figure out how to take power away from her, not to figure out where it came from. I remind myself of that, even as my brain has ideas about every possible way this could have happened.

However she got these Nightingales, whoever worked on them for her, they're tiny screaming speakers singing out her agenda all over the sky, and they're using Aza and Caru's song to sing weather and transformation. With the additional benefit that they can apparently drop explosives on those who don't comply in Magonia. And up here, I'm guessing, that's revolutionary in itself. Earth weapons deployed by a Magonian.

I take the precaution of disabling its song file. I have no interest in hearing this drone sing something suddenly that makes this ship into water, a thing Aza and Caru's song is fully capable of doing.

I go into the network and reprogram the captured drone's signal so that it talks to my phone instead of to anything else. It's fairly straightforward once you know what you're doing.

All this war. All these things made for killing and destroying. These thousands of years of vengeance, and now these, creatures that can kill without you ever seeing them coming.

Sweat is dripping down my back. Cold sweat. I wipe my

forehead. My skull feels like it's splitting and my arms feel like they don't quite belong to me. I feel like my skin is about to boil, my chest a screaming volcano of pain. There are still things seared to my skin, burnt shirt, burnt soul.

I keep working.

"What are you doing?" Jik asks me. Suddenly she's right there and I have the uncomfortable feeling she's been listening to me quietly singing digits of pi for the last hour and a half.

"Tech," I say.

"What will you do with it?"

"Make things better," I say, and she looks at me. She looks exhausted.

"*Try* to make things better," I amend.

"I'll take that," she says.

Pi circles in my head like a bunch of runners on a track, but I'm running alongside them, and the drone is submitting to my reprogramming. Submitting. Like it's something living. It *has* to submit, because it's a little bit of metal and wire. It's at the mercy of its machinery.

And I'm at the mercy of my own mortal body. I'm pieces of flesh and bone all ready to relent depending on what attacks me. So it's in my interest to make this drone into something that works for me rather than against me. And what do I want this drone to do? I consult the SWAB surveillance network.

I'm myself again for this moment, in a way I haven't been in a year. I'm the Jason Kerwin I'm supposed to be, the guy who learned how to do this shit when he was eleven. Hacking it out. Like not exactly a badass, but like someone who kind of knows something.

Does it redeem me?

Can anything?

I replace the panel on the bird's belly. I put its camera back in. I smooth its fake feathers into place. I instruct it via phone to wake up, and there, it does. I check it with my phone, and it's back online.

Ancient wing, the middle ground between a dinosaur and a modern avian. And here, the one in my hand, is the middle ground between a modern bird and a full-on shiny metal robot. It's something made by men trying to play god over this kingdom in the sky.

Of course, as happens every time, the humans lost control of their creations. You only have to look at the history of the world to know the stories about that. There are plenty of them.

Now the sky is full of drones, and I think SWAB has no idea that the drones they think they're controlling are actually under Zal's sway. I'm pretty sure the song they're singing has been altered enough by Magonian magic that it can do whatever Zal wants it to do.

Mine, though, is missing its voice.

All it is now is a flyer on a mission. *My* mission.

CHAPTER 23

{AZA}

*I wake up in strange surroundings, a little room with trans-*parent walls, where I'm looking at a flock of birds surrounding my bed, hovering all around me, hanging in the air: falcons, swallows, and swifts, and I'm swaying in a hammock, where a tiny bat is singing into my ear.

I'm on a ship called *Glyampus*, and my heart is pounding.

But it wasn't real. I rattle through my skull. That was a nightmare, a vision. It didn't happen.

No.

It did.

Heyward's dead.

This, for once, isn't something my brain invented. I look at my hands, but there's no blood on them. I feel like there should be something visible, something that shows everyone I'm not the hero I'm supposed to be.

I failed her.

Chosen one. Chosen by whom?

Chosen by Jason to be his best friend. Wrong choice.

Chosen by Zal to be her weapon. Wrong choice.

Chosen by my mother and father to love, chosen and kept alive by them.

They're the ones I think about now, when I think *chosen one*. When I think they thought I was worth saving.

I have to be worth saving.

The bat sings a weird little trill.

"You sound like Elvis," I whisper to her.

"Vespers amuses herself picking up radio frequencies from the science station below us." I jerk my head up and see the Flock walking into the room. "She likes to sing with all the other creatures that sing. Bats, whales, humans, the tiniest things on earth. Everything has a song."

I sit up, hearing that. It reminds me of my mother and her singing mice, and that reminds me of the fact that I'm here for real, not there, and that everything below me is in danger and I've been sleeping through it.

Vespers flies off, singing all the way. I hear the bat shift her signal to talk radio, a news station.

"Flooding," says the talk radio through Vespers. "Ten thousand dead."

"Where?" I ask the Flock. He shrugs.

"It's Zal," I tell him, but I don't know for sure. It could also be everything below messing with everything up here. It could also be chemicals and catastrophe. It could be anything, any of the possible terrible things on earth or in the heavens, and I have no idea which it actually is.

I can't stay here sleeping in the middle of a lost part of the sky, no information, no one but us out here. They sent that ship after Heyward and me. We've already been attacked. Does Zal know the Flock is out here? Her old enemy?

Some enemy, this singer who has no intention of teaching me to sing. Maybe he's my enemy too.

"You have to help me," I plead again. "Teach me how you sing the way you do. Teach me how to fight her."

"Did Zal send you here to take me back to her? We are long done with singing, she and I."

"But . . . you sang *with* her? You know her song? Then you can help me defeat her. Just teach me how! She didn't send me. I came here myself."

"Don't ask me to have dealings with Zal," he says.

I flinch at those words, but he keeps talking.

"Without the drowners' earth, there are no nests, no caves, no hives. My song depends on the things of the world as well as the sky. She would drown the world."

The Flock looks increasingly wizened and ancient. Me, I feel increasingly dark. He won't teach me. He won't help me fight Zal. He's barely here. He wants to sit out the entire conflict from his safe perch in uninhabited sky.

"She sent that warship that caught us. It was hers, but she must have been sending it at you! She didn't know where we were," I try, even though I have a deep suspicion I'm wrong about this. "Why else would she send a whole warship, full of Nightingales?! You're her enemy."

"She sent it for YOU," he replies. "Not me. She doesn't know I'm here, and I wish it to remain that way. I wish her to imagine that you dropped into the sea with your shipmate, a dead thing. If she is to cease pursuing your song, she must think you're dead. She thinks I'm dead, and that's how I wish it to stay."

"Does she really think *you* are? Are you sure?"

He looks steadily at me.

"I am as good as dead," he says. "I don't touch Magonia, and Magonia does not touch me."

I won't give up.

"I'm not asking you to SEE Zal," I say. "I only want you to show me how to sing like you do."

"So you can kill your mother?" says the Flock. "She is your mother, is she not?"

I don't say anything. What is there to say? I want to kill her. I want revenge. Who wouldn't want that? On someone like Zal? She's a dictator. She's a murderer. Never mind how she got that way, never mind that she's my mother.

"I don't wish for you to kill her. I don't wish any of this. I never expected to live this long, to watch the sea broken, to watch the sky broken. The squallwhales are dying and the oceans beneath us are full of poisons. The ice is melting. There are gaps in the sky."

Vespers glides through the room singing a quick song in a newscaster voice about thousands dead somewhere else, this time because of a huge storm that came out of nowhere and flattened half an island. My stomach lurches.

"You know who's doing this!" I say. "How can you just do nothing? She's calling down a flood, and she's using my heartbird's song to do it. And my song too. She has him captive, and everything about it is going to end with all of us dead. Do you *want* to be dead?"

He walks away from me.

"I can make things better!" I shout after him.

He looks over at me, his eyes gleaming and golden. "But will you choose to?" he says. "You are *her* daughter."

"I'm myself," I say. "I'm trying."

Am I? My brain is full of visions of Zal, of taking Eli back, Caru back, getting vengeance for all the horrible things she's done, all the horrible things she WILL do if I let her. I have to get to her. I have to stop her.

I have to kill her. It's HAVE to. It's not a matter of what I want.

My brain is full of Jason too, of showing him that I never needed him to be strong, that I can do it alone. I'm strong enough with or without his love. My brain is full of finding Dai and showing him the same things, these boys who both lied to me, these boys who both pretended to love me.

And Heyward. Dead because of something I did. Dead because of something *all of them* did.

I want to throw myself at it, to sing a song that will tear it all apart, make it all right again. Sometimes, to find balance, you have to hurt rather than heal, isn't that true? It must be true. Use her own technique against her. If she's singing a destruction song, then my only option is to sing one that is stronger than hers. To outsing her.

The Flock stares steadily at me, then sighs.

"Sing, then," he says. "Sing the song you have to sing to do this. Can you find it?"

"I obviously don't know how," I say, losing every bedraggled bit of patience. "OR I WOULD BE SINGING IT RIGHT NOW."

The Flock taps on my lung door, and it opens for Vespers. WHAT?

Oh my god. This isn't what I was planning. A bat in my chest? Vespers flies into my lung.

A bat in my belfry. That's how this feels. It feels like I've just inhaled something that's gone down the wrong tube, but worse than any other version, much worse than Milekt down my throat. This feels like I just choked on gasoline, or like the end of the world is showing up, inside my lung. A tiny lung-pocalypse. I feel all wrong, doomed and dimmed, and insecure that even as I hate the feeling of the bat, the bat hates the feeling of me too. Will she hang upside down? Is that what's about to happen?

"You asked to learn this song," the Flock reminds me. "It requires more than one canwr. You'll get used to it. This canwr knows how to sing with you."

I swallow, trying to be okay with it. I inhale, and go as Zen as I can go. Which is not the most Zen, but it's something.

And so Vespers and I sing together. Not sing exactly. Vespers vibrates a song, something I can't even hear, and I try to sing alongside it, wrapping my song into the bat's voice, a voice that is twitching my skin, from inside out. I feel like a guitar string.

The Flock was able to command thousands of birds with his song. I look out alongside the ship, watching for a flock of sparrows rising, and instead, I see one old seagull. He gives me a dark look before he moves on.

The Flock is watching.

"You have to try harder if you want this," he says. "It's not the song you've been singing in Magonia."

I don't have time to wait. I want a hack! I want the learn-a-little-and-do-it version, the way things usually are for me, the way I've lived my whole life. Factoid expertise in narrow slices equals the illusion of larger clarity.

"What song is it, then?"

"You are singing sky. But this song is everything," the Flock says. "Not just the sky. The earth alongside it. You're singing only Magonian notes. And you're singing notes you learned from Zal. It's no surprise the song will not come for you. It requires . . . purity."

The Flock sings two notes and a thousand sparrows arc across the sky, spelling a word, in fancy calligraphy, which only makes me feel more frustrated:

T R U T H

Seriously?! What life is this? What kind of life, where even the birds are spouting things from greeting cards you wouldn't send to your enemies? What kind of life where there is no sarcasm, no cynicism, no reasonable suspicion of romantic gestures—

And then I think . . . *purity*?

Oh, wait. Oh, hell no.

I'm full of mortification and fury all over again. This is made of trite. This is typical. This is bullshit! I feel myself almost levitating off the deck, because this is ancient crap used to control girls since the beginning of time, since the legend of unicorns and blah blah blah, this whole notion that—

"Purity. You mean I have to be a virgin?"

The Flock looks at me, with a look that says I'm missing nine degrees of the point.

"What is *a virgin*?"

"It's a person who's never . . ."

I discover that I don't really feel like explaining my sexual history to some old man on a glass boat in the sky, thank you.

He looks at me, and the look reminds me of so many things, makes me miss so many people.

"I see," he says. "And no. That has nothing to do with it. The only way to sing with so many canwr is to sing peacefully. They sing your truth, and if that is fury, they show it. It will destroy you, and them. It's possible to cause an entire flock to die mid-flight. To sing with a flock successfully, you must sing joy."

Blushing is a thing. I have no idea what color I am. And also—

Maybe the idea of *having* to sing joy pisses me off as much as the idea that I couldn't sing this song if I'm not a virgin. How can you sing joy if you have no joy? How can you sing love if you have no love?

"I know your song. I've sung it. Had I continued singing that way," the Flock says, "my canwr would have taken me and torn me to pieces. As they will you."

I look out at the sky, the misty miserable white, and I know he's right.

He sings another note. I do my best to echo it. We trill it out into the sky together.

The smooth wave of birds twists on itself and dives rapidly toward the sea, freaking me out. Are they—

The Flock sings a sharp note that somehow manages still to be full of the sun, and Vespers sings it too. The Flock's birds shift direction, arcing across the sky, now smooth again. Caladrius comes out of nowhere and prods my ear with her beak.

"That is what happens," says the Flock.

Vespers unhelpfully trills a little bit of radio. Some random pop song about love and longing.

I sing a note that causes the tremendous, calm flock of birds to spread out from their murmuration, and into shooting stars of frustration. All of them shriek and drop in midair, flipping, twisting, and crashing into one another.

The Flock patiently sings another note, bringing the birds back together, calming them.

I sing again, trying my hardest to dim the problem elements of my soul, and the birds just whirl over my head like a tornado of feathers, screaming, until Caladrius and the Flock sing them into a soothing wave of lighter than air.

Vespers makes a disgruntled sound from inside my chest, but I can't help it. I'm reminded of Milekt, and of Caru. Milekt hating me, judging me, singing fury from inside my chest. And then . . . I don't even want to think about what happened to Milekt when we parted. We were bonded. There's no way Milekt is okay after that, no matter what wrongs he did to my song.

Caru, though, is the one I ought to be singing with. Caru is wild and filled with danger, but he understands how to sing with me, and I understand how to sing with him. I never had to learn it. It was just there, the moment we heard each other's voices. Isn't that how it's supposed to be?

Are you supposed to have to work this hard?

Vespers comes out of my chest and gives me a look that tells me this bat would never trust me to sing the stars across the sky with her.

I'm crying, but crying doesn't help me sing any kind of joy. Crying only makes me worse. And it only makes me think about how much I miss the days when I knew nothing about Magonia, when I was safe on earth, when I knew that people loved me—

Never mind that I was dying back then.

Never mind that some of the anger I have lurking in my throat, fucking up my song, dates to fifteen years of dying out loud.

Never mind that. Never mind the whole truth, this giant mess that I've been trying to turn into a less complicated story, a story in which no one died so I could live, in which no one's life got stolen, and no one's destined singing partner forcibly controlled her voice, and no one's mother was a psychopath, and no one's only totally trusted person lied to her.

Never mind that I understand the reasons for all of it. Never mind that I get it. Never mind that I know what's wrong with me. It doesn't make anything less painful, knowing its origin.

I'm still angry, and it comes out every time I open my mouth. The birds look at me, and Vespers looks at me, and the Flock looks at me, and for a second I just want to give up on all of this and roll off the deck, down through layers of icy air, and into the ocean. Maybe a frozen version of me can be brought back in a hundred years, and maybe then there won't be fury hiding in every note I sing.

That might be what it takes to erase seventeen angry years from my song, a full reboot. I already had one of those, though, and here I still am, stewing and fucked up.

"Again," the Flock says.

And again, singing drills, until I'm gasping, until I'm singing notes I've never sung before, but they're all still full of wrong.

Finally, after hours, Vespers sings . . .

Well, Vespers sings vespers. Or an equivalent. An evening prayer anyway. Some kind of prayer. To no one. To everyone.

Starlight, she sings, and I'm pretty sure she's about to sing "Twinkle, Twinkle, Little Star," which would be ridiculous but would also kind of make me happy.

Instead, though, she just sings a lullaby that brings all the birds in the sky into full voice, a flood of rapture, all the birds rising up, and then falling through the air. All of them singing snow as I shut my eyes, exhausted.

The last thing I feel is the Flock picking me up off the deck and carrying me to my cabin. And I feel, for a moment, totally safe.

"Wait," I say.

The Flock pauses in the doorway, Caladrius on his shoulder.

"You sang with her?" I ask. "I just want to know what it was like. No one's ever told me what her voice actually *sounded* like. I never heard it. Or, at least, I don't remember it. I was tiny when I was taken from her ship. I only remember being on earth. They put me with the drowners, in a skin, and they left me there."

I'm telling him more than I should, probably, more than is wise. Does he hate drowners? I don't know. He looks at me and I can't tell at all what he's thinking. His face is troubled.

"I did sing with her," he says, and sighs. "A long time ago. She had a voice like no one else in the sky back then."

"And you don't?"

"I do. There was a reason we were well-met," he says. "I was on *Amina Pennarum*. I was a cabin boy. Assigned to scrubbing, mainly, every plank, feeding the sail, untangling ropes, and mending nets. She was lower even than I was, the cook's girl, and so she saw the hunger firsthand. She was in the galley, watching provisions come into our ship from below, seeing things broken by the ground, and stretching our stores to feed the ship, until, one day, she stood on the deck and sang out in frustration. She created a wave of wind and storm to tear the corn up from a field below us and bring it onto the ship. The drowners, she said, were polluting the crops, ruining the feed, spraying it with things that poisoned insects, eagles, Magonians. She knelt in the corn she'd stolen and cried. Her voice was so powerful that the captain, Ley Fol, noticed her. I noticed her too."

I jolt. Ley Fol is the pirate Zal made walk the plank last year. She's also the Magonian who sent me to earth when Zal was punished, when her chest was sealed so that she would never again sing with a heartbird. I have a history with Ley Fol myself. She's the reason I had a life at all. She was ordered to kill me, and instead she saved me.

The Flock smiles, but his smile is sad. Now Vespers is in the cabin, hanging from the top of the invisible ceiling, stretching her tiny silver wings. I can't even imagine this version of Zal, my age, younger? Or of the Flock, for that matter. He seems ancient.

"What happened, though?"

"She was a wonder of the sky," he says. "She sang, and I sang with her. She rose. I rose alongside her. Eventually, she took over the ship. She became the captain, but being the captain of a single ship did not make the forage better on the ground. Singing the songs she sang did not keep her crew fed, and the capital had strict regulations about forage, and how it was managed. Her anger and frustration grew. Her first and most powerful songs were songs of destruction. Those were the ones she sang naturally. The rest, she sang with effort, and practice, but they were never the easy songs for her. She made enemies in the sky, singing those songs, but they were the ones that seemed they could change everything, at least to her. At last she returned to them, singing without a partner, using only her heartbird—"

"Caru?" I ask.

He looks even more troubled with the mention of Caru's name.

"She used him to sing songs no heartbird should sing. No bird at all should sing those songs. That is what I know now. I did not know it then."

"She was punished," I say.

"I know she was," he says, and winces, his own hand over his heart. "But she was not always so made of night. She could sing creation songs too. For a time, long ago, Zal Quel was the light of the sky. There was a time, but that time is done. She made a choice, and her choice was destruction. Her choice was to flood."

"Why?" I ask.

He doesn't answer me. He just strokes the heartbird on his shoulder, his face furrowed.

"Because she knew how. I made choices of my own. As will you," he says. "As does everything living, everything singing, everything in wind and weather. Sleep now, singer. There will be another morning."

"I hope so," I mumble.

"There will be," he says, and he pats me awkwardly on the head. "Caladrius sings of it already, and Vespers too. All the birds in this sky have been around the earth and seen tomorrow, and we will see it too."

"Is that a lullaby?" I ask.

"It's only the truth," he says.

His golden eyes shine as he leaves my room, Vespers singing a soft song of stars and constellations, Caladrius singing with her, and finally the Flock joining in, all three singing with one bright voice.

I fall asleep hearing their voices wrapping around the ship, a song of crackling ice and singing whales, a song of birds riding the wind and the ocean washing itself into brilliant frozen waves, each one of them full of the voice of the sea, and of the songs Vespers sings from the radio, a combination of love songs and temperatures, all of it merged into one thing, the voice of the world.

CHAPTER 24

{JASON}

I careen my drone back in the direction I think it came from, boomeranging it toward whomever sent it at us.

That would be Zal and Dai, and wherever they are, Caru is. That's what I'm hoping. Guessing.

I've pulled up its origin coordinates, and that's where I send it, steering it through a vortex of wind currents, and weirdnesses. It makes sense to me on some level, these flight simulation video game–style controls. The drone is showing me video as I move it through the sky.

I can see warships. None of them look major, there's nothing that seems to be Zal. And none of them are moving. They're just . . . waiting for something.

It occurs to me that maybe they're waiting for Aza to show up. Maybe they're waiting for her to be unable to stand it. Or they're waiting for someone to bring her back. Maybe she's already been captured somewhere else in the sky and that's why she didn't answer when I called and—

Stop.

There's a lurch and my drone spins furiously in the currents, flips upside down, and flies backward for a moment. I see other drones, flying fast in the opposite direction of mine, a high-pitched clicking sound. My drone swerves upward in a draft, and down, and then barrel rolls, and another drone passes, beeping.

Now, through drone camera eyes, I can see the vague edges of Maganwetar, the nothingness that is its camouflage, and the definitions of its WHERE—all guarded from every angle. Nothing else would need so many guards.

But. What does it mean that the drone came from Maganwetar?

A wall of whirlwinds, surrounded by lightning-full storm-sharks, their teeth bared, their bodies made of sparks and dark. There's a humming of song all around it. High above the blankness, I see a ring of additional drones, hovering in the sky, protecting the perimeter. These drones are bigger than the archaeopteryx I'm piloting, their wings flapping slowly, mechanized, their toothy beaks open. These are the size of eagles, their black feathers a serrated edge of metallic gleam. There's a halo of them hovering over Maganwetar.

Why the hell are they there? They should be with Zal.

How many drones did SWAB send up here? Or did Zal somehow manage to gain access to drones from elsewhere in the sky? There are at least fifty of them, and they are wing to wing, the blades at the tip of each wing making a fence of barbed wire to keep out anything that might be coming toward the invisible capital city.

Maganwetar is powerful. There's more to it than just a mass of invisible ships and invisible buildings. The capital of Magonia is full of magic, but it seems like I can't see anything coming out of it. The ships are quiet. The city is quiet. The sky, despite all the guards, is quiet.

There's no ship guarding it precisely, no ship I can pin down as the one they're on.

Where is Zal Quel? Where's Dai? Where, most importantly, is Caru?

Magic and science. The drones are from earth, but the song they're singing is the heartbeat of Aza's song turned into something evil and destructive, twisted into something that could turn solid to liquid, rock to water, flesh to blood. Destruction.

Zal's song, in other words. That's all I can think, hearing it twisting around the city. Which means she must be—

And then.

I see it.

The faint tops of the buildings, a glassy city. It looks like the most beautiful thing I've ever seen, an ice palace, a Disney version of splendor.

There are towers shaped like birds, and towers shaped like phoenixes, towers shaped like airkraken. Creatures from the sea and sky converge into the shapes of the city of Maganwetar, and all the buildings seem to move, swaying gently in the wind. I can't see any people from here, and no guards either, beyond the stormsharks and the little flotilla of drones.

It blinks in and out of visibility. The city seems to be sailing with a fleet of manta rays as sails, and *ray* is an accurate word, as in sun's rays. These are sending out rays of dark, not light. I can see their huge wings moving, and there must be thousands of them. They fold the city up in a cloak of wings, and then unfold it. I see the city flicker in and out of view.

My jaw drops. *These* are what keep Maganwetar invisible. Not some kind of tech. These.

The city itself, from below? It must be . . .

I think about weather reports I've seen over the years, about the way storms move across water, pulling up strength, the way they soar until they make landfall.

Maganwetar is a superstorm. It's a destroyer. Even with all this beauty inside it. It's concealed by weather, and for now, the weather is dormant.

I don't want to be around when it's not.

I see the manta's chains, dark as their wings. They're lifting all of Maganwetar, and carrying it through the sky.

Enslaved. And the same thing that Zal's been using to sail her ship. Which means—

I send my drone in closer, propelling it through the edges of buildings, and into Maganwetar.

Then I'm staggering. Eli's beside me, looking at the screen of my phone where my drone's footage is showing me what the city has been hiding from us, camouflaging with manta rays and storm clouds.

"Wow," she says.

That's all there is to say. The city is teeming with Magonians in uniform, thousands of blue people in all kinds of uniforms, all of them the colors of the sky at night and morning, their hair twisting ropes. They're armed to the teeth. They have swords and axes, ropes, knives. All the things I've seen in SWAB's archives are up here in reality. I've seen Magonians before. Aza, Dai, Zal, a glimpse back in Svalbard of the *Amina Pennarum* crew, but this is different.

"That's an army," Eli says.

I follow the drone's passage over the buildings, looking

through its eyes, searching for Dai, thinking he's what we're going to arrive at.

Finally, finally, the drone banks on an air current over a tower, and I look down through its camera. It's back to its original coordinates.

Its original coordinates are Zal Quel.

I'm looking down on her from above. She's commanding the city, like she'd command a ship. I can see her bent over a giant sky chart, and she's pointing and gesturing to Magonians.

And I see what's attached to Zal.

Caru. Caru, being used like bait on a fishing line. He's flying above the city, attached to a chain, and screaming. I can't hear his song, but I know what he's singing. It's pleading. It's *help*.

It's like I'm seeing Aza's heart chained to someone else. It's like I'm seeing all of my nightmares about her not loving me anymore, except in the form of her heartbird stolen from her, taken against her will.

I have a clear shot. There's nothing to decide.

"Go," says Eli. "Do it." I can feel her supporting me as I instruct my drone. I'm hardly standing, and she's holding me up. I can't think about it. I'm so barely here.

I see Zal looking up from below, but my drone is there, ready. I waver, waver, and the city beneath me is shaking and my hands are shaking, and I target through the sight just as I see Zal point at the drone. Other drones come spinning fast right at mine, but it's too late—

I press the button and deploy my drone's explosive.

Not at her—no, though I want to—but at the chain holding Caru to her, and to Maganwetar.

Maximum strength, right at the chain. There's a huge burst of light, and my drone lurches, attacked by other drones, just as I lurch too. I'm slammed into by someone, and then grabbed, someone leaping over the edge of this ship, off a launch and into the Rostrae nest ship.

Across from me, Eli's getting grabbed too.

Within moments, both of us are tied and shoved into the bottom of a fast launch boat, screaming and fury all around us.

I look up and see Dai looking down at me.

CHAPTER 25

{AZA}

I'm shrieking at a city in the sky, singing my song into it. I'm going to break Maganwetar open. I'm going to destroy it. Caru and I are singing together, our voices a fine-pointed weapon flying up into Magonia's capital. We blast them.

The sky's full of silver sails and sharks. Thousands and thousands of them. Manta rays soar, their wings rippling. I can't see the chains that hold them to the city, but I know they're there, glittering and silver. They've been captured by Zal. My mother doesn't care who she hurts. She never has.

I don't care anymore either.

I sing fury at her.

I sing

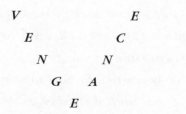

She's my enemy.

I see Dai beside her, Dai who betrayed me, and I sing at

him too. At everyone I couldn't trust, who lied to me, who tried to control me without ever asking what I wanted.

I'm singing with a flock, a huge wave of birds, a tsunami—

Singing death at everyone who assumed I wanted what they did.

In me, something is rising up, a dark power. It reminds me of Svalbard. Of that crest I felt with Dai. His power taking over mine.

But this time it's my power, my own choice—

This is what I want. I'm going to kill them both. This is my choice. MINE.

The birds rush around me, their beaks sharp, their talons out, and Zal's singing a storm made of knives, a storm made of arrows.

The world starts to change below us. The ground begins to turn to liquid. The street becomes a river. Feathers are on fire, and I can tell that above me are miles of dead, broken bodies, killed by my mother, falling—

She's singing me to the end of the story. She's winning—

NO, I'm going to sing the end myself. I'm going to destroy everything she wants revenge on, before she can. I won't let her do it. I'll destroy her too. She wanted to control me and I will NOT BE CONTROLLED.

My own birds start to dive at me, attacking me, tearing at me, and my body isn't my own, my heart isn't my own, my song is full of death and horror.

I feel my body starting to turn to stone, first my fingers, and then my arms, until it reaches the bottom of my lungs, and I feel them starting to seize, morphing into some sort of dark rock, my body becoming not anyone's—

I wake up, someone shaking me, my throat feeling blistered, like it's sung notes I don't know. The Flock is sitting beside my bed, his canwr all around me. He's watching me carefully, and his hand is on my shoulder.

"You were singing in your sleep," says the Flock. "A dark song."

I look around. Nothing's broken. No one's hurt.

"It was an endsong," he says. "How did you know it? Did Zal teach it to you?"

"No. I didn't know I knew it at all."

"It is nothing you should sing."

I hesitate. "What's an endsong?"

"Your deathsong," he says. "But more than just *yours*. It's a deathsong in which you kill not only yourself, but every other thing in proximity. You un-sing them and yourself at once." He pauses. "Do you wish yourself dead?"

"No!"

"What do you wish, then, Aza Ray?"

I glance at him. This man with golden eyes, and an exhausted face.

Heyward. I can't stop thinking about her dying, and about how it wasn't me. It should have been me. I think about Ley Fol now, executed by Zal because she saved me. I think about all the people I've hurt, all the people who've starved in Magonia, all the people who are at the mercy of Zal, people who'd still be alive if I had just surrendered to her and given her what she's always wanted. She wants me to be her daughter, her heir, and instead, I—

Chose everyone else.

"I don't know," I say. It's the truth. It's as close to the truth as I've ever gotten. I thought I knew what I wanted, and it was Jason. It was both of us alive, and in love, and in one place. And then?

No plan beyond that.

I thought I knew what I wanted, and it was home with my family, on earth, but—

Then I came to Magonia, and when I returned, I wanted more.

Maybe I'm like Zal. I think about the songs that are easy for *me* to sing. I think about the things that have been easy for *me* to do. Sing with Dai. And what we sang was—

Destruction songs. I'm like her. I'm so much like her.

Maybe I'm worse than she is, because I've been better. I've had a happier life. And yet, I'm *still* this angry, this confused.

Vespers is on my shoulder now, singing a song that makes my heart hurt. She's singing the world, singing the songs humans sing, but in her own voice, the songs of people falling in love and falling out of love and trying to understand one another.

"Dying would be easier than THIS," I say. "Dying wasn't hard. It wasn't horrible. I've done it before. It's living that's hard. Who *chose* me anyway? Why am I supposed to do any of these things?"

I can still feel the endsong all over my body. I feel like I did something I may never be able to take back.

"Chosen or not chosen," the Flock says. "All you can do is what you are strong enough to do. You have a song. You can only sing it. It doesn't matter what others think of that, whether they think you have any power at all. Everyone has power, every person, every bird, every bat. *Chosen* is only because it makes things simpler. The world is like a ship, and you can climb the mast, or scrub the figurehead. You can keep the charts, or plot the course." He stares deep into my eyes. "You have a song. Sing it."

He looks at me, his golden eyes shining.

"What if I can't? What if I sing something horrible instead? What if I destroy things when I'm trying to save them?"

"Dying without song because you don't know which life you want isn't brave, Aza," says the Flock.

"I don't want death. I just want—"

"You just want someone *else* to die," he says, and nods. "That's easy too. You could sing death into the body of anyone you wish. You could sing it into me. You're strong enough."

I am. I know that now.

"But if you do that, if you merely sing an endsong, you'll be like she is."

I don't feel like there's much to me beyond anger, frustration, and misery right now.

"Who wouldn't be angry at Zal? Aren't you? She made me— She's your enemy. That's what I know about you. That's what they told me."

"She wasn't always my enemy," he says, and laughs a sad laugh. "I was her ethologidion," he says. "I am still. There's no removing that bond, no matter how much one might wish to. But I will not sing with her again."

I thought he was just part of her crew. I thought when he said he sang with her, he meant he sang in service of her song. But this is—

He was her . . . *Dai*? Which means . . .

Not only is he made to sing with her . . . he can control her song.

"You look like her," he says. "And you sing like her. We sang the stars into alignment and sailed across the sky, before she was broken."

A white tattoo appears on his skin, the face of my mother, a long time ago.

And beside her is Caru, perched on her arm.

I watch the tattoo move, the ghostly inked Zal open her mouth and sing, but there's no sound. She reaches out her hands and laughs, looking at someone who isn't there. Looking at someone with love. I've never seen her look this way, never seen her look so—

So trusting.

Rain tattoos its way down over her head, and covers her with ink dots. A disappearing woman, there on his skin.

He looks at it, considering, and all the white lines undo themselves and disappear again.

The old man stares at me steadily, silently, for a moment.

"We are long since finished with our singing, Zal Quel and I," he says. "That time is done. But my song? My flock? You need no teaching. You have it already. It is your inheritance."

Wait.

I stare at him.

"Are you—?"

"I was done singing with Zal, but I did not leave you. I was told you'd died. That you'd been kidnapped, that they'd killed you. That is why I'm here. That's what made me leave Magonia."

I say it, because there's nothing left to say. I discover that I knew it already.

"You're my father."

"Daughter," says the Flock. His face is startlingly gentle for a moment. "Perhaps your mother taught you your song, but I heard you sing it. Your song came from me too. And from who you are. Believing anyone else is in control of that—living in such anger—will not let you sing the song you're meant to sing," he says. "You are strong enough to sing as you wish, not as your pain has forced you to. You aren't your hurt. You're other than that. You are not the broken things you've been. Look at yourself. You're living, not a singer in the midst of her deathsong."

I'm sputtering, still feeling that endsong, still seeing Zal before my eyes, still in pain, and now. Another father. Out here on the edge. A father who ran from Zal. A father who won't help me fight her—

"Zal was my only love," says the Flock simply. "But she was capable of horrible things. As am I. As are you. That's something you'll learn if you live a long time. Everyone can break things."

I jolt, because I already know that. On every level.

"You're strong enough to heal things too," he says, his hand on my shoulder, pressing hard on it. "Not just break them. It's simply that breaking is easier."

"What if I can't help it? What if I just destroy? What if I don't know how to do anything else?"

After a moment, he smiles.

"You remind me of myself. I wasn't strong enough to sing beside Zal," says the Flock. "Not without destroying us both. The love we had wasn't enough. I was angry too, and the anger would have destroyed us both. You are her daughter, not her singer, though. You ARE strong enough. You just have to choose to be."

I sit with that for a moment. I've seen what's wrong with the world. Once you've seen it, you don't get to go back.

"Please," I say, sitting beside him. "You told me you were the last of your kind, but you don't have to be. Teach me. I'll do what you say. I'll try to figure it out."

The Flock nods and opens his mouth to sing when—

FLASH. I suddenly see through Caru's eyes for the first time in days. I shake, frozen.

AZA! Caru screamsings.

I see him. Caru's loose, flying free, flinging himself through the spires of Maganwetar, frantic, searching for me.

He twists past the last of the stormsharks, and throws himself into the air outside the city, flying as fast as he can, but I can tell he has no sense of direction, no idea where I am. He's lost.

Aza, he sings, desperate.

Oh god. I stop and stand in the center of the deck, singing, trying to strengthen him.

Vespers starts singing her beautiful bat song, hard with me, and I'm so grateful.

I feel Caru's pain. Tiny bones in his wings are fractured. He wonders if he should dive out of the clouds and die, but he doesn't, because he's hunting for me. He can feel our bond, but he doesn't know where I am. He's panicked. He's been tortured, and they've forced his song from him, twisted it into other songs.

The Flock is beside me now, and he's singing too, with me, with Vespers. Now Caladrius joins too.

He's singing to Caru, to guide Caru here.

I feel Caru taking it in, sensing it. I call again to him and feel him hear me at last, with a blasting trill of relief and exhaustion.

AZA, he sings. AZA.

Suddenly there are hundreds of other birds in the sky around

Caru. The Flock's sending all the canwr in the area to help.

I glance at him, but his face is only focus, intensely singing with his heartbird and heartbat, and with me.

I tentatively start to sing with them. Because this is Caru. This is the rest of *my* heart.

I have a vision through Caru of a string of birds leading him to us, and of those birds all around him, supporting his song. Caru is barely flying, but the birds bring him, hiding him in their midst.

The Flock sings the whole time, calling in more of his birds, through the dark and into the grayness that heralds the dawn.

It lightens, and the sun starts to blaze the sky into orange and pink. I see a black speck out on the edges, followed by a wave of wings. Caru is flying fast, a vibrating song of terror coming from him.

Then I see what's wrong. He's being pursued by one of the birds I've seen attacking us over and over, the black ones. Mechanical. Singing machines.

All around us the air vibrates with that monstrous song, the song of an entire city screaming for Aza Ray, the song of the deaths of everyone on earth I love, and everyone here too. I see the vibrating vision of the earth flooding and burning at once. I feel the sky dividing into something that's basically all on fire.

It's Zal's song. Zal, and also—

The robot bird is singing a note that I last sang when Dai and I first sang together, a note that made the ocean rise beneath us and consider turning over, and another note that melted earth into water. It's mechanized and skewed, but I know my song when I hear it.

It's my song. For the death of the drowners. Sung by

something that is changing it, making it stronger, and worse.

Caru sings over that, as loudly and furiously as I've ever heard him sing, and the Flock's birds rise up to surround him. Vespers and Caladrius take off from the deck and put themselves on each side of my heartbird.

The thing chasing him is huge, as big as Caru, and it has wings tipped with blades. It's diving and spiraling in the sky.

The Flock's birds are up and around Caru and the predator is attacking them. They scream, and the Flock screams back. When he screams, his birds get stronger, singing *protection*, singing *shield*, their bodies between Caru and what I now realize is a drone. The Flock's tsunami of birds keeps the predator from Caru, but some of them are dying in the process.

TO ME, QUICKLY, I sing, HOME, sending Caru my strength.

Vespers and Caladrius sing it too, ferociously. Vespers shrills a note I can hardly hear, and the drone tilts on one wing, screaming too, its voice vibrating wrongly and twitching its entire body.

Caru dives out of the clouds and into my arms, screaming, bleeding, but he's here. I hold him tight.

I look up just in time to see the drone spinning in the air and screaming out a furious string of notes that flips all the birds in range in the wind as well.

JASON AND ELI ARE HERE. TO MAGANWETAR OR THEY DIE.

Then it flies fast as a jet plane out of range, and into the clouds, fleeing the Flock and his song.

Aza, Caru trills, in my arms, my poor heartbird, wing in pain, beak scarred, body trembling. The Flock sings the birds out of the sky. They perch all over *Glyampus*.

"Thank you," I whisper to the Flock. I'm shaking all over with the effort of the song, and with fear for everyone.

The Flock puts his hand on Caru's head. Caru whistles at him.

"Caru is an old friend," he says. "I did not think to see him again."

Broken string, says Caru sadly, and looks at Caladrius, who tilts her head at him and sings a few beautiful notes. Caru sings with them. Of course they know each other. This was what they did with Zal, long before I was born.

My poor heartbird can't stop shaking for hours after he arrives. The Flock helps me splint his wing, which is fractured and bent. I tend his other wounds.

All the while Caru sings to me about Zal, a muddle of panicked songs about her plans, about what she's doing. He sends visions into my brain of her killing Rostrae and killing other things too. Canwr, and creatures from other parts of the sky. I see a phoenix, and I see a batsail.

Broken heart, sings Caru. *Broken string.* But he can't explain. I twine my heart to his and we sing together, me trying to heal him.

He tucks his beak, then his head under my arm, and I feel something open up in my heart. I feel it crack, for Caru if for no one else. All the guard I've had up. All the protection. I feel it start to melt, and the song I've not been singing comes out, a little. It's quiet, but it's full of love, and strong enough to knit bones.

The Flock comes out of his cabin and watches me.

I sing the healing song, and Caru cries out in pain.

It hurts me to hurt him, but I can feel the bones mending. Caru submits. I sing his wing into calmness, sing it into wholeness, and he screals, but he lets me do it. When I'm done singing, he opens his wings and trills uncertainly. It's okay, I think. He's still weak, but no longer broken.

Caladrius comes toward me and tilts her head.

Fly, she sings. Caru sings it back to her.

I look at the Flock. I feel stronger now, with Caru, at least, even if I haven't mastered the Flock's song. I have to go to them. If I can sing a healing song, that's something. If I can sing any song that isn't destruction, if I can do that, I have at least a little of what I need. I don't have time to wait for more.

"Will you lend me a launch?"

He stares hard at me.

"So you can sail to your death?"

"That's not my plan," I tell him, but I can tell he hears what I'm not saying, that plans can change. That sometimes people change them for you. I try to look like I know what I'm doing. I don't want to sail to my death. But I might be about to do that anyway.

"No," he says. "I won't allow it."

"She has my sister," I say. "She has—"

"Your ethologidion," he says.

"No," I say. "My . . . I don't know what the word is."

"It's the same word," the Flock says. "Maybe you have two singers. Maybe you're bonded to both of them. I have two heart-birds. Maybe you have two bonds, two who sing with you. There are different songs to sing, Aza."

"I have to go," I say. "They know where we are. We might be able to defend this piece of the sky against warships and

Nightingales, but against Maganwetar and Zal? No. I have to go. Otherwise I'll bring Zal here and that will be worse."

"You're not ready. You have to be able to sing against her."

I look at him, but he doesn't change his mind.

So I wait until the middle of the night, creep guiltily onto the deck with Caru on my shoulder, take provisions from the galley, and pack them into a sack. I slink over to the edge of *Glyampus*.

It's strange to imagine Caru and these canwr, all part of the same song, with Zal and the Flock, together and possibly . . . happy?

I imagine Zal and the Flock singing together. My biological parents. They are why I'm here. I have to be grateful they found each other, even if it ended up like this. Zal in love. The Flock young and not gray in the skin. Both singing, and canwr are all around them.

I feel a jab of loss. I don't know how to heal Zal.

I have to do this. I shift ropes, untangle lines.

I turn and the Flock is right behind me. Of course he is. The sky is silent out here, and he pays attention to every noise.

"I have to," I say.

"I see that. Sing one note, then," he says. "Sing the one that will make the future possible."

I stare at him. I don't know the note. That's all I can think. I'm supposed to be the *chosen one*, but why? Who chooses someone who messes everything up?

Caru starts to sing.

And what he's singing?

It begins with the song of the mice from our kitchen at home. Then the song of the lonely whale.

I—

He sings the song of the batsail from *Amina Pennarum*.

He starts whistling. I know what he's whistling.

I don't want him to be. I don't want to remember this. It's in Silbo, the whistled Spanish from the Canary Islands, the song I sang at a talent show, it seems like a million years ago.

I sang it for Jason. It's full of words only Jason and I know, jokes only we have, all the love I couldn't figure out how to talk about. All the things I didn't know how to say. He didn't even know what I was singing. He couldn't understand me. I did that on purpose, because I was too scared to say everything, too scared to give him everything. Maybe too scared to know it myself. So I sang it in a language only a few people speak, and I made it too hard for him to translate.

But Caru knows it. Caru is the part of my heart that has to tell the truth.

Caru is singing them, all these things at once, and I feel something give way in my chest, because now he's singing my apology list, he's singing the things I was sorry for, the fact that I was going to die and leave Jason alone, the times I'd looked at him and not seen him. He's singing the things I'd never told him, and all the rest of it too. He's singing my worry at being imperfect Aza, and then Alien Aza, at being this wreck of a girl who could never heal any of Jason's pain, but only create more for him. At being someone who couldn't save the person she loves.

I feel my heart tilt, I feel my lungs full of song, my body full of song, because finally, Caru is singing the whole thing, all my love for all of my life below, all my love for my life above, all of it, and I join him.

I can't help myself. I have to.

This is everything. All of us at once, stars in dark rooms, parents singing me to sleep, hospital beeps and wind in the trees, Eli laughing, Jason whispering to me in my sleep. Squallwhales and batsails, Wedda teaching me to fight, to dress, to braid my hair, Jik telling me the truth about Rostrae. Stars shooting out across the sky, and all of it, everything, part of this existence. The sorrow and the joy, the guilt and the pride, the failures and the accomplishments.

This is the whole thing, and we sing it together, until it comes out of my mouth in one pure note.

Caru sings, and I sing my harmony back. It becomes one note, a note I don't recognize at first until I realize that Caru's singing me my parents, all four of them, my history, my heart, my future.

We're singing the sound of my heartbeat and my breath, the sound of bright blue blood running through my Magonian veins, the sound of someone trying to be everything at once, trying to save everyone at once.

I sing it with him. The truest note I can find. I'm not just someone's chosen one, it says. I'm myself. *I* have to choose now.

I watch the sky shift.

A whooshing surge of starlings, a murmuration, a cloud of them dancing in the air, their bodies swooping and twisting, folding the sky and singing with us, a note that summons a veil of wings, a black lace curtain of words and song. They fly around the ship, a soaring roar of glory, a million birds moving as one body.

The Flock looks at me. "Daughter," he says.

Tears are running down my face. I'm shaking, and I feel like

I'm exposed. The world has just seen everything I'm scared of losing, all at once, written in shifting letters in the air.

"You will take my ship."

"You don't have to do that."

His smile broadens. "We all have songs to sing, Aza Ray. I didn't know I had a daughter. Now that I do, I have no wish to lose her. My ship is faster than any launch, and I'm coming with it."

Vespers lands on one of my shoulders, and Caladrius on the other. Caru sings from the Flock's shoulder. We're a strange family, all the canwr, me, and my father together.

I fumble in the pocket of my flight suit. I bring out the compass Jason gave me.

The needle points.

I head north.

*3.14159265358979323846264338327950288419716939937510
58209749445923078164062862089986280348253421170679821
4808651328230664709384460955058223*1

"Jason! Look at me!"

72535940812848111745028410270

"The burns on his chest are infected. I don't know how long they've been like this. Can someone help us? Please?"

*193852110555964462294895493038196442881097566593
344612847564823378678316*52

"Don't go to sleep. Jason! JASON!"

712019091456485 someone slaps my face *669234603486104*

"Do you want him to die? Is that the goal? A dead hostage? Is that what you want? He's burning up. I DON'T KNOW WHERE SHE IS. If you want Aza, you have to keep him alive."

Cold hand on my forehead. Cold hand, colder than human—

*543266482133936072602491*4

I open my eyes and someone's leaning over me. I'm at the level of his chest, looking up. There's a tattoo of Aza Ray. White lines on dark blue skin, and it moves and shows her singing.

"Jason," Dai says. "Welcome to Maganwetar."

This guy has already burned me half to death, and before that, he nearly obliterated Aza. He's a liar (and?), a betrayer (and?), someone who chose the wrong side and stayed on it because Zal offered him power. He is, except for a few differences, just like me.

The tattoo on Dai's chest shifts to Aza singing with him, leaning against a sail, an ocean rising below the ship they're on. She's wearing captain's insignia. So is he. They're sailing together. This is their future.

12737245870066063155881748815209209 6282

I forget about the way my body is spinning and broken, the way I feel like I'm pea and sun, shriveling and expanding at once.

All I can hear is my own heartbeat, pounding, and then I grab Dai with both hands, and bring him closer to me.

"I met her when we were five! You don't even know her!" I yell.

I hear Eli yelling too.

"What are you doing? Jason! You're hurting yourself! Stop it!"

"*You* don't know her," Dai says. "She died in your care. You lost her. You should have been keeping her safe."

I lose track of everything around us and everything beneath us.

"I tried to save her!"

"She sang with me. She's been mine since she was born, and I hers," he says. "We share one voice."

Dai's leaning over me and his tattoos are showing me Aza's name and face and body, over and over, and his canwr's singing what can only be insults.

"You don't even know her. You don't know what she is. You don't know who she is. You don't know what she sings in her sleep," I whisper. "You don't know how much—"

I exhale. There's a moment of stillness during which I try to make this all make sense.

"How much what?" he asks.

"You don't know how much I love her," I manage to say, but I'm dizzy, in so much pain, and the edge of his sleeve drags across my chest, open wound, burns, broken skin, broken heart, broken, broken broken—

I'm blinded for a moment, blacked out in agony.

9254091715364367892

I close my eyes. It's black and calm behind them, peaceful. Everything hurts. Nothing hurts. Feathers fan across the darkness.

91227938183011949129833673362440656566430

"This is her drowner, then?" someone says in Magonian, the Magonian I understand from sleepless nights steeping myself in sound files from SWAB. At least they've given me something.

I open my eyes and see Zal Quel looking down at me, her face like Aza's, her hair like Aza's, her voice like Aza's. Here I am with Aza's worst enemy, and with the reason Aza exists at once, and I don't have any strength to fight.

"Jason Kerwin," she says, and bends over me. Aza's mother's face is close to mine, beautiful and strange, like a sky seen through dark glass, and her hair twists in the wind.

She raises her arms and I see what I didn't see before, through the drone camera. Her arms are strung with wires, and her throat is wrapped with them. When she opens her mouth the Nightingales open their throats and sing for her. Her skin is laced with song circuits to compensate for the loss of her canwr.

She looks exactly like Aza Ray, and for a moment I confuse the two of them. I see Aza, and then Zal, and then Aza again, I see the girl I first met in kindergarten, clipping ships out of paper. I see her heart and bones and her face, the way she looked at me and knew I wasn't enough for her. I wasn't.

No, that's Zal looking at me.

That's Zal staring into my eyes.

"What did my daughter see in this weakling?" she asks Dai.

"I don't know," says Dai, but I see him glance at me, and he looks uncertain. "He says he loves her."

Zal's given herself a voice out of the stolen voices of Aza and Caru. She's twisted it with her own silenced song. This is what she's done. This is what she's made.

And it's still my fault. I'm not strong enough to change it.

"You're her drowner, then," says Zal. "And you can save Aza. Do you wish to save Aza?"

I can't move anything, but it's okay. The sky is full of stars. There are songs rising all around me.

"I love Aza," I say.

"Then do this for her," she says.

"What?"

She opens her mouth. AZA AZA AZA AZA, she sings, and the Nightingales attached to her voice sing it for her. The sky vibrates with hundreds of voices in chorus singing her name.

"Give me your voice," Aza's mother hisses. "Tell my daughter she is wanted here."

Dai moves one of the wires from a Nightingale and presses

it to my throat. He sings a strange note, a blistering sound that welds the wire to my skin. It hurts, but everything hurts. Everything is agony.

There's a dry screaming creak, a hissing, and the sky's suddenly full of greenish smoke, crackling, lights. Shooting stars?

A meteor shower.

It's Aza coming. It must be.

For a second, I'm full of joy. I forget about every reason Aza should hate me, everything that's probably gonna be broken from here on out, and I just look up at these thousands of shooting stars falling all over the dark, like heaven's exploding, like the sky's a birthday cake topped with sparklers, like we're looking up at the sky on the Fourth of July, normal teenagers in love.

I watch a meteor come straight at me, and then another. Flaming boulders are falling all around us.

"JASON." Someone slaps my cheek. Cold water pouring down.

"He'll last long enough to call to her," says Zal. "She approaches."

"He's dying," says Dai.

"He has enough life left," says Zal. "She won't want him. Look at how weak he is. She needs you. She can't sing without you. We know that. She only needs to remember."

Her voice has a scathing beauty, the song of someone who's spent her life screaming orders, and screaming pain. She smiles a smile I'm unlikely to forget. A combination of rage and longing.

Aza's mother.

Aza's nightmare.

Aza's abuser.

Aza's captain, but not one she chose.

"He's hallucinating," I hear Eli say, and Dai is over me for a moment, looking at me, his face creased with something that might be . . . worry. I look up at him.

"I love her," I say. I hear my own whisper echo through Zal's Nightingales, way above us. "Tell her I'm sorry."

The Nightingales shout it into the sky.

My words.

I love her. Tell her I'm sorry. I hear them sing it, and I feel frozen and then like I'm made of glass. The air is whistling around me, and the stars have stopped falling. I start listing my apologies.

I don't ask her to come save me.

I don't ask her to come. I don't deserve that.

"Somebody help us! Please!" Eli's crying somewhere, but she's far away from me. I don't know where I am. In the sky. Aza's coming for me.

59036001133053054

I feel myself being picked up, lifted up from where I'm lying, carried. I feel myself floating over the deck, maybe flying. Beside me someone is holding my hand so tightly I can't move my fingers.

"Aza?"

"It's Eli."

The air around me is filled with song, and there are clouds full of rain, and I can hear Eli talking, and yelling at someone far away from me, and birds screaming and wings in the air.

"She's COMING!" shout a million voices, all over the city, a million Magonians, a million Nightingales, a million echoes of echoes.

86021394946395224737190702179860943702770539217

17629317675238467481846766940513200056812714526356
08277857713427577896091736371787214684409012249534
3014654958

And this is the end. The world is full of miracles. At least I've seen some of them.

CHAPTER 27

{AZA}

We fly past constellations, past shooting stars, past asteroids, past parts of the sky that are burning. The wind is high and it burns my face. We tilt and then slide fast across clouds, just us and our flock of a million birds, out in the sky.

We go faster.

As we go I feel what we're doing to the sky we're leaving. There are waves in the air, and ripples, and shudders of wind in our wake.

A giant wave of birds is carrying us across the sky to Maganwetar. I try not to think about what's waiting there. If we have to raise an ocean to drown Zal, we can do that. If we have to die fighting her, we can do that too—

I don't want to die.

I think about Eli all the way to Maganwetar, and I know some things about my sister. She's not weak. She might be hurt, but she's brave.

I think about Jason.

I can't think about the Jason I know right now. I'm still too dark, too hurt, too guilty. So I think about his alligator costume. In my mind, Jason on skates, spinning in his suit, spinning, and spinning and spinning in the middle of the roller rink.

If I die, I will still see him spinning. If I die, he'll spin there forever.

I think about Dai, who has them both. Dai, who could be better than this. Dai, who could be the other half of my voice. How could someone who could sing with me so perfectly, so clearly, so easily, be so different from me? How could he end up trying to turn my song into some horrible thing?

It feels so right to sing with him. It always did. But I can do it without him. I have new songs now.

And they are MINE.

We fly all night. I look up at the stars, and think about something I read, back on earth, about how the stars can vibrate like bells (astroseismology, in case you were wondering) and some astronomer started making their noises into symphonies. I wonder. Then I stop wondering.

I twist and braid my hair into the knots Wedda taught me, the style she called my own battle style. It feels so long ago that I was on *Amina Pennarum,* scared and still feeling like a dead girl, trying to learn to be *this.* So long ago that I found Caru locked in a cage in Zal's cabin, screaming his ghost song.

A poem I learned—it's a poem everyone learns at some point—is in my head, rattling around, weirdly comforting. "Invictus," it's called. I don't know the whole thing. It's probably about something other than going to war against your mother in a sky kingdom, but I'll take what I can get. I yell it out at the sky.

> It matters not how strait the gate,
> How charged with punishments the scroll,

I am the master of my fate:
I am the captain of my soul.

Caru perches on my shoulder, looking out into the distance, me singing with him, maneuvering the Flock's birds, moving this murmuration across the sky.

The sun's rising when I finally see Maganwetar, and I can't help but think the whole city is in battle stance, just like I am. One girl, and her heartbird.

I'm still worried this isn't enough. I'm shaking with terror, not for myself, but for everything and everyone around me, earth and sky, air and ground, sea and stars.

Maganwetar's not like I saw it in Svalbard, not anything like what I saw there, the underbelly of something tremendous, hardly seen at all.

No. Now I see much more.

It's a terrifying sight, each building with a figurehead of birds and bodies, each sail a tremendous ray, wings rippling.

There must be thousands of Magonians in that flying city, along with Zal. She has crews. All of them can sing.

Small Nightingales are on the outskirts, and they hum around our heads. So much for surprise. I watch the robot birds click photos above me.

It's now or never. I blast a note out into the air.

"ZAL QUEL, SHOW YOURSELF! I'M HERE!" I shout.

Caru sings the bottom note in my scream. Not just Caru. I hear something else. Other birds, from far away. They sound like . . . I don't let myself hope.

A raft approaches, speeding through the sky, a blue jay at its helm.

Jik, Wedda, and the Rostrae of *Amina Pennarum*. The raft is bristling with weaponry, Jik with a sword in her hands, Wedda too, and both of them are rising up from the deck, their wings wide, their feathers on end.

"Aza!" shouts Jik.

"Nestling!" shouts Wedda.

I look around frantically, hoping they have Jason and Eli, but they don't. It's Rostrae only.

"Have you seen Eli?" I ask them. They're the first ones to know what I'm talking about. They're the only ones who will understand about earth, about Jason. They were with me when I was saying good-bye to all of it. "Is she here? And Jason? We were told they were here."

I'm hoping it's a lie, all of it. Except that north led us directly here.

"Dai took your sister," says Jik. "And your drowner. They're in the city. Our ship was set on fire, and we've been fighting since."

Other Rostrae are coming toward us. Some on their little ships, some of them flying. All with their wings spread, their talons out, their ships mobilized. They war the way birds war, with rocks and branches, with knives and song. Our ship is quickly surrounded by Rostrae.

I hear song coming fast from other parts of the sky, beautiful and strange. I look up, through the whirlwinds and madness of Maganwetar, and see batsails. Dozens of them. Their wings are as wide as the mantas' wings, and all of them are singing.

They're echolocating one another, and none of them are attached to ships with chains, but many of them have ships with them. They're towing of their own will.

Each ship is full of things I've never seen, and some I have, people from the edges of the sky. There are things here I saw in the prison, and I'm flooded with gratitude. Maybe some of them came because I set them free. Maybe not. Maybe everything here is here because this is Zal Quel trying to destroy the world, and there are many things in the world. This is the reckoning for Zal's rebellion. These are the forces she will face.

Thousands of batsails. Millions of birds. There are raft after raft of Rostrae.

We're not alone. The sky is full of silent ships. All waiting for something to happen.

For someone to sing it.

Two sides of the sky.

The capital city of an empire, buildings and people, ships and sharks, manta rays, frozen and hovering in the sky waiting for an order from my mother or a feint from me.

The remnants of its camouflage, the veil created by song and by the manta rays drops, and I see it for real now. All of it.

A dazzling metropolis emerging from fog, all spiky buildings, and streets full of Magonians.

There are Magonians carrying dark storm clouds in their hands, and Magonians singing spirals of snow. There are Magonians holding oblongs of stationary rain, and Magonians carrying strings of ice, each piece formed into a spike. The city's energy is focused entirely on the place in the sky where we're floating.

Stormsharks circle, spitting lightning. The air creaks with

thunder, but nothing's louder than the voice booming out of every building, out of every Nightingale, every stormshark, every ship.

I know that voice.

It's Jason. Oh god. I quiver, hearing him, over and over, his voice, his pain. He's hurt. He's REALLY hurt. Something's wrong. He's gasping. Over and over it repeats, out of every mechanical bird's throat, out of the whole city.

I LOVE HER. TELL HER I'M SORRY FOR EVERYTHING.

THE TIMES I TOLD HER WHAT TO DO.

THE TIMES I DIDN'T TRUST HER TO KNOW HER OWN MIND.

THE TIMES I THOUGHT SHE TOOK TOO MANY RISKS.

His apology list. That's the format. I know it well, because this is my whole childhood, my whole list-making version, all of us trying to keep each other safe.

This means he's *dying*?

I open my mouth, my lungs full of fury, full of deathsong for Zal, wherever she is, full of blast—

The Flock grabs my hand from where he's hidden inside the transparent camouflage of the cabin. "Steady," he says.

Maganwetar is low, I suddenly realize. I glance down, and I'm stunned. Last I looked, we were over the ocean. Now?

I know my hometown.

I know what it looks like from above. I know what it looks like from every angle. I know what it looks like when we're watching my funeral from a ship. I know what our house looks like, and Jason's house. There are cars in the driveway.

Maganwetar is full of weapons. I watch as the Magonians wielding them shift away from the Rostrae and me, and begin to point downward. I feel rather than see the energy of my city looking up at us. What do we look like? A giant dark cloud full of danger? A hurricane? Do we look like the storm to end all storms? That's what we are.

I sing my vessel closer to the edge, and finally, finally—

I see him, standing on the edge of the city, my ethologidion, singing out to me.

Dai looks like someone punched him. Black eye, bloodied face. He looks ragged, like he looked last year, except much thinner, and much older. Like he's been hurt, a lot, for a long time. He looks made of misery.

Dai. I helped him rise in Magonia, and then I made him fall. All I really want to do right this moment, across from Dai for the first time in a year, is cry.

This is the end of something. Maybe I don't need an ethologidion. I can live without him. But can I kill him? Or is he the other one I'm bonded to? Do I need two heartbirds, and two ethologidions?

Can I kill Dai?

No.

His voice is still the voice that partners mine, the voice that feels like it should be coming out of his chest and mine at once. We're joined in this stupid bond, this thing we didn't choose, this harmonic language of power. Someone chose US for it, and I don't even know who it was. We're meant to sing together, even after everything that's happened. It's a year later and I thought I'd chased that bond out of my soul. My heart is mine. It belongs to me. And it hurts.

I'm terrified the moment I see him. He has power over me.

He knows my song better than anyone but Caru.

I swallow.

He doesn't know what I've learned. He only knows what I knew when he last saw me. I can do this. We're close enough.

Then I see something else. Eli, tied up, her face made of fury.

And Jason. Very still. So still. His chest is covered in bandages, and there's blood on them, and he looks—

He can't be.

Maganwetar doesn't need you, Aza Ray, sings a drone in Zal's voice. *But I want you. Join us, or they die.*

The rest of the Nightingales join in, singing me the twisted version of an old song, an element-shifting song, sung in harmony.

I see my mother, at long last. She walks out from behind a building, and stands, looking at me. Her face is furious and her tattoos are everywhere. Her skin is covered with white ships, white lights, the sun and moon and stars.

I'm not the only one who's changed. I'm not the only one who has a new song.

"ZAL QUEL!" I shout.

"Daughter," she says, and smiles at me. "Choose."

I look down and in the rivers and lakes surrounding my town, I see waves beginning to stack themselves into columns. The rivers are stirring, twitching up from their beds, and it's the song that's doing it. Out at the northern edge of the city, on the lake, I see something else happening. A piece of land liquefies and slips into the water.

The Nightingales have my song. They can turn land to

water, and water to stone. They can do whatever I can do. Not all of it, though.

They don't know all of it.

Zal's making a hurricane. She's stirring up a storm surge, a windblast, a disaster. I watch as the sky darkens, as wind begins to whip up from everywhere. We're above it, and I can see garbage and dirt, trees and bits of buildings, things blowing and joining the song. We are the eye of the hurricane, Maganwetar, and below us, the whole world is a spiral of furious song.

"You're my daughter," Zal sings out over the space between us. "You belong to me. Your song is mine."

Zal opens her mouth and all the Nightingales scream at once, with her voice. She was silenced, but now she's not. This is her, mixed with me, mixed with Caru. This voice is a cacophony of metal and fire.

She doesn't know everything. She doesn't know what I have. She doesn't know that I know who I am now.

All of it.

All of me.

I'm here.

We're here.

I start to sing the song the Flock taught me, a song that can bring everything to this battle, a song filled with blazing light and all the canwr in the sky.

I feel things starting to shift, a movement, a startling ripple everywhere, and beside me, Jik takes off, and rises up, fighting another Nightingale, and Wedda too, taking another one down.

A strong note, a blistering note of communion, and on my side of the sky, things start to almost glow with it. I feel my father with me, and Vespers and Caladrius, feel them calling out to the world and everything it contains, and I wrap my song around theirs—

Zal looks bewildered by what I'm singing. I'm singing a song I inherited from someone she hid from me.

I'm singing a song I learned from my father. She has no idea he's here.

But Dai's singing too now, and I hear another voice. A shrill, maddened, yellow voice. The door in Dai's chest opens, slowly.

Tiny, missing feathers, ragged. Golden less gold than it should be. Slowly, Milekt turns his head and looks at me.

Broken string! he shrieks.

I know the song of a canwr that's unbonded with its Magonian. I know it from Caru.

KILL ME! shrieks Milekt, and my whole body shudders. I did this. I broke our bond. It shakes my song. Dai looks at me.

I remember the Aza Ray who was meant to be with him. The Aza Ray who didn't love him, but who was promised to him. Everything political in that, everything forced, and still, there are some things you can't fight. This is one of them. We were bonded. *Are* bonded.

My voice still thinks Dai's the one I'm supposed to move the sky with.

Dai's voice presses to my other ear.

He's singing beneath my song, and my song is stronger, but wrong. He's making it into Zal's wishes all over again. MY song's bringing planets out of alignment. He's singing the rest of my song, the ends of each note belonging to him, and his canwr, Svilken, is singing too. Milekt is singing them into my heart, into my chest.

Caru shrills, attacking Milekt with beak and claw, with song and breath, but it's not working. There's a brutal shriek and I lose my voice for a moment, confused by emotion, gasping in pain.

Milekt whips out of Dai's chest, not the weakened, dying thing he seemed.

Traitor! Milekt screals. *TRAITOR! TRAITOR!*

He's fast as a dart, like the one that killed Heyward, coming at me so quickly I almost can't see him. My lungs are burning and my throat is cracking—

There's one second where Milekt is right in front of me, close to my face, and I look into his bright black eyes, and he's screaming curses at me, and that second hangs forever.

His beak, black, his wings spread wide, and he's singing *AZA YOU RUINED YOU RUINED ME YOU BROKE MY SONG AZA DESTROYER!*

Milekt torpedoes into my singing mouth. I choke on my former canwr and he stays there, in my throat.

Silencing me.

Strangling my song.

"Get her," I hear Zal snarl.

CHAPTER 28

{JASON}

Aza Ray's standing on the deck of a ship maybe thirty feet in front of me. She looks, through my slitted eyes, like something made of light.

She looks like someone I don't even know.

Maybe I don't. I'm almost not here, and everything around me is blurry, waves of pain, brightness, screaming from every part of the sky, and Aza there, right there, close enough that I can see her, I can feel her—

How does anyone stand it, when the only person you're ever going to love doesn't love you anymore? How does anyone live through this?

Even in the middle of a war, I can feel it, the same feeling I had when lightning was about to strike me, except that it's across the whole sky. It's like the ceiling is about to fall, like it's a dome, a fresco coming down in an earthquake.

Everyone's up here. Everything.

There's a hurricane below us, and up here, a still, desperate eye to the storm.

I start to notice fighter jets. They're coming to Maganwetar. Maybe SWAB's pushed the button.

I see planes peel off, twisting around the edge of the city.

There's screaming song under the chopping of helicopter blades and the sound of jet engines, and I can't quite hear the words but—

Something's changing. Stormsharks and whirlwinds begin to twist and spark, long streaks of electricity and wind in the sky. Cannons fire from one of the ships of Maganwetar, and I see ropes with hooks flying out toward the jets and copters that've come from SWAB. The jets themselves are having trouble in the weather, twisting and lurching, and I wonder if their navigation is messed up by the storm. The storm is huge. I feel the whole sky turning black, and all over it is fire and fighting, and Aza, Aza, in front of me, singing a song I've never heard her sing before. There are millions of birds. There's too much and I can't see it, can't feel it, can't—

I think about the helicopter, last year, taken down by Magonia. I think about the black box I listened to. Magonia is about to kill these pilots. Magonia's about to crash these planes.

There's a fierce wind kicking up all around Maganwetar, and the shormsharks are spitting bright white light, searing fire. The whirlwinds are full of dirt and garbage.

this is real

this is real

this is real

Aza's singing a wave of wind and storm, rising up out of the air and rolling hard all around Maganwetar.

Aza Ray Boyle, the girl I've loved since the beginning of my memories, the girl I've been trying to keep safe, the girl I've been trying to understand?

That girl starts to sing a note I don't know, but somehow . . . *do*. It feels like everything I've ever heard her say over the years. It feels like every moment we've ever spent together, every back room of a museum, every library shelf, every time I looked at her and felt stunned that I was standing there at all.

All those times when you're blinded by joy and you can't even tell why. All that, and her too, this core that sings her own song, the song she sings when she sleeps, the song she whistles when she's not paying attention, something with no melody, no chorus, no sense to it, but entirely Aza Ray.

It's stronger than I've ever heard her, sweeter and more ferocious at once. The note she's singing almost hurts, and I can't separate it from my own physical pain and the pain in my heart that I've never noticed how she really sounds before.

I always heard myself too loudly, alongside her. This is her with no backup, her *self* in song form. This is Aza without me.

If I die? She doesn't need me. If she doesn't need me, it's okay to go.

It's a relief.

All those years, all that dying, and I thought I was keeping her alive. I thought I was supporting the universe, but I was just supporting *my* universe. She was Aza the whole time.

So I listen.

I've got nothing but that. All I can do is hear her.

I listen to her bend the sky. I listen to her, and I know this song will break Zal, win over anything. It has to.

But I hear Zal shouting directions at Dai, and Dai shouting back.

I see Milekt fly across the gap between Maganwetar and Aza's ship.

Aza chokes, and her song is gone, with a strangled cry.

I don't know what happened, because I can't sit up. I can't stand up. I can't see her anymore. The light around her is gone.

"Get her!" Zal shouts.

There are millions of notes suddenly, Magonians singing with their canwr, and each Nightingale is singing too, a robotic approximation of Magonian song, a high-pitched razor song.

Aza's mother is as strong as Aza is. Stronger?

Surreal, sky on fire, the smell of gasoline and ozone, birds screaming everywhere.

I catch a glimpse of something, and I don't even know what it is. A squallwhale? More than one squallwhale? I'm lost here, a sprawled human stuck too far from home, and off the edge of the deck, which is tilting, I'm seeing buildings.

```
            A       J
          Z       A
          A       S
        R       O
        A     N
      Y   &   K
      B     E
        O       R
          Y       W
          L       I
            E       N
```

are supposed to be connected by an &, not two forms of nothing, dying on separate ships.

This is not the plan. This is not what we've been working for, for all these years. And here we are anyway. Maybe that's how it always is.

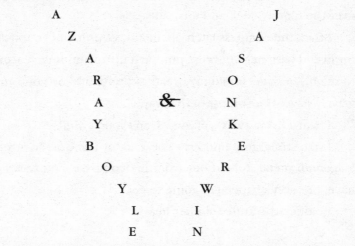

In my hand I feel the round shape of the compass, its weight and smoothness. I feel the latch at the back, the thing I had built in, another thing I never told Aza about. I should've. I thought we'd have time.

But here I am.

"Zal!" I call, croaking it out, making a particular sound like a death rattle, a sound I once heard the girl I love more than anything make.

Here I am right now, still here. I can do something for Aza, even if it's the last thing I do. The SWAB archive had things in it. Some of them were tiny. Some of them could be palmed.

Zal leans over me.

"Is the drowner dead?" she asks.

Tomorrow, on earth, there will be reports of weather events. Of flocks of birds falling out of the heavens. Of a super-storm. People will worry about bird flu and about catastrophe, about the heavens falling, in all the ways people always have, and should, and do.

I squint through almost closed eyes out across the clouds, over the bloody deck and torn sails.

I flick the compass latch open. Zal is leaning over, touching my eyelid with her fingertip, pulling it up, examining. Checking to see if I'm gone. I hold my breath. I pretend to be gone all the way, instead of just most of the way.

I hear Eli, far away, yelling, "Don't touch him!"

I stab straight up into Zal's chest, a tiny knife made of stolen Magonian metal, folded out from my compass, and that's all I have, the only chance I'm going to get.

I plunge the knife into her heart.

CHAPTER 29

{AZA}

I can't make a sound. There's nothing. Milekt is in my throat, binding my song. Milekt himself. A suicide mission? An end-song? He's taking me down with his own body? I feel like I'm choking, but there's enough room for me to breathe, a tiny bit. Not to sing. I'm mute. Not the way I was on the prison ship. A new way. No tech. This is a living thing, inside my voice, stopping my song like a cork.

My broken canwr. Motionless. I—

I cough. Like a dying girl. Like Aza Ray Boyle, blue in the lips, blue in the fingers, broken in the soul, missing her family in advance.

And below me is their house. Below me is everything I knew when I was learning about the world.

Lightning strikes my backyard.

Lightning sets a tree on fire. Right by the bedroom windows. Wind is coursing over the landscape, flattening it.

Rivers rise up and I watch them begin to flow over the ground, flooding the land where I live, the places I wanted to pick flowers, but couldn't, because I was Magonian and couldn't breathe. The places I wanted to play, but couldn't, because I was this, and the earth was not my home.

Zal steps onto the deck of my ship.

I'm on my knees.

"There's no deathsong for traitors, Aza Ray," Zal says, but her voice is strange. She's holding a spot on her chest, wincing. The same spot Heyward's dart was.

"Your voice was a gift I gave you, and now it returns to me. It was mine."

I whisper, "Why?"

This is worse than the last time, on the prison ship. A dead canwr in my throat. MY dead canwr. I want to scream, but nothing comes out.

"A healing song," she says. "Sing me a healing song. Sing what you were singing before. I heard you. Sing that at me."

There's no healing what's broken in Zal.

I can't sing to the birds all around me, all these birds who came to die for me, and I can't even see Eli and Jason.

I'm sorry, I think at them. *I'm so sorry you're dying up here.* Caru isn't in my line of sight and I don't dare turn my head to look for him.

Come closer.

Come closer, Zal Quel. Come closer, you captain of nowhere who birthed me. Come closer.

I can't hate her.

I have to feel her pain. It's not hard to feel it. The sky is full of it. Her throat is covered in wires and her face is a frozen thing. There are Nightingales singing out in the distance, and her throat is singing with them. She's broken.

I can almost feel the pain in her chest, some wound there. Her face is agonized.

I don't know how to heal Zal Quel. I only know how to sing to her. I open my arms to my mother, this nightmare, this broken thing who is stronger than I am.

What happened to her to make her this? Why is she still here? I can't believe she wants to be.

Zal takes a step toward me, her face bewildered.

"That song you were singing." Her face flickers. Sadness? Fury? I can't tell. "Where did you find it?"

"It's mine," I choke, the last of my voice around Milekt.

"Which deathsong would you have sung? What funeral would we have given you, if you'd died with honor? There would have been sunsets and clouds streaked silver. There would have been new stars. Daughter of the ruler. But you choose to die dishonored, and disowned. A traitor."

She's an inch from me.

"If I die," she says, "the world goes with me. If I die, I've taught my Nightingales a song."

I can see them spitting all around the sky, singing weather, singing with my voice.

I still don't know the song that will heal her. It's not this one.

I look at the hand she's holding to her chest. It's blue with her blood.

She takes a step forward and I step backward. One more. Another. I think about how I'm going to have to take her with me. Maybe that's the end.

"I can't," I choke, Milekt there in my throat. I feel him spread his wings.

Not dead. Not—

Zal looks at me, her face furrowed with pain, every part of her radiating fury.

"Then you're no one's daughter," she says, and shoves.

Milekt flies out, leaving the shipwreck. Caru screams, and catches Milekt in his talons, killing him with one clasp—

And everything changes. The ship tilts and the sky glitters, and there is a roar of a million voices, a rush of song. Of whale-song. Of birdsong. Of everything.

Something supports my falling body. Something wide and strong. I'm on a squallwhale's back, feeling its body vibrate as it glides up again, beside a launch ship made of birds, all flying together, all flying hard and fast at us as though they're one body, and standing on their wings is—

"She is MY daughter!" sings the Flock from all around me. "MY DAUGHTER!"

All the birds sing it. All the whales. There must be hundreds of squallwhales, here out of nowhere, here to join us.

I turn my head, and there he is, his birds perched on his arms. He's covered in brightness, and his lung doors are both open. Caladrius and Vespers. The entire sky is full of his birds.

Our birds.

Zal's face is aghast. Her mouth is wide, her eyes blazing, staring at the Flock. Her hands shake.

"You're dead," Zal says. "YOU'RE SUPPOSED TO BE DEAD."

"I didn't die. I disappeared," he says. "That is a different thing."

They're silent for a moment.

"How could you leave me?" Zal whispers.

"You broke our song."

"No, you left me when they *took* my song." Her expression is pleading. "But I have it back! Sing me a healing. I'm dying."

He looks at her.

"We are all dying," he says. "And your 'song' is the sound of murder. Your song was taken from you because you sang to kill. You always have."

"Not always," she says. "I didn't, not with you."

His eyes on her might as well be full of lightning. "What happened to you?"

"The world is full of hunger," she says. "No one helps. No one but me," she says. She looks at him pleadingly again.

I watch them, wary.

They look at each other, and the look that passes between them is old. It's the look of history on fire. It's the look of love, regardless, love no matter what has happened, love despite betrayal. It's the look of love that will never make sense.

But here I am.

And here they are.

The Flock takes a step forward, and Zal does too, and for a moment I think he's going to heal her, that he won't be able to keep from it.

Instead, the Flock blasts out a note so loud and ferocious it shakes everything.

Then they're both singing into each other's lungs; Zal's voice is all Nightingales, and his is all the birds in the sky.

He sings *with* her. He's as strong as she is. As fierce. This is a battle of equals.

The Flock's voice, a voice compounded of all his birds, is underneath Zal's, pushing it to be larger, singing it into a flood. This is what happened to me. I know what this feels like.

And it's my song they're pushing. My stolen song.

"STOP!" Zal screams, managing to make it over the song, managing to be louder than her Nightingales for a moment. She chokes, then flexes her fingers, controlling the voices of the birds above her. I see her tighten her throat to sing a high pitch.

The Flock tilts in the air, in pain. Her song, the Nightingale song, hurts him. But he keeps singing.

Lightning bolts, flashes of twirling northern lights and comets. There's a glow around them both, and it hurts my eyes and my head.

He's singing shooting stars and sunrises.

I'm close enough to them that I can see their faces. Zal's eyes are entirely orange, lit on fire, her face bright and her skin covered in tattoos of the things she loves and lives for.

He's written on her skin. And she's written on his.

I see the points of Zal's teeth, the love and murder in her eyes.

Caladrius is sagging, long crane neck wrapped around the Flock's shoulders. He's weakening.

Zal's sagging too, bleeding, holding on to his hands. Both of them are barely staying in the air.

The two of them, even wounded, are equally strong. They are bonded, and they sing as one thing.

They sing a note that is so ferocious that I can't even hear it. Right into each other's bodies, into each other's mouths, into each other's lungs, and as the note happens I realize I know what the Flock is singing.

Zal's face crumples, and she gasps, choking on the song she's singing. The Nightingales above her are twisting, tangling, and the note the Flock is singing is horribly beautiful. It's high and sweet and savage, and Zal is singing the other half of it.

He's singing Zal's note.

Her Nightingales twist in the air, flying out over the city

below us, and Zal is singing a note she doesn't want to sing, a note of joy instead of destruction. The Flock sings with her, shifts her song into creation instead, and for a moment—

I see a flash of recognition on her face. A softening. She sings a trill that is her own, a trill that is full of things I've never heard her sing. She sounds like the recordings I've heard of that.

Astroseismology.

Her song is nothing earthbound. It's a vibration. It's the song of a star, a quivering warble that comes from elsewhere.

My mother's real song is the song of a star sending light?

I look at her. She's beautiful suddenly, and her skin shines. She's glowing, trembling as she sings.

The Flock is barely hanging in the air, and he's singing with her so hard that I can tell he's about to fall.

He inhales. She inhales too. I can tell they're both preparing for a final blast, a last note—

And then everything goes still.

They stare at each other.

The Nightingales whip across the sky. Zal twists, screaming a note she must have kept inside herself for years, tugging the wires that hold the Nightingales to her.

The note is a blinding obliteration, the opposite of the Flock's song, a song of unbelief, of distrust, of fury and sorrow.

I'm paralyzed, watching the father I only just found writhe in agony, his face contorted, his voice tight and broken. The echoes of her note reverberating out into the sky, into the Nightingales, across the city, shaking everything, turning all sound into catastrophe. I see Magonians clutching their chests, and in the planes orbiting us, I see pilots convulsing.

She's singing death for everyone, an endsong for their

partnership, their love, their world, and ours too. Vespers screams and Caladrius screams with her.

Zal's singing the Flock's endsong, trying to collapse his heart. And it's coming right at me. He has to sing his own note back at her, he has to call his birds, he has to—

The Flock looks hard at me, and sings *my* note instead of his own.

He sings *LOVE* for me, and my name, and his belief in me, the entirety of me, the part that came from Zal *and* the part that came from him. The part that came from earth, being raised by my parents, loved by them, having a sister, having Jason. He sings it all. He sings certainty that I will be able to do anything I want to do.

And that I can do it right now, without him.

The Flock sings me not extinct.

He grabs Zal in his arms, in the middle of the sky, the two of them equally matched, the two of them still strong, both of them mortally wounded.

And he sings one last ferocious note with her, a note like nothing I've ever heard before. It balances her completely. It silences her.

It silences him too.

The Flock takes Zal in his arms, and together, they leap. They're falling, and falling, and then I see the vultures come for them.

The whole sky stops.

Caladrius makes a mournful call, a call that says it's over, and Vespers sings with her. Caladrius folds her wings midair, and falls, even as I hold out my hands trying to stop her.

I hear the vultures calling out in triumph from underneath the ship.

Deadthings. Deadsongs. Deadsingers.

The air is a mist of blue blood and echoing notes, and I'm sobbing, gasping, bent over on the back of my whale, but my parents are gone, both of them, and below me are a mass of black wings.

Black wings of vultures, and of Nightingales.

Zal's remaining canwr rise around me, all of them singing horror. All of them singing ruin.

Waters appear below us. Land turns to lake. Storms are crashing down upon the city, and cars float, winds tearing down trees.

The Nightingales are singing by themselves now, agony, starvation, grief, death. I can see all of them, making their way across the sky, tiny dots of disaster.

The captain's Nightingales sing a song full of the wide eyes of children on the ground, the outlines of buildings about to be flattened by weather events. They sing parched ground and holes in it, and in their song are corpses, heaps of bodies, graves.

The Nightingales sing a song of a dead ocean, gray and flat, and a dead earth, gray and flat, and a dead sky, nothing living in it.

I swallow.

I try to feel my own song.

The only song I can sing to fight this.

I try to find it.

But it's gone.

CHAPTER 30

{JASON}

There's a sound of screaming change, a shift in everything, and I open my eyes.

"Oh my god," says Eli.

"NO!" screams Dai. "NO!"

He's running to the edge of Maganwetar, sprinting, and his hands are outstretched to catch anything, but there's nothing left. Zal is gone. The Flock is gone.

Is it over?

Is everyone dead? Aza? Where is she?

I look across the gap between Maganwetar and Aza's ship, and I see her, looking like she's in shock, on the back of a tremendous squallwhale, pale and speckled, the size of a bus.

It's singing. The whole sky is full of singers. There are squallwhales everywhere, and the underneath is whipping with storms. Magonians are running in all directions onboard this city, and I can hear screams of the dying, fighting with Rostrae.

"What's happening?" Eli yells as drones appear all around us, all over the sky. "Jason? What's happening?"

One drone after another beeps and yelps. I can see them

fixing on targets. Who's controlling them? They're all around Aza, and all over the sky.

I hear a ticking sound, a ping, and then I see something rising up from the center of Maganwetar.

I've seen something like it. On the monitors at SWAB. It's *Argentavis magnificens*. The *magnificent silver bird* with the twenty-three-foot wingspan, extinct I don't know how long ago.

It rises.

It rises.

It spreads its wings, and it looks at her. It's like the Nightingales, but fifty times their size.

Aza's standing on the whale's back. She turns and sees it, and stops. She doesn't sing. Why doesn't she sing?

A red dot appears on Aza's chest. The drone is looking directly at her, and I can tell that it's fixing a target. What does it have? Explosives? It's the size of a small plane, not a blackbird, not anything like the small ones. This is a SWAB drone. This is why they're here, ready to deploy their weapon.

No one moves.

Aza's standing on the back of the squallwhale, and slowly, others join her. There must be fifty squallwhales now. A hundred.

But it won't matter. What does that drone have?

I look around frantically.

This was what SWAB must have been preparing. This is what they had up here, smuggled in. This is why they had the bones of the bird in the headquarters, why they had a live version in the prison. Maybe it wasn't live at all. Maybe it was a prototype.

Eli clutches my hand, suddenly beside me. Dai is here too, standing, his jaw dropped.

Aza looks up at the tremendous bird, and it looks down at her, this non-sentient thing, this monster made by some mechanics, some engineers, some metalworkers.

Somewhere inside it is a red button.

I feel Eli twitch beside me. No idea what her plan is, but I can tell it involves jumping off the edge of the city, and straight at anything attacking Aza. I catch a glimpse of Dai beside me, and I swear he's thinking the same thing.

Then something moves. A screal, a fast flying shriek, and Caru comes out of the blue, a dive-bomb of black and scarlet wings.

DEATHBIRD shrieks Caru, folds his wings, and dives at top speed right at the silver bird. Not just Caru. Caru and a tiny silver bat. They're both diving, both flinging themselves through the air and at the drone.

The tremendous drone bird begins to sing. It raises its voice and I watch as the rivers leap from their beds, as the sky shakes, and as the water below us becomes land, and then water again. The air bends around it. It has as much Magonian magic as it has science from SWAB.

Something changes in Dai. I watch it happen.

"No more of this. No more."

His tattoos change abruptly, becoming only birds, only canwr, and his skin shifts until every inch of it is etched.

He starts to sing, and his song changes something. Aza looks up. She focuses on him.

"AZA RAY!" he shouts.

I watch as the planes kept outside our radius by weather begin to make their way over Maganwetar—

Is SWAB trying to create an event? Something that will make

their funding certain? Something, no matter how many people it sacrifices, that will make it so their mission isn't in jeopardy? They want to destroy Maganwetar, but they want it to be the kind of destruction that makes their name in the government.

Planes begin to fly through the chains that hold manta sails to Maganwetar, killing the mantas as they do. Maganwetar tips like a ship in a major storm.

This great slab of city, this huge whirlwind of song and sound, is moving toward falling like a nuclear bomb from the sky. This is a Book of Miracles. This is an asteroid hitting earth.

We're on it.

This is everything I ever read about, everything I studied, and I don't even know who's doing it, Zal's final orders, or SWAB, or both things, with the same goal of creating a huge war between heaven and earth.

I have my phone in my hand. I hold it as close to my face as I can, trying to access the huge drone's signal, trying to find its song and stop it.

Caru flips midair, grabbing the drone's skull in his claws, beak open in a savage falcon hunting posture, but he's not strong enough. The bat is clawing at the drone's eyes, yanking at its panels, its metal feathers.

Jik and Wedda join them. I see the Rostrae take flight and land on top of the huge bird, both of them ferocious, both of them dismantling it. Jik pries at another set of panels with her talons. Wedda's beak finds the central power.

Jik tangles her talons in the explosive case, shredding power cables, twisting metal.

Caru sings a deathsong for the bird. The bat joins Caru, their voices twining.

I see Aza standing, staring up at Caru with tears streaming down her face.

Her heartbird and the bat sing joy for the bird's brief existence, for its extinction, for its fall.

They sings a song of sorrow for this bird/not bird, this thing, and then Caru twists its neck with his talons and impales its power source entirely with his beak.

It falls out of the air in a heap of feathers and wiring, broken panel, broken metal wings.

Aza gasps like someone who's been holding her breath, and finally, she's singing again.

Dai is singing with her, not against her, not in opposition. He's broadening her reach, focusing her notes. It's a new song, something I've never heard before.

It's a healing song. Even I can hear it. It's a roar, but a different kind of roar, the roar of breath being taken for the first time, of things being born, of water rushing up after being dammed. It's the sound of wind through trees and birds chirping, a song of something other than chaos, a song of order, with repeating verses, things that twist back and find earlier themes, building on them, rising in strength and volume as Aza and Dai sing together, looking hard at each other. The bat is singing too, and Caru, and Dai's canwr too, everything in a chorus of instruments.

Below us is the whole world, and I look down for a moment and see a lot of disaster. Burning wreckage. There are carcasses of things all over the place and vultures are eating them.

We're very low. I can see waves roiling, and the sky darkening. Only in a few places is the song beginning to work, beginning to roll back the waves and bring the trees up from their flattened state, push the river back into its banks. It's not fast enough.

I hold my phone up and hit record.

Aza's shaking with the song she's singing, and she looks almost exactly like Zal, but the opposite, somehow. Her wild hair twists into the air, and her skin is covered with white lines of light.

Dai's veins are bulging, his throat tight, and his song is unmaking weather with Aza's.

Maganwetar is stabilizing, even as planes are being roped by Rostrae, twisting in their flight paths, and Nightingales are being flipped through the air.

Aza and Dai clench their fists across the gap, until they're singing into each other's lungs. This is what she meant when she told me they were bonded. They sing with one voice. They sing one blinding note of joy.

I stop recording and start moving the sound files, adding things. I move the song Aza is singing into the voices of the Nightingales, pushing it over the network and into each drone.

Aza and Dai are restoring the ground. I make the Nightingales do it too.

Now the Nightingales sing a creation song, restoring it with them. The sky fills with other creatures, and all of them are singing with her.

I look down.

In the water below us, there are whales and dolphins, rising up from the deep. I see a mass of them, dark and silver, in the waters that are close enough, nearly to touch. They surface in a riot of splashing and song, high sonar waves reaching up to drag the remaining darksinging Nightingales down into the depths where their circuits will drown.

Another Nightingale begins to sing with Aza. And another, and another, through the system. I override their instructions. I break their orders.

At the last, a single whale rises up from the ocean, a tremendous whale with dark blue flesh, not the same as any of the others, three times their size.

I know its strange voice, amplified through the Nightingales. Like a screaming owl. It's the lonely one, the one I've been obsessed with for years, following its sound files around the ocean. It's the song I added to this mixture. It sings up to the whales of the sky, its counterparts, and now the squallwhales sing at full strength with Aza and Dai, with the lonely one below.

Aza's singing with all of them, all of them her canwr, and Dai is singing with them, restoring broken things.

Smallest creatures, Aza sings.

Smallest creatures, Dai sings.

I hear a song amplified through them, and it's a song I don't recognize, a high, intricate jangle, something like a small bird or a music box.

A tiny silver mouse is looking up from right beside me. Eli's holding it in her palm. She smiles at me. It's singing.

"Just in case," she said. "It came with me for luck."

I'm overtaken by the song I heard on earth, in Aza's kitchen, her mother's mice trilling out their music.

"There might be a few of them with me," she says. "Mice breed fast."

This mouse has joined in, singing songs to reverse damage. I see other mice scattering around the deck of the ship.

They launch themselves up the wires that connect

Maganwetar to the manta rays, and into the engines of SWAB airplanes. They sing themselves into the breaking of SWAB.

The sky and earth and air are singing, all at once.

The last of Zal's remaining Nightingales lurch and jolt in the air. I look and see the mice are chewing their wiring into nothingness, shorting out signals, forgotten songs of dead electronics.

That's the song it is. That's the magic it has, that of making song rather than destroying it.

Below us, our city has suffered a hurricane and water is washed up over the edges of everything, but the buildings are standing. Whales and dolphins are swimming back to their places, away from the edges.

I make sure.

Our houses are still standing. We're still there.

I lost Aza a long time ago. I'm not her singer. She's not mine. Maybe it wasn't meant to be forever, but it was real.

I can't do what Dai can, and I understand why she wants him instead. I can't grieve it now. I can't think. I can't do anything else.

All I can do is shut my eyes. We're still here. We're still living.

That's all I can ask for.

{AZA}

Dai and I are standing on opposite sides of a gap between a ship and a city. We're holding hands. We've just been singing into each other's lungs.

Now we're both gasping with the effort of that, of things across the sky still changing.

"Dai," I whisper.

"Aza," he says, and tries to smile at me. I try to smile back at him. Neither of us has it in us.

"What happened? Milekt and you and Zal? What happened?" I ask him. Magonian isn't a good language for someone who's crying.

"Everything," he says.

I stare at this blue tattoo of a boy. I can't hate him. I've never been able to hate him. He's part of me.

He just sang life out of death. He just sang joy out of catastrophe. He did it for me.

The ground is in bloom beneath us. It was snow and now it's green and flowers. The water is clear. The storm is passing. Our song, the one we sang together, did that. The airplanes that were coming into Maganwetar are here, not crashed, and their crews are looking startled out from their seats. Should they be dead? Maybe.

Should we be dead?

Maybe.

Do we need to say things to each other? Yes. But not now. Not when the world is whirling around us, our song the thread that has stitched it back together. Not when I have a heartbird and a heartbat on my shoulders, and the sun is coming out above us.

"Zal was wrong," Dai says. "I thought I knew her, but she was broken. I broke her out, and all she could say, all she WOULD say, was *drown the drowners for good*. That song, the one she sang with him? That was a healing."

"She died," I say. "And he did too."

"Death isn't the worst thing," Dai says. "She was suffering for too long. Sometimes death is the only outcome."

"What happens when I die?" I ask him. "To you?"

"What do you think?"

I look at him. He squeezes my hands.

"You have to go to Maganwetar," he says. "Your drowner is there. Your sister too."

I pause. He holds out his hand and picks me up as I leap across the gap.

I say good-bye to the two of us singing together.

He is not the life I choose.

I am not the life he chooses.

But we keep living anyway. Maybe that's how it always is, wherever in the universe you are, sky, earth, in between. Maybe you come back to all those people when you die, and there you are together again, all the choices you didn't make, and those you did. Maybe love is just that, and only that. The choice you make. And so, you choose to love. You choose to give it all up, to surrender your scared self and live in this mystery.

Jik is standing on the edge of the city, blue and shining. I can see Rostrae everywhere. An entire country's worth of nomads landing in a new home. The sails brought from rafts are being hitched to buildings, and Rostrae from all corners of the sky have come to crew the city ships.

From this angle, Maganwetar looks like a nest of buildings, ship masts and sails. Maybe it belonged to someone else before it belonged to Magonians. Maybe it was a Rostrae city. The buildings take sharp angles, and have birds in statue form flying from their heights.

Caru sings a screal, and together we sing *Rise*.

All the birds in miles sing it with us. Maganwetar rises, a whoosh of air behind it, a song in its wake. Around it, I sing a wall of clouds.

I see Wedda peering over the edge of the city. I see all these Rostrae who fought, all these Magonians who were taken unwillingly by Zal, and by this version of certainty.

There are lots of versions of certainty. There are things happening in every corner of every world that look like this. *On earth as it is in heaven.* Is that the saying? It means something else, of course. It means the heavens are good, and earth is less so, that earth should strive to be like the sky.

I'm not so sure. I think about what goes on everywhere, and . . . everything happens. People trust leaders they shouldn't trust. People listen just because someone is singing loudly.

"You could stay here," says Jik.

Carpe omnia. I want everything. But I don't want to be

anyone's ruler. I don't want to be anyone's queen. I don't even want to be anyone's captain, except my own.

That's my choice. I want to go between.

Then I see my sister in front of me, free. She holds out her arms, and the look on her face—

Jason's at her feet, horribly still.

There's no version of *everything* without him in it. Some things are forever. This is one of them.

I leap.

I'm a million miles across the sky. Pi, but beyond it. I've found the end of an endless number. I've gotten to the final digit. It's beautiful there.

Someone's shaking me back into my body. A raw whisper. "Jason. Jason. Come on."

The voice it sounds like isn't who I think it is. I'm still here, barely. Hallucinating still, probably. Too far gone to come back.

Something lands on my chest. I feel wings, feathers, pain, too much pain, and then even more, because a beak nips my nose.

I open my eyes. It's Caru, right there, staring at me with falcon pupils, and singing a low trill. And then a bat. A strange, silver bat, looking into my eyes and singing with Caru.

And then it's Aza. I'm looking at her, finally, touching her again, finally, even if this isn't real.

Her eyes are gold and indigo and orange, her skin blue and tattooed in white lines, ship rigging and sails, anchors and swords. All the things she loves, that's what she told me once, that's how Magonian tattoos work.

I'm not on there.

This is her coming to tell me she's leaving. I'm ready. I can do it.

Her skin is covered with Magonia. Squallwhales and bat-sails, a tentacle from an airkraken wrapping around one arm and onto her neck. She's got a flock of canwr flying across her shoulders, and on one cheek I can see a shifting constellation, which shines as brightly as any star.

"Jason," she whispers. "Jason. You can't die, okay? I need you."

"I'm fine," I say. "I've been dying for days. I'll just keep doing it."

"Liar," she says, and the word contains all the versions of liar I've ever been. "You're not fine. Even when you were fine, you weren't fine."

She rips open my shirt and looks at my burns. I see on her face how bad it is.

"I don't know how to sing this," she says, and looks up at Dai. He shakes his head.

"I have something for you," I say.

She looks at me, her eyebrow up, in a very Aza Ray expression.

"A weird fact. I'm going to win with this one."

"You don't have to win," Aza says, and she's crying. "We're not competing."

"I've been saving it," I tell her. "For a special occasion. But now I don't know if I'm going to make it that far, so you get it now."

"You're blatantly not dying," she tells me. "You have sixty, seventy years to win—"

"So," I interrupt. "This is a thing that happened during World War II. An inventor created a plan involving bats. A lot of bats were captured, and rigged out with tiny bombs. They were chilled and put into a cargo drop, in the anticipation of dropping tiny bats on Japan and setting the country on fire. Everyone was sure that the bats would do their bidding. The idea was that bats would roost in flammable areas and create firebombs in barns. The rural country would be panicked and everyone would surrender, thinking there were soldiers hiding everywhere. That was the plan. It was diagrammed out. It was even tested, but the bats had their own opinions. They chewed through their cords, flew away, and set the testing facility on fire."

Aza's looking down at me, her face covered in blue-black tears.

"The bats did what they were meant to do," I say. "No one could make them be anything they weren't meant to be. All they wanted to do was roam the sky."

"I don't want to roam the sky, Jason," she says.

"You might, and that would be reasonable," I say.

"Everything is possible," I say.

"Carpe omnia," says Eli to Aza, and Aza looks at her for a moment, and then smiles.

"Everything," says Aza as she turns to me.

"You don't love me anymore," I tell her. "And I don't need to give you permission to leave, but you have it. I screwed you over. I thought I was doing the right thing, but the right thing was complicated, and I was stupid. Now? I don't know what any right thing is anymore. I'm sorry."

She holds up her hand—

"Let me apologize," I say.

"You already did. You apologized with the voice of, like, a

hundred Nightingales. But look," she says.

Aza holds out her right arm and shows me the inside of it. It's a tattoo of a wing. I recognize it instantly. It's one of those wings we broke our ankles with when we were kids, jumping off the garage. These dumb wings we made from Da Vinci diagrams.

We're not kids anymore, and something about that makes me want to cry more than anything else.

Back then, we both thought if we were together we'd be able to fly. But love isn't enough to save you from everything. It's not even enough to save you from yourself.

I want to tell her that. I don't want to tell her that.

She holds out her other arm and shows me the other wing. Both these wings were busted on the ground outside her garage.

I almost can't look at her, except that I don't know how to stop looking at Aza Ray. I can't imagine my life without her. Even if falling for her is like falling for a shooting star.

What am I supposed to do?

Here she is, in front of me. Here she is, the same girl she always was.

I have one photo of Aza, the real Aza, taken secretly on my phone, when we were in Svalbard. I took it as she ran back to the ship to put on the Beth skin, and I never told her.

I spent the last year looking at that picture of Aza, wishing I could see her like that again, wishing I knew everything about her the way I did the moment I took it. Wishing she knew everything about me too.

Because something that can happen when you know everything about each other is that it takes only a little bit of time to know nothing again. A few months, a few lies.

She's blue and wild in the photo, her skin deeper than lake

water, her hair in knots around her, her eyes red, orange, and indigo. She's alien, but I know her so well. She looks like Aza in this photo, not like anyone or anything else.

And here she is again.

I can't stand it, and yet here I still am, with this girl I met when we were five and didn't know anything about the world.

Before we knew how hard it would be to be together. Before we knew how much we needed each other. Before we knew anything except that she was going to die, and I was going to try to keep her alive.

Here she is. Alive. I didn't keep her that way.

Here she is, and it wasn't me who kept her going. She did it herself. She can't keep me alive either.

"A skin!" she shouts suddenly.

What?

"Dai! Get a skin!"

Dai takes off running.

Aza's eyes are full of dark blue tears. She tenses her jaw and swallows. She's as scared as I am.

"Do you still love me, Jason Kerwin? At all?"

Aza Ray is an idiot just like I'm an idiot. I was born to love her. I was born to do all kinds of other things too, but this part? This part I can't avoid.

"I still love you, Aza Ray Boyle."

"Do you love me if I'm Aza Ray Quel?"

"I do."

"Do you love me if I'm neither of those names? If I don't believe in anything sometimes? If I don't trust anyone? If sometimes the whole sky goes dark inside my head and I try to tell you that everything is nothing?"

"What about you?" I ask her. "Do you love me even if I lied to you? If I ask for forgiveness?"

"If I ask for forgiveness," she says.

We stare at each other for a moment and then we say it at once.

"I forgive you."

"I'm a mess," she says, "but I choose you."

Dai hands her something.

I'm flat on my back, screwed up, half ruined, and Aza places the skin onto me, and I feel it join with my skin, move around me, change me to fit.

I have no idea what's happening. No idea why this is working. This is something that makes no sense, has nothing to do with science. This is me inside of magic.

This is not the first time I've been surrounded by magic.

Caru is singing loudly with the bat, and Aza and Dai start singing too, and I feel her hand on my chest, where my heart is, where my canwr would be singing if I had one.

I feel myself starting to come back.

I'm made of pieces that could assemble the sun, or a pea, and it could go either way. Love is not this simple thing. Love isn't this obvious thing.

It's not about that first moment of knowing. It's about what you keep doing after you break each other's hearts. It's about choosing each other on terrible days as well as on beautiful ones.

It's about picking each other up off the floor and then laughing about it later. You can go pretty far into disaster as long as you're willing to look at each other again. You can fix a lot of failures.

You can fail as long as you keep trying.

It's a long journey up from below the ground, up into the sky. It's a long journey through a life I had, which is now totally changed.

Aza sniffles and wipes her nose. Nothing about it is beautiful. Everything about it is beautiful.

I stand before her in my new skin. What do I look like? I have no idea.

Am I human? Am I Magonian? Am I both?

"You hold no horrors for me," she says.

I pick her up off the deck and hold her as tightly as I can. She holds me back.

We're two lost things becoming one found thing again.

And here we are, me, Jason, Eli, and Dai, standing in a city none of us came from.

We step into a ship, given to us by Jik. There are skins in the hold. Supplies for our journey back to the ground, and for me to return when I wish.

Vespers orbits, trilling, singing some radio frequency love song, some half magic involving music brought from below and from the stars as well. I can hear her drawing from every edge of everything. I thought Vespers would die when the Flock went. But now I have another heartsinger, not a bird this time, but a bat. I inherited her song, and she chose me too. Along with Caru. Together now, the three of us.

With Caru, Vespers sings, the two of them old partners. I feel things moving all over the sky, clouds and rain, sunsets and sunrises. Squallwhales. They sang with me too.

Dai's given me his song, and in his song, I can tell there's nothing left of his fury.

The sky has edges and he's familiar with them. He's going to where he came from to see if there is a city there still, to broker with earth if there's not. He's been sent by Jik, and he will be a first mate to Wedda.

And this isn't the end of us singing together. Why should it be? You only have one of these lives, these precious, wild, strange lives. I don't have a version of my life where we never sing again. Why would I be that dumb? When I can try to have everything?

I can try.

There are still problems.

The agency Jason worked with, SWAB, and their warfare against the sky. The world below, hating the world above. The world above, hating the world below. Hunger and confusion, starvation and fury. I have plans, but what do I know about plans? Crop science plans, Jason's mom. Breathing plans, my mom.

Things that can be solved.

Healed.

Hoped for.

I look down off of Maganwetar and consider our houses, from high above. Weather crises. Our parents at home, wondering what's happening up here. Jason, now changed. Maybe not forever. I don't even know what he looks like now. He looks like himself to me. I see him inside of anything.

We're on our way home. But we have other places to go too, or at least, I do. To my parents, to tell them this is okay. To Jason's parents, who are going to have to learn things from the beginning. Though, if you ask me, I'm not sure they don't have some idea about things. I look at them, and I wonder. They're not the usual parents.

Whose are?

There is so much I don't know. There's so much everyone

doesn't know. It could all go wrong again. The thing about trusting someone is that you have to do it anyway, even if you know it might end in disaster. Not being able to trust anyone means you spend your life alone.

I don't want to be that version. That's dying girl all over again. So now I'm girl between worlds. I'm all the things I've been, and none of them, at once.

Maybe I don't have everything, but that doesn't mean I'm not reaching for it. Good morning, world. This is the new version of Aza Ray, walking between the edges, balancing on the impossible still wearing a flight suit and a pair of unlikely boots.

Below us, off the coast, there are still boats moving, and whales. Our ship goes low, sung over the sea by me and Caru. The skyship glides over the cloud waves for a moment, and then I feel it touch the sea itself.

There are things in the ocean. I saw them in the prison. I saw them, and now I know that if I want the world to be better, I have to do some things. Sing some things. All over it. Flying fish are here suddenly, leaping over the edges of the ocean, over the ship, and I hear their song.

Some birds, they've proven, navigate by means of magnets in their beaks. Not magnets exactly but ferrous deposits, which function as compasses. There was a test years ago, in which they tried to see if humans had magnets too, if any of us had directional sense that worked that way. Apparently some people maybe do. They can walk miles across a landscape, always knowing where north is.

Other birds navigate by means of star maps. They sit in their nests as chicks, staring out until they find the North Star. I'm serious. They then memorize the shit out of the sky. Once the star maps are in place in their bird skulls, they are free to fly anywhere, always knowing where they are.

Me, I know where north is, because everything else gets memorized from that position. If the people I love are in front of me, I know the whole sky.

My past was flight. Maybe my future is everything at once.

I look at Eli. I look at Jason. They each have one of my hands, but no one's keeping me here.

"All good?" I ask Eli. I take off my boots and unzip my suit.

"If you don't take me down there at some point, there will be hell to pay," Eli informs me.

"I need to see a kraken," says Jason. "I warn you now. Air-kraken, seakraken, I don't care, but it's going to have to happen."

"Noted," I say.

This is a clear sky, and the entirety of it is covered in birds and clouds, squallwhales singing nothing but their own songs, no rain, no darkness. I take off the flight suit.

I take a step forward. I look at the tattoos on my own arms, the wings. I spread those wings.

I feel a tattoo getting written across my collarbone right now, the words Jason wrote to me a year ago.

I {   } you more than [[[{{{((   ))}}}]]].

But this time it's not just about the two of us. It's about life, and the size of the world. It's about being part of everything at once. It's about all the worlds, all one thing. It's about singing one song, and that song, that song—

With my wings spread, with my arms open, I dive into the ocean, singing my own flock, bringing flying fish and whales and dolphins, singing a roar into the depths of the world, just as I sang one into the heights.

I sing joy into the dark.

I sing my heart into saltwater, and with me, all the fish in the sea, and all the birds in the sky, with me all the song in the world. We sing an entwining song.

We make it up as we go, all of us living things singing together, bringing light back into the bodies of the living. We sing against collapse, against despair, against shipwreck.

All of us breathers

All of us swimmers

All of us flyers

All of us sailors

In the dark, I see the flash of a tail, a woman swimming into the depths, and I follow her down.

And I listen to the sound of singing. Everything, everywhere.

ACKNOWLEDGMENTS

As ever, *Aerie* and her sister, *Magonia,* were inspired by historical glory and lore about the world above us, and in this case, by lots of new and wonderful science about climate and creatures. The story about the bats being unsuccessfully deployed as bombs is true, and there are plenty of other elements in the book that are like that one—peculiar, unlikely, grabbed from our world. Gratitude to all the explorers who've written in-depth pieces on the wonders, and on the horrors. Exploration is necessary. There are so many things about the way earth works that can and should be changed into something better.

My gratitude to my true-believer, nothing-startles-her-at-this-point agent, Stephanie Cabot, as well as to Ellen Goodson and Will Roberts and everyone else at the Gernert Company.

At HarperCollins, my editor, Kristen Pettit, who lets me be as weird as I want to be, and who always insists on deep love and strange glories. How lucky I am to have worked with her on two books now! Elizabeth Lynch, assistant editor, who keeps my ship sailing, and the entire divine Harper crew: Kate Morgan Jackson, Suzanne Murphy, Jen Klonsky, Alexei Esikoff,

Veronica Ambrose, Alison Klapthor, Lillian Sun, Elizabeth Ward, and Gina Rizzo, and to Craig Shields for the once-again-stunning cover art. Also, thank you to the Epic Reads team of fantastic readers, book pushers, and brains!

On the wine-pouring, complaint-hearing, oyster-buying, soul-feeding fronts, gigantic thanks are due to Marina Merli at Arte Studio Ginestrelle in Assisi, where I did the final draft of *Aerie*, John Joseph Adams, Sarah Alden, Libba Bray, Martha Brockenbrough, Belinda Casas, Haddayr Copley-Woods, Ellen Datlow, Rupa Dasgupta, Nathan Dunbar, Kelley Eskridge & Nicola Griffith, Larisa Fuchs, Neil Gaiman, Barry Goldblatt, Liz Gorinsky, Theodora Goss, Liz Hand, Mark Headley & Meghan Koch, Adriane Headley, Molly Headley, Nancy Hightower, Roger & Deborah Hodge, Kat Howard, Lance Horne, Genevieve Leloup, Ben Loory, Chuck Martinez, Sarah McCarry, Francesca Myman, Patrick Farrell, Billy Schultz, Sxip Shirey, Tracey Solomon, Caitlin Strokosch, Michael Damian Thomas, and Lynne Thomas & Christie Yant. Once again, my family of friends: Zay Amsbury, Jess Benko & Kate Czajkowski, who were next to me with every page. Thank-yous to Sarah Schenkkan and Joshua Schenkkan, as always, as ever, because hello, what ridiculous joy to have them in my life. And last, again, China Miéville. I thank him for the shrills of late-night mandrakes, for the Flock, and for the co-spine-plotting. There's a particular joy in sharing an imaginary world with another inventor, and I wouldn't have written these books without him.

Thank you, finally, to every single bookseller, librarian, reader, parent, kid, and wanderer who read *Magonia* and wanted more. You kept me writing and kept me inventing. I am inspired because of the things you said to me, everything from bonding with Aza to hating Dai, everything from crying over death in your own lives to living bigger in your futures.

I would be very much less without you in my life.

Thank you for flying with me.

JOIN THE
Epic Reads
COMMUNITY

THE ULTIMATE YA DESTINATION

◀ **DISCOVER** ▶
your next favorite read

◀ **MEET** ▶
new authors to love

◀ **WIN** ▶
free books

◀ **SHARE** ▶
infographics, playlists, quizzes, and more

◀ **WATCH** ▶
the latest videos

◀ **TUNE IN** ▶
to Tea Time with Team Epic Reads